Lock Down Publications and Ca$h
Presents

I0679134

FOR THE LOVE OF BLOOD 4

Playin' 4 Keeps

By
JAMEL MITCHELL

First Edition 2024

Printed in the United States of America

This is a work of fiction. Names, characters, places, and incidents either are products of the author's imagination or are used fictitiously. Any similarity to actual events or locales or persons, living or dead, is entirely coincidental.

Lock Down Publications
P.O. Box 944
Stockbridge, GA 30281
www.lockdownpublications.com

Like our page on Facebook: Lock Down Publications
www.facebook.com/lockdownpublications.ldp

Stay Connected with Us!

Text **LOCKDOWN** to 22828 to stay up-to-date with new releases, sneak peaks, contests and more…

Like our page on Facebook:
Lock Down Publications

Join Lock Down Publications/The New Era Reading Group

Visit our website:
www.lockdownpublications.com

Follow us on Instagram:
Lock Down Publications

Email Us: We want to hear from you!

THANK YOUS

I want to thank my belove-it family for years of support and understanding. Truly, Thank you. Mommy, Meela, Lynitrah, Jamey, Jordyn, Queen, Empress, Wayne, and King. Thanks for the love, support & criticism.

This book is dedicated to my Three Knights: Ethan Nappier, Ke'mante Gravely and Tan'Keem Brown.

Words can't explain the way I love you three young men. I'm so proud to have you in my corner. At some of my roughest times the thought of you alone has pushed me forward. Over the years I haven't been perfect, but never have none of y'all ever turned y'all back on me. All I want to do is make y'all better. I want different opportunities for y'all than I had. You are who I strive for. I'm very proud of all three of you. I love you niggas, it's only up from here...

To Joshua "Killa" Meregildo, feel we made it, ya heard. Like my boss told me, this shit like cooking in an oven. It's gone take time and after all these years, I have become great friends with patience. My nigga we waited long enough, it's our turn now! For real, your diligence is profound blood. To have been faced with death if you blew trial, you still stood tall with sixteen codefendants and never muttered a word. Keeping ya G intact. I really commend you, nigga. Not many built like us, especially in this day and age. No matter what life brings our way, my goon, I'm here. I know you heard it all before, many...many times. Shit gang, I have to. But on dead homies killz when I finally touch soil, my nigga, I'm gone do what brothers supposed to do. Take care of team.

I'm screaming free you till I free you. Remain sturdy and stay dangerous, gang.

It's Courtlandt Ave over everything. We all we got!

With each book that I have written, thoughts lingered that needed to be addressed, yet I have suppressed them time and time again. Not no more…

First, let me start off by saying if I forgot you in my last few shout outs, I sincerely apologize. If I have, you already know the vibes! But when it comes to thanking people for being my rock and actually being a factor in life is hard. Because in this shit me and millions of men and women call life behind these walls, people tend to forget about us. No matter the caliber or statue you hold outside these bricks. So, this thank you is solely motivated for those who forgot about what type of niggas we are, and how we bring it for those we love. My motivation is fueled by your lack of love and empathy. Y'all mufuckaz made me into a beast! I bet mufuckaz looking crazy reading this, but you know who you are. If the shoe fit, wear it. It's time to run it up, ya heard.

All praise is due to the most high, Allah. I know I haven't always been the best me at times, but who has? You live and learn, right? Right…Allah is all knowing and most forgiving. Thank you for giving me such a talent, this came out of nowhere.

I told myself on many occasions that I wasn't gone go crazy with the shout outs. But how the fuck can I not! You mufuckas are amazing. I'm truly blessed. For those that have been here since the beginning, I appreciate your advice, criticism, and consistency…much love and respect to the following…

Braheem, Skino, Sachmo, C, Thug, Big Kev, Lil' Kev, Zion Mitchell, Zion McCauley, Jody Wright, Loso tha boss, Rayshawn Byrd, Blk Tay, Ivory, E Wezzy, Munchie, Donnell, Jaynce, Malik Edler, Mario Goodson, Starkfam Buzz, Shalor Gore, Trey Schooley. Dej Russell, Jamal Davis, Dana Stevenson, La La, Amanda Durchsprung. Hassan

Cleveland, Mare Mare, Desmond "D-dope" Clark, Brandon Sherrod, Taja, Drevo, Joshawa Clark, Eric Sneed, Odell "Killa" Parks, Jamar Walton, Corey Samuels, Nairo, Double R, Marcus Penrose, Les Pittman, Kyrell Davenport, Tasshie Davenport, Takiese, Asavean, Pay Pay, Ping, Kevin Goodman, Santana Rose, Vito AKA Von Dutch, Tanajuah Brown, Naeshia Gravely, Keona Brock, Morgan Smith and last but not least my nigga, Anthony Fields, you are a beast at what you do. I couldn't ask for a better mentor, ock, words won't be enough, but know you also will be taken great care of when my time comes. Keep ya head high. I'm patiently waiting on that next banger…Peace be upon you!

I'm sorry this shit seems all long and drawn out, but I had to recognize my strengths that keeps me afloat…If I forgot you, I do apologize, my mind draws blanks at times. I'm not perfect, it happens.

Last but not least, I would like to thank my boss, Cash, and my editor, Kiera Northington. Words can't explain my gratitude. Cash, thank you for seeing the vision. I'm coming for that best seller's spot, believe that!

Courtlandt Ave, stand up…

Ounnie, Woogy, Nalevi, Jason, Nevel Rock, DJ Hardy, Pyscho D, Duke, Sha Ek, B-Lovee, Zach, Kiua, Skeet Box, Mel Balla, E-Wezzy, A-Butta, Ivory and Lil' Jordan (RIP)

It's a Melrose, Jackson, thing ya heard…you know da vibes…

Ooh way is the movement, all day, Broadway, AK long as a pool stick.

–Oun P

IN LOVING MEMORY OF
HUNTER "NARDO" JESSUP

TRACK LIST

Mozzy "If You Love Me"
Celly RU "Frozen Hearted"
Tsu Surf Feat Leaf Ward "Vip Lap"
Tsu Surf Feat Leaf Ward "Percs & Paranoia"
Meek Mill feat. Vory "Think It's a Game"
Leaf Ward "Deal With Death"
Mozzy "Never Tell 'Em Shit"
Mozzy Fear. Tsu Surf "Symbolize"
B Lovee "Dishonest"
Oun P Feat. J Quest "City On My Back"
StarkFam Blizz "Krosses"
J Quest "God Got Us"
Lloyd Banks "Till Da End"
Tee Jay 3 "Middle Child"
Mozzy "Turn Your Book"
Mozzy "Not the Same"
Mozzy "Murda on my Mind"
Stunna Gambino "Dying 2 Live"
Nippsey Hussle feat. Kendrick Lamar "Dedication"

Chapter 1

"Ummmmm...damn, nigga...Ummmm...Santana, please. Fuck!" Kat crawled up the bed away from Santana. He pulled her back into him, sucking on her swollen pussy lips. He had fantasized about this time after time since being in West Virginia. He licked his tongue up and down her clit slowly and sensually. They both were in heaven. *Damn, this bitch taste good as fuck*, Santana thought as he moved his fingers inside of her, slow and deep. Kat yelled again.

"Tana...Tana...baby, please st-st-stop." She moaned again, motivating his cause. He looked up at her and smiled when he saw her eyes were closed and her mouth gaped open. He flicked his tongue faster, driving her further up the bed. Kat pushed his head away but gripped it, all in the same motion.

"Uggghhhhhh...daddy, I'm ummmm...I'm…cumming..." Kat gripped his head firmly and rubbed her pussy up and down on his lips as she came long and hard. Santana sucked her pussy sloppily. He licked around her pussy, licked the crevice between her thighs and pussy. He licked teasingly and sexily. He was driving her crazy with his sensual touch. This time when he looked up, he made eye contact with her. She was elated, he could tell. Kat rubbed her hand through his hair. Santana finished cleaning her with his tongue and mouth. He rose from the bed, licking his lips. Kat smiled. Santana's lips were glistening with her juices.

"Come here, baby," Kat said, summoning him with her index finger. Santana got back on the bed and laid over Kat's naked body.

"What's up, ma?" Santana asked softly, hovering over her. She pulled him into her and kissed him deeply. Their tongues met and they explored each other. Kat grabbed Santana's belt buckle, trying to gain access. Santana got lost in her kiss, he didn't want to stop, but he did to aid her in her feeble attempts. He took his shirt off showing his muscular frame, all the pushups he did at the Hickey School paid off. Kat bit her bottom lip as Santana undressed for her. The gun on his hip made her stir, but just as fast as she saw the gun, the worry vanished. Santana took the gun off his hip and sat it on the nightstand closest to them. He pulled his pants off and kicked his sneakers off, all in one motion. Kat gasped at Santana's naked body. God damn, this little nigga... Kat shook her head side to side. The size of his dick fucked her up. He was definitely going to be able to hit her pussy whenever he wanted.

"Damn, nigga. I see you." She smiled, thirsty for the dick. Santana smiled and rubbed his dick to full mass.

"Do you? What you see? Show me." He moved back towards the bed. Kat rose up and positioned herself at the end of the bed. She pulled him into her, she rubbed him as she kissed and licked his dick. Kat inserted him into her mouth and sucked him deeply. She rolled her tongue on the head of his man, driving him even crazier.

"Damn, ma." Santana exhaled. He grabbed her head, trying to guide her, but she moved out of his grasp.

"You'll have time for that, I wanna taste you right now," Kat said, trying to snatch his soul. *Damn, this bitch the truth.* He smiled and nodded in approval. Kat pulled him back towards her and guided the tip of his dick into her mouth with only her tongue. She sucked back and forth slowly, all while not losing eye contact with him. That shit was driving Santana crazy, though he held his composure. He closed his eyes and let Kat go to work. As his dick strengthened, so did her pace. Kat sucked him to her own rhythm. Santana jumped when he felt Kat's hands begin to rub his ball sack. She got the reaction she was looking for.

"Now is ya time," she spoke with a mouth full. Santana guided her head deeper on his dick and her throat adjusted to his size. When he felt the back of her throat, he began to thrust forward, trying to go as deep as he was allowed. She moaned. Kat was loving the taste of his dick. Santana could feel the pressure building in him.

"Ma, I'm bout to cum. What ... damn ... what you want me to do?" Santana asked as he fucked her face long and deep. Kat never answered, she was so gone in him, she just sucked and played with his balls. "Ahhhhh... I'm cumming, ma," Santana said as he exploded in her mouth.

Kat stopped sucking for a second, she looked into his eyes until he was done filling her up. After she was sure he was completely done, she sucked slowly, swallowing his cum down her throat. She used her hand to milk him for the rest of his sperm. She licked the tip of his dick clean and licked her lips as if she just finished one of her favorite meals. "Little Santana ain't so little no more. Damn boy, you was serious, wasn't you?" Kat sat at the end of the bed like she was going to eat him.

"Ma, you ill. I had to try. I can't front, you so bad I was satisfied with just sucking on ya pussy for you." He laughed but whether she knew it or not he was being dead ass serious.

"Well, how was your experience?" she asked him seductively.

"What! Ummmm, is all a nigga can say. This shit not over, bend that ass over. I wanna bust this dick all in ya pussy." He rubbed his dick, trying to get it back to attention. In response, Kat laid back on the bed and began rubbing her wet pussy. The sound of her pussy alone got his dick hard again. Santana moved toward Kat with his dick extended directly in front of him at attention. She followed his lead and bent over at the end of the bed. Santana rubbed his dick up and down her pussy lips, gathering her juices upon entry. He entered her slowly, pulled out and pushed back into her.

"Ohhhh, my God," Kat moaned as she pushed back on his dick. She wanted him inside her. She was geeking for the dick. Santana gained complete access and hit her slow but deep. He wanted to feel her pussy walls grip his dick.

"Fuck this pussy, Santana… Santana ... ummm." Santana picked up his pace, fucking her faster. He hit her sides, he dipped and even fucked her in circles. He was giving Kat all she wanted.

"Who pussy is this? Huh?" he asked cockily. He smacked her ass as hard as he could.

He had seen that in a porno. Kat was a freak, so he knew she probably would like that and damn, was he right. She started throwing that pussy back on him. They were both so lost in ecstasy, they didn't hear Santana's phone ring. He continued digging Kat out. His phone rang nonstop. Finally, he heard it after they attempted to switch positions. The ring tone was Darla's. Santana picked the phone up and ignored it, but before he could set it back down, she was calling back again. Something was wrong. He looked at an awaiting Kat, then at his phone. He ignored the call yet again. He climbed back on the bed with Kat. She climbed on top of him, she could sense the urgency of the call, so she wasted no time. She stuck Santana's dick inside her and rode him hard. His dick was touching cobwebs she hadn't had dusted in years. She closed her eyes grabbed his chest and threw that pussy on him. Santana grabbed Kat by her hips and matched her energy. He couldn't take too much more. The grip and wetness of her pussy had that nigga weak. Santana rubbed the fullness of her ass and straightened out. Kat knew he was on the verge of cumming. She sped up.

"Cum in this pussy, Tana. This ya pussy right? Cum in this pussy, daddy." Kat spun around so he could see his dick gripped by her pussy. She threw her pussy at Santana faster and faster. She watched as his toes curled and felt him explode deep inside her. He just laid there out of breath. Kat got up and walked to the bathroom. Santana could hear the shower turn on. He laid still for a minute, second-guessing what just happened. He had wanted to fuck Kat since he been in West Virginia, he never figured it would happen, so he left well alone. Putting Kat in a position to get money with him showed her he was something other than a child. He was grown, or he was playing grown man games at least. Kat walked out the bathroom with a wet washcloth. She walked up to Santana and wiped his dick clean from their combined juices.

"So where do we go from here?" Kat asked as she continued to wipe him clean.

"What do you mean? We still do us. Don't let this complicate shit, ma. Whenever you want me to cater to you, call me. I'm here. Unless you want this to be a one-time thing, then I have no choice but to oblige. This whole thing falls on ya call, ma," he replied. Kat sat on the bed and said nothing, it seemed as if she was lost in the thought of what she really wanted to do. Santana let her sit in her silence and began to get dressed. After putting his shirt over his head and getting his bearings together, he picked his phone up from the floor and saw he had ten missed calls from Darla. *Man, what the fuck?* Santana never received that many calls from Darla back-to-back, something was out of place. Forgetting where he was, he called Darla in concern. Darla answered her phone on the first ring.

"Tana, where are you?" Darla cried hysterically.

"I'm on the east, sweetheart. Are you good, what's good? What happened?" Santana asked, genuinely concerned.

"Somebody killed Nessy!" She was distraught and he could hear it all in her voice. She was hurting. He knew Nessy was her sister's first cousin, but they all grew up together, so she considered Nessy to be her family also. Darla, Sofiya and Nessy were more like sisters than anything. He remembered how mad Darla was at Nessy for running her mouth about the shooting with Santana. They hadn't talked since, so he understood why she felt so fucked up. She felt guilty, but she was hurt, nonetheless.

"What? How the fuck that happened?" Santana kissed Kat on the forehead. Kat could see the conversation regarding them would have to wait.

She mouthed, "Go," to Santana. Whatever he was dealing with would take precedence. Santana nodded his head in understanding. He wasn't trying to leave Kat on these terms.

"When can you pull up on me?" Darla asked. He picked his gun up off the nightstand and popped the clip out, checking the magazine. A habit he learned from his mother's paranoia.

"Now. Where are you?" he replied, tucking his Smith & Wesson into his waistband. "Hold on for a second, ma." He put the phone down and walked to Kat. "I'm sorry. I—" Santana tried to explain.

"No need. Handle ya business, baby. We good. Don't be a stranger." Kat got up and walked to the bathroom. Santana shook his head, knowing she was disappointed. He shrugged his shoulders and rushed out the door to Darla.

***

Zach and Santana pulled up to the Washington Manor complex, located near the downtown part of the city. Santana was wary about leaving his gun in the car, but with the amount of cop cars that had the block flooded he had no choice. No bullshit, the gesture even surprised Zach. He followed suit and they both put their guns in the glove box. They got out the car to find Darla. The atmosphere was wild. There were family, friends and curious onlookers everywhere. Santana spotted Darla in the middle of a crowd, holding on to her sister Sofiya. Santana could tell Sofiya was broken from Nessy's loss and his heart went out to her. He knew firsthand what it felt like to lose someone you not only considered a friend, but family.

"Come on, son. Looks like they needing us right about now," Santana said to Zach. This wasn't Zach's scene. Santana could tell that much by the look on his face. Santana walked to the crowd. "Excuse me," he asked politely. The crowd of onlookers reluctantly moved to the side to let him and Zach through. Even though they didn't know him, they knew he was a friend of Darla's. Santana walked up to Darla and Sofiya and without notice, he hugged them both. Santana's presence alone startled them. Darla looked up, meeting eyes with Santana. Her eyes were red from the constant crying.

"You alright?" Santana asked her, knowing she wasn't. He just didn't know what to say. He was honestly lost for words. Darla nodded her head up and down with strength she really didn't have. He whispered in her ear. He didn't need anyone else to hear what he had to say. "You find out who did this and I promise to end him where he stands." She knew he meant the words he spoke. Nessy had told her how he killed Breeze the day he was shot. He hugged both women tightly. "I love y'all, my nigga. I'm here. Spend time with ya people. Me and Zach gone be posted right over there." He pointed to the parking lot where Zach parked his truck. "Whenever y'all ready to leave or ease ya mind, I'm a call away."

"Okay. We love you too. Thank you for being here for me and my sister," Sofiya said, looking up from Darla's shoulder.

"Always. I got you," Santana assured them. He kissed Darla on her forehead and walked away with Zach in tow. He looked at Darla and put his hand to his ear in the gesture of a phone, reminding her to call whenever she was ready to leave. She blew him a kiss, her way of relaying her appreciation. He smiled and caught it, placing his hand over his heart. The gesture was so genuine, it took both Darla and

Sofiya by surprise. It brought a smile to their faces for the first time that night.

"Awwww. Now that nigga right there something else," Sofiya said, hugging her sister tighter.

"Both him and his mother are," was all Darla said in response.

***

Remy and Von looked on in awe as Santana interacted with Darla and Sofiya. Von didn't know Santana was tapped in with Darla and Sofiya like that. Nessy had never mentioned knowing him prior, or after the killing of his brother. That was neither here nor there now because Nessy was dead. Von didn't know if he was responsible, or just an innocent nigga in all of the bullshit, so he took the green light off his head momentarily and had one of his men observing on occasion.

"Who that nigga hugged up on Darla and them, bruh? I could have sworn I seen that nigga before," Remy asked, head tilted in thought.

"That's the lil nigga Breeze shot in the back that day he got killed," Von said painfully. Remy started snapping his fingers excitedly and pointing at Santana as he walked down Daniel Boone Drive.

"Bruh, that's the nigga that saved N.O. the night we had him coming out of Keke's house. I know I knew that face. He saw me and Lil Leek sitting near Corey Brother's, we began to creep up the street and he opened fire on us. We banged back but got the fuck outta there." Remy was hyped. He was itching to catch a body, but little did he know, so was Santana. Von rubbed his beard and pondered on his next move.

"Say less. In due time, all will be taken care of," Von assured him. But Von also knew anything Remy said or spoke of he had to take with a grain of salt, because he was a bad liar and his flaws ran deep. Von went into his pocket and dialed Torrey's burner number. It was on now. His hatred for Santana grew by the seconds. Someone had to pay for his little brother's death, and if Remy was telling the truth about the night he and Leek went on that mission, Santana was a dead man. Von looked over at Santana and Zach laughing and carrying on like there wasn't a bounty on their heads. He laughed. Von just knew he had three easy confirmed kills.

While he laughed and smiled, Santana watched the men look and gander at him and Zach. They were stupid, the emotion showed all over the men's faces. He used Zach in a way to show his weakness of being green to the situations around him. But in all reality, he was very much on point. Santana constantly nudged his hip to feel the comfort of the pistol he held there. *These niggaz got me fucked up.* He was thirsty for a nigga to try him. *When you embark, shorty, dig two graves ... this won't be an easy body to catch*, he thought as he gritted his teeth and made eye contact with Von.

Chapter 2

The rest of the night went uneventful. No one was hurt, but the feelings of those who lost Nessy Garland. Santana and Zach stayed posted in Washington Manor as promised. Haseem popped up briefly to show support for the grieving. Santana knew the city was going to be in an uproar over Nessy's murder. Especially the DT's. Everyone knew who and what Nessy was, but the manner in which she was killed was gruesome and overbearing, for the most part. Santana could see Darla would need him, now more than ever. And he promised himself he would be present when she needed him most. Darla was someone his mother held dear to her heart, though his love had already transcended Simfany's. Now it was his time to step up and show he could be a good friend in her time of mourning.

As all the women cried for Nessy and the men grouped up as if all hell would break loose, the reaper lurked in the shadows, waiting to scratch names off his list of revenge. Fatty Man walked away satisfied with the outcome of the situation. Now, it was on to the next. There were a few souls that he still needed to claim. "These bitch ass niggaz thought I was gone just fucking leave. Ha ha ha ha ha," Fatty laughed to himself as he hit the cut and disappeared into the darkness.

Fatty Man held visual outside of Remy's mother's house. It was a house he knew all too well. He had played tag, lost his virginity, fought and boxed with the homies there, this was the house they had all really became men at. But as the years passed each man grew differently and grew apart. Fatty Man shook the memories away, he didn't need to concentrate on that right now in this moment. His mission was to crush Remy's bitch ass and get on to the next. After killing Nessy, he was going to leave Charleston for a few days, but decided against it. He went to the place he had been calling home for the last month or so, he changed clothing and slid back to the streets. He sat posted only a few doors away from Remy's most beloved family member. He sparked a cigarette and inhaled deeply. Fatty Man was stressed, nervous, anxious and paranoid.

The Naked Lady ecstasy pills he popped after killing Nessy was running his mind rabid. He was fighting the demons within himself. At times, he thought he could see Breeze's face looking back at him when he looked into the mirror. He was tripping, that much he knew for sure. All Fatty Man could hear were the words Nessy spoke in the basement. Her words shot daggers to his heart. He knew he was supposed to aid and assist his brother. The stories Fatty told Von on multiple occasions were fabricated or false. At no point did he and Breeze talk about escape routes or splitting up after the skit. In all truth, the men had no plan whatsoever. He couldn't tell Von that then, and he for sure wasn't going to tell Von that while he had a gun pointed in his face. Fatty cursed Breeze daily for his careless actions. He always told Breeze not to be motivated by emotion, it could be the death of them. Fatty Man repeated that to Breeze on many occasions, more than once.

He always said that, trying to beat reality into Breeze Saunders' head, the most impulsive being he had ever met. Everything Breeze did was off pure emotion. All the people Breeze terrorized throughout the city was done strictly from impulsive or just erratic behavior. Fatty smiled. Breeze was a loose cannon, but he loved that nigga more than he loved himself some time.

Now as he sat and pondered on the truth in his heart, it broke daily. He watched his brother get shot in the face and he froze. The image alone brought tears to Fatty's eyes. He wasn't mentally or physically prepared to be a part of that. Any time he had ever gone on a mission, he felt like it was a no brainer he would come out on top. But not this time, and it cost him a great friend for the lack of their preparation. Though Nessy fabricated some parts, the majority of her story stood firm. The truth as he knew, he had bitched up and let his man from the sand box die in vain.

Fatty Man dropped his head at yet another thought of Breeze's untimely demise. He knew he had to redeem himself, and he had to redeem himself fast. The headlights that crept up the street caught him by surprise. Fatty slid down into his seat, trying to conceal his presence. Being seen wasn't an option. Fatty peeked over the dashboard and instantly got excited. Remy was pulling into his mother's driveway. Fatty smiled and popped his clip out to make sure his gun was fully loaded. When it indicated it was, he popped the magazine back into his gun. He opened his door and made his way across the street. The shadows concealed Fatty as he ran alongside the parked cars. When he got to the driveway where Remy was parked, he stationed himself behind the parked car on bended knee. He wanted Remy to get out the car so he wouldn't be exposed to the eye of a lurking witness.

When Fatty Man didn't hear Remy exit the vehicle, he looked around from his hiding spot, Remy was in the car rolling what seemed to be a blunt while talking on the phone. *Fuck it*, Fatty thought. He pulled his ski mask down over his face and rose from his knee. The light that illuminated the driveway would be a problem Fatty knew, but he still didn't care. Remy had to die. Remy was too lost in what he was doing to see Fatty creeping up behind him, gun in hand. Fatty wasted no time, he fired into the car, hitting Remy in his shoulder. The blood from the wound sprayed against the window. Fatty then ran up to the driver's side door and opened fire, shooting Remy in his face, torso and neck, until his clip indicated he had no more bullets to give.

"Bitch ass nigga!" Fatty said and spit into the car. The scream that came from behind him pierced his ears. He turned, gun raised, ready to end the noise. When he pulled the trigger, his gun clicked. He forgot his magazine was empty. He looked Remy's mother in her eyes for a split second before he took off. He ran full sprint to his parked car. He could hear the sirens nearing the scene. He needed to get the fuck on and fast. Fatty put the rental into drive and sped off the block. After he got a safe distance away, he pulled the mask from his face. Another soul had been claimed, the city of Charleston was drowning by the day.

***

Santana laid across his bed. He was exhausted from the day's events. His mind played back all the events that had taken place in the last few months. It'd been a wild year so far, and the damn year just began for the most part. He closed his eyes and inhaled deeply, taking in the fresh conditioned air that circulated the room. Through all that was going on, he hadn't had time to relax. He hadn't had time to enjoy the fruits of his labor. Santana shrugged the thought off and pulled his phone out. "You can sleep when you die, nigga." Santana loved the lyrics by Young Jeezy. That shit resonated deeply inside him. He texted Darla, he wanted to make sure all was well her way.

Awaiting her reply, Santana got up from his bed and logged into his *MySpace* page. He read about Nessy being in a better place and all the shit that came with death. What caught him by surprise were the "Rest In Paradise, Remy" posts everywhere. He didn't know who Remy was, but the whole city of Charleston seemed to be hurt over his demise.

He pulled his phone out to call Darla but was interrupted by a call from Haseem.

"What's good, my G?" Santana answered on the first ring.

"Shit… chillin, cuz, where you and Zach been?"

"We chilled with Nessy peoples last night. Paying respect, why, what's good? What you got on ya agenda today?" Santana wasn't trying to rush him off the phone, but all in the same breath, he wanted Haseem to get on with what he wanted. He had other shit on his mind that took precedence.

"You were with whose peoples?" Haseem asked to make sure he heard Santana right.

"Nessy's. Why you acting all extra for? My nigga, get to the point you trying to make. I got shit I have to do." Santana was getting irritated. One thing Haseem did too much of was fucking play. No matter the mood, all Haseem wanted to do was play and joke. Majority of the time, Santana had no issue with Haseem' s humor, now was just not the time.

"Oh… okay, bruh… that's how you bringing shit? Ight, bet. Anyway, shorty was the one that spread the rumors about you smoking the little nigga Breeze in front of Shop-N-Go. Why the fuck you consoling her family? That's weird shit, bruh." Nothing about Haseem's demeanor indicated any humor. He was dead ass serious, because he was lost. Santana looked at the phone and laughed. *You got it, son ...* those were the only words that came to mind.

"First off, my G, what… you calling yourself checking me about something?" Santana asked with an obvious attitude.

"Nah, bruh. I was just asking—" Haseem tried to explain.

"Wasn't you out there with us consoling shorty peoples?" Santana vaguely asked. He was lost. "You know what, my nigga? This not us. How you living?" Santana changed the subject. The last thing he wanted to do was argue with his nigga about some shit that had no true importance in his life.

"Shit bruh, I'm good. I went O.T. last night and one of my cluck's wanted to spend a few hundred. I tried calling Zach but didn't get an answer. You want the play?" Haseem asked. Santana thought about it, he was being lazy. The money sounded good. Damn ...

"Aight, who I have to meet?"

"Doug." Haseem laughed.

"The old army nigga?" Santana sighed.

"Yeah ..." Haseem busted out laughing.

"Oh, yeah ... ohhh you think you funny. Now, you know I don't mix with that weird ass nigga. His old ass be tripping. Man, how much he speaking bout?" He wasn't excited, that's for sure.

"He said he got four hundred. He with his people's Gary and them." Santana knew Gary as being the source behind the money. He was the one Santana wanted to get ahold of. It was rumored his family was either owners or connected to owners of a few oil companies.

"Is Gary supposed to be there?" Santana asked.

"Shit, I don't know, for real. Bruhhhhh...are you going to meet the nigga or not?" Haseem asked, irritated. Santana heard the frustration in his voice and laughed at him.

"Finally, you can feel my pain." Santana clowned. "Let me know where to meet him at."

"Bet. I'm bout to hit him. I'll text you the information." Haseem hung up. Santana dialed Darla's number. She answered after a few rings.

"Hey," Darla answered the phone.

"How you feeling, ma? How sis holding up?" Santana asked, concerned.

"Shit, for real, she holding her emotions to herself. You know I thought about what you said the other night about the person who killed Nessy, and I feel like this isn't your or my issue to handle. That girl had a lot of shit with her, and I wouldn't feel right if I let you either harm yourself or your future behind her bullshit. As you know, I wasn't on the best terms with her before her death. When she put that shit out there about you being the nigga that ended Breeze, it not only pissed me off, but it baffled me. Every account about that situation I have heard was you was shot first. What do people expect out of a situation like that?"

Santana loved the fact that she was so green to the violence and bullshit. That to him meant she had a little purity still in her. "Whether that be the case or not, she should have kept her mouth shut. I called her on many occasions, Messy Nessy. I love you and your mother genuinely, me and Melquan both do. We are very grateful for y'all and to put you in a situation of that kind is not what I will do. I hope you can understand that. The thought alone lets me know where we stand," Darla said lovingly.

"That's up to you, ma. I told you on more than one occasion I have you and ya people's if needed. Listen to me on this though, if any harm ever comes to you or ya child, I will do what I see fit. Can we agree on that?" Santana asked. His phone chimed at that moment, indicating he had a new message.

"I can agree on that. Mr. Santana, it sounds like you are beginning to like me. Is that what I'm hearing from you?" Santana's face turned red as if she was standing right on front of him.

"You okay. You sexy and all," he teased.

"Ummm...I know that's right." Darla became silent.

"What?" Santana asked.

"Nothing, I just haven't had a nigga that fuck with me like you do, without wanting something in return. You and your mother are a different breed of people though. I ask myself... how did I get so lucky to meet y'all? Ya momma has helped me in so many ways, repaying her is something that would be impossible. And you, the way you look at me and the way you interact with my son blows my mind. You are the epitome of a real nigga."

"Well now, Ms. Darla, it sounds like you are beginning to like me," he joked with her.

"But what if I am, is that crossing a line for us?" Darla asked seriously. Santana realized it was no longer laughs and giggles, these were real feelings talking.

"Look Darla, I pride myself on being a good person through and through. I've done my bullshit in life and have my own demons. Some of those things I sleep and have peace with, while others hit my mind from time to time. Do I like you in a romantic sense? Absolutely! You are beautiful, intelligent, a great mother, for real. I can keep going on about the pros you bring to the table. Yet, I have remained a friend because sometimes, that's the best people can bring to the table. It gets complicated after the intimate part of shit. I fuck with you the long way, and I want to be able to hold a friendship with you forever. I don't want to take you through the bullshit, beauty. I've never really been in a real relationship. I was in one when I was younger. That's been a while though." Santana tried to explain as easy he could without putting her down. Did he want to be with a girl like Darla? Fuck yeah. But he wasn't into ruining her or her son's life.

"Oh. Okay. Well, what if I wanted to try. Like take it slow. if I don't like what I see or vice versa, we can pull away and still remain friends. How bout that? Can that work?" *Damn*, Santana thought. She sounded so sexy. She was so sexy.

"If you're willing to give me the time and patience, how can I say no? But before we decide this, I wanna talk to you and let you know what I have going on in ya city." Santana's phone chimed again.

"I'm good with that. What you have going on tonight? Can you slide this way?" Darla asked.

"I have to go handle something for Heern and then I'm free. I can come through there some time after that. How that sound?" Santana got up from the computer, knocking his laziness away.

"That sound good to me. I'll be waiting. Be careful. I love you."

"I love you too, beauty." Santana hung up from the phone call and checked his messages.

Haseem had hit him twice, one message pertained to Doug and the other pertained to the Remy nigga he kept reading about everywhere. He made a mental note to speak on dude and why he was of any importance. Santana grabbed his gun from the nightstand next to his bed and put it on his hip. He went into his walk-in closet where his fire safe was located and grabbed two already bagged up 8-balls. He put them in his pocket, turned his light off before leaving his home. He hopped in his mother's truck and drove to the corner of Lewis and Beauregard. He parked and surveyed the scene for a second. He texted Haseem to let him know he was there, to let him know what the next move was. Santana was wary about the meet, so he took the Glock .27 off his hip and laid it across his lap. The windows of Simfany's Tahoe were tinted so he wasn't worried about anyone being able to see who the driver was of the SUV. He waited patiently for Haseem to text back. Santana was growing impatient. His phone finally chimed, indicating he had a new message. He opened his phone and read the message.

Doug scary ass sitting in the gold Corolla in front of his house with Gary. He is waiting on you.

This was one of the reasons he hated fucking with Doug's paranoid ass. Santana was one to call the kettle black. He sighed and hopped out of the truck. Forgetting that he sat his gun on his lap, it hit the ground. Lucky for him it was dark outside, and the street was deserted. He shook his head. He picked his gun up, placed it on his hip and looked down the street for a Gold Toyota Corolla. When he spotted it, he jogged to the awaiting car. When he got to the car, he knocked on the window to be let in. When he opened the passenger side door, a cloud of smoke rose out of the car.

"Nigga, what the fuck! Why would you start smoking that shit in the car before I got here?" Santana was irate.

"I didn't know you would be here so soon. I do apologize. Just leave the door open for a second," Doug said smugly. Santana realized he was holding his breath trapping the smoke inside his lungs. After a few seconds, Doug blew the smoke out the driver's side window. Santana looked in the back seat and saw it was empty. *I thought this nigga said Gary was with this nigga*, Santana thought, finding it odd, but let the thought go as fast as it came. Santana sat in the passenger seat and closed the door.

"Spin the block, I don't like to sit still," Santana said as he reached into his pocket and pulled out the two 8-balls of crack. Doug did as he was told.

"So, how much do you have?"

"I have the four hundred dollars, but I should have more before the night is over. Will you still be good?" Doug asked as he pulled back onto his block.

"Just hit Heern and I will come back and take care of you. That's cool with you son?"

"Fine by me, youngster," Doug agreed, in anticipation of getting his crack. Santana handed Doug the two plastic baggies and Doug handed Santana the money. They both checked their possessions to make sure all was well. After Santana counted his money, he opened the door.

"You good?" Santana asked.

"Yes, thank you very much. I'll hit—" the crack of a gun exploding deafened the still night. Santana ducked into the car as he pulled his Glock off his hip. He couldn't see where the shooter or shooters were coming from. He just raised his gun from his crouched position and fired out the back windows. The bullets made contact with the body of the Corolla at rapid successions. Santana could hear the bullets flying past his head, hitting the door frame in front of him. He shot until his clip was emptied. Santana hastily ejected his magazine and entered another. The shooting had stopped, but he rose with caution. His heart was beating out of his chest. Looking both up and down the street, he saw no signs of any shooters. Santana could see people peeking through the blinds of their homes, trying to see what was going on. Santana was shaken, he looked down and saw that his shirt was covered in blood. He put his gun up and checked his body for bullet wounds. He felt none. He then looked into the car and saw Doug covered in blood, groaning in pain. Santana had to think fast. *Think nigga, think ...*

"Move over to this side, Doug, I got you. I'll drop you off at the entrance of the hospital. I'll give you ya dope back when you come out that bitch. If you make it."

"I'm okay. You hit me in the shoulder when you crouched down. We good. Take me inside. I can fix this." Doug coughed. Santana looked at Doug like he lost his mind. He helped him out the car and up the stairs to his home. "Go before the police come. Thank you. You saved our lives back there." Gary and a female were waiting at the door, faces full of concern as Doug walked into his house wounded.

Santana didn't waste time. He hopped off the side of the stoop and ran up the street to his mother's Tahoe. Santana hopped in and sped off. The games had begun, and Santana knew he had cheated death yet again. *Fuck! These niggaz got me fucked up.* He knew he could possibly be blitzed from all angles once the money was put on their heads. He took note mentally that the shooter or shooters weren't for the walk down. They were looking for an easy body. One he promised himself they wouldn't get from him.

Chapter 3

Detective Ramos walked through the precinct in stride. He had finally gotten the surveillance video from Windsor Valley on the questioned date of the murders. He should have listened to his late partner. He had embarked on a surreal connection of murder and mayhem. Ramos sat down at his desk and entered the DVD into his computer. The camera he requested was positioned on the main street in the complex, where Simfany and Santana resided. Ramos fast forwarded the footage until he was able to see movement from the address his murder suspect occupied. At the early hour of 8:00 am, Santana could be seen running from his home with no shirt on, chasing a female with dreads. The conversation was brief, Ramos fast forwarded to another form of movement. Only minutes after Santana ran back into the home, Simfany made her first appearance on the video. Ramos could see her jumping into an SUV-style truck.

He grew excited as he waited on Santana to follow, but no one left the home with Simfany Vasquez. Ramos was now confused. He fast forwarded the footage further into the day. The next activity came from a cherry red Caprice. The Caprice pulled up to the residence and waited for a few minutes before Ramos saw Santana walk out the home and get into the car. Ramos looked at the time Santana was picked up. It read 10:43 am. He paused the video and checked his file for the time the 911 call came in from Monument Street. "Oh shit," was all he could say when he realized it was impossible for Santana to be the killer of the two deceased men. At the time he was getting into the Caprice, only minutes later the murders occurred in Baltimore City. Ramos knew it was impossible to make it to Monument Street from Windsor Valley in ten minutes, to commit the murders he was now wanted for.

He jotted down notes in his pad, made a copy of the video before he left and went and saw his superior. He didn't know at this point who he was fighting for. But he knew the killer or killers would still be out there if Santana went to jail for a crime he didn't commit. The brazen kills that connected the city's and county's drug trade scared many. The war that started after the killing of the five victims was epic. And in order to find out what started the war, he knew he needed to find out who the real killer was of the two men on Monument and Port. Ironically, the steps he took to get him to this point had pushed him back. He was content with that, he was never into ruining lives. He picked his phone up and dialed his superior's number.

"Davis," his boss answered.

"This is Ramos, I have some important evidence regarding the Santana Vasquez case. May I come up and talk with you?" Ramos waited for his response. He hated the man and Davis knew it.

"Yes. I have time," Captain Davis replied annoyingly. Ramos said nothing further. He hung the phone up, grabbed his newly found evidence and made his way to Davis's office.

***

Tez-Mo cried hard as he watched his baby sister being lowered into the ground. As the oldest, he knew he had fucked up in protecting them all, even Kevin. His brother loved and looked up to him so much, he followed his footsteps in every way possible. He felt the guilt tremendously. Tez looked from his mother to his brother, then to his precious niece. He took Sasha's death hard. He wasn't in the right mind set to seek revenge as of yet. Tez knew all too well about killing in an emotional state. Mistakes were bound to happen in that instance. So, he'd let his mind clear as much as possible before he rose to the occasion and slid on behalf of his beloved. Tez wiped his eyes and grabbed his sobbing niece. Tez-Mo bent down in front of Diamond and looked her in the eyes, he wiped her tears away from her swollen eyes.

"I love you, mommas. I always want you to know that. You hear me?" Diamond nodded her head up and down. Tez-Mo grabbed Diamond and hugged her tightly. When he opened his eyes from the well-needed hug, he saw a car he had recognized from earlier in the day circle the cemetery. He rose off his feet slowly, he wanted to warn Kevin about his suspicion.

"Go to ya Nana, beauty." Tez squeezed Diamond's shoulder lightly. Diamond did as she was told. Tez, never taking his eye off of the gray sedan, began to walk to Kevin. The caravan's side door slid open and three men hopped out, guns in hand. Tez pulled his gun at the sight of the men and fired.

"Get down!" Tez screamed. He fired in hopes of backing the men away from his family. The three assailants fired back, overpowering Tez tremendously. When Kev realized what was going on, he joined the gunfight.

"Shorty, what the fuck!" Kev yelled from behind the tombstone.

"You go left, I'm gone go right. We need to split these niggaz up and do ya work. I love you, bro," Tez said and took off to the right, firing his pistol at the men. Kev took a deep breath and ran to his mother and niece.

"Get the fuck outta here. I'm going to shoot. You and Diamond run until you can no longer hear these shots. You hear me?" They both nodded. Kev rose from his hiding spot and fired his gun.

"Go!" he yelled. Ms. Nancy and Diamond took off up the hill and out of sight. Now that the two most prolific people in his life were out of harm's way, he advanced with each shot.

"These niggaz gotta die." Tez-Mo and Kev were no match for the assault rifles the men had, and they knew that but were still willing to die behind the cause. The sirens sounded in the distance, changing the game for all involved. The three shooters fired a few more shots and hopped into their van and sped off. Tez-Mo and Kev chased the car up the road firing their guns into the caravan. Once the van hit the corner, they stopped running. Kev bent over to catch his breath. He was tired.

"We don't have time to rest, lor bro. One time around the corner," Tez said as he pulled on Kevin's shirt.

I love you, sis, Kev thought as they ran away deep into the cemetery.

***

Ramos laid his and Lawson's notes along the table of Captain Davis's office. The look the captain gave Ramos was one of pure anguish. The falling out they had after the death of Lawson took a toll on the department as a whole. The captain blamed Ramos for Lawson's untimely demise. Ramos never could understand why, but he did. At first, he was hurt about the whole ordeal. Davis was a person he used to consider a friend. A great one at that. He shook the thoughts out his head and got to the task at hand. If Davis hated him now, he would probably hate him more after this conversation. *Fuck it, here goes nothing,* he thought.

"So, I was going through the notes of Detective Lawson as he freelanced, worked the Vasquez/Parks case—" Davis cut him off.

"Stop saying that shit, he wasn't freelancing. He was doing his duty as a great detective!" Captain Davis shouted.

"My apologies, sir... and as he was your friend, he was certainly mine also. But the truth of this is, he was working under his own personal agenda. Why? Because he felt it was more to the story than a close case of Simfany Vasquez not knowing her shooter. He compiled a lot of evidence from a few conspiracies, which at best could all be circumstantial." Ramos looked down and pulled a noted page from Lawson's folder. Spilled coffee stained most of the page, but his writing was still legible. He handed it to his captain.

"That page confirms and links Simfany Vasquez to the infamous Carlos Rivera. As you read, Lawson noted after the meeting, a figure came from out of the shadows with a modified style rifle and fired on him. He barely escaped with his life. Whether that was or was not related to the meeting that took place, it draws concern. So, I continued to search for the connections of all the people he was investigating. After a few weeks, I went to Windsor Valley and requested the video surveillance of the day all the murders occurred, and this is what I found. May I?" Ramos asked, DVD in hand. Davis said nothing, but moved out his way so he could enter the disc into his computer. When the surveillance picture popped up, he began to explain.

"Okay, this is the home and residence of Simfany and Santana Vasquez. At 8:13 am, Ms. Vasquez left the home in a SUV, but not the same make, model or color of the SUV involved in the killings on Monument Street. Now, as you can see, there is no other movement in or out of the home." At that moment, he realized he didn't get the camera footage that could show the patio side of the homes. He continued anyway. "Now, as you see, this cherry red Caprice pulls up, holding unknown occupants. Are you with me?" Davis agreed smugly.

"What are you trying to get at, Ramos? Goddamn! Get to the point." Ramos could tell Captain Davis was getting irritated. He didn't really give a fuck about how bored or irritated he was. This shit was important.

"Okay, now at 10:43, you can see Santana Vasquez leaving and getting into the cherry-colored Caprice. Do you see what time that says?"

Davis leaned up and stated the time. "It's 10:43 am." Ramos dug through his file.

"Now, the time stamp from the 911 call came in at 10:36 am. We can even say it came in ten minutes late. It would still be impossible for Santana Vasquez to be the shooter on Monument Street that fatal morning. So that means there is another killer out there. The hunch I have is this Blood gang got into something dangerous with either Brian 'Byrd' Parks or his little brother Jimmy 'Jimdog' Parks, ending in bloodshed. Sir, if you look at the people killed and how it is all connected, there is no way we can overlook this. I looked up Hassan Jamir for Lawson the same morning this all happened. He lied and told me he was just trying to connect some dots. I wasn't aware he was following behind these figures. Anyway, the person Jamir was most connected to, besides his gang, was Brian 'Byrd' Parks." He let that settle a second.

"Okay, look at this." He pulled the beginning notes from Lawson's file folder. "Simfany Vasquez was a known associate of Brian 'Byrd' Parks. After Parks was found in the Harbor, Vasquez was shot in her home on Edmondson Avenue only weeks after. After that her son Santana sought revenge by shooting Jimmy 'Jimdog' Parks. The noise died down for months. Now the gang had their own issues going on in-house. A man by the name Narvel 'Blaze' Harris turned state's evidence in a murder case. Harris and his mother were later gunned down in the Harford Commons sector of Edgewood. As the notes I have state, Lawson did research connecting the gang to both Parks brothers. That's the only connection I can make that can connect the bullets at all three scenes. This is a shit show. But the reason I felt we needed to have this conversation is because of the murder warrant that is out on Santana Vasquez. Cap, I don't want to let this shit go either, but I'm not into letting innocent people go to jail for crimes that they didn't commit. I just hope I have you on board with—" Davis cut his words short.

"Leave me the tape, give me some time to review all possibilities and I'll call you back in here. Good work, Ramos."

"Thank you, Cap." Ramos handed Davis the DVD and the combined files. Without another word spoken, he walked out the office. He hoped Davis did what needed to be done with the information he gave him, because if he didn't, he would go to a higher source. And he prayed he wouldn't have to do that. He could only imagine the backlash that would cause. He took an oath to be an overseer of justice and he would do just that. Ramos walked out the front door of the precinct and lit a cigarette. He inhaled, letting the nicotine grab ahold of his lungs for a short second, then exhaled. The stress temporarily relieved itself. As he leaned against the railing, his radio sounded. The operator had just put all cars in the vicinity onto a shots' fired call at a cemetery in the West Baltimore sector of the city. Ramos threw his cigarette down and sprinted to his car.

"Dispatch, 3045. I'm in route, 10-4," Ramos called into the radio. Ramos wasted no time and pulled into traffic. The city was getting out of control. They were only four months into the year, and the murder rate was proving to be one of the deadliest since the early 90s. Ramos sped into New Cathedral Cemetery and parked behind the other patrol cars. The scene was crazy. He walked up the grass to the roped-off crime scene. The K-9 unit tried to follow a scent he knew wouldn't amount to nothing.

"What happened here?" Ramos flashed his credentials to the lone officer.

"What the witnesses are saying is, a family was in the middle of burying a loved one and a van pulled up and started firing into the crowd." Ramos looked around. He could see close to a couple hundred shell casings. There were some in the grass where he stood, and the majority of them near the drive. The placing of the shell casings told its own story. There was a gunfight between the family and the assailants.

"Do you know the name of the family that was burying their loved one?" Ramos walked towards the grave and was astonished at what he saw. The casket that was being lowered into the ground had been flipped onto its side, spilling the body from its final resting place.

"We need to find out who this family is now! Do you not see this?" The officer walked over to the hole in the ground and looked at Sasha's corpse as if he'd seen shit like that on a regular basis. He looked at Ramos as if he was tripping.

"Why the fuck you looking stupid like that? What, you must see shit like this all the time huh?"

"No, but she is already dead," the officer answered nonchalantly. Ramos shook his head and walked over to the program director.

"Can I please have the name of the deceased?" Ramos asked politely. His head was spinning from the thought alone. The botched shooting was bold to say the least.

"If I'm not mistaken, the deceased woman's name was a ... Sasha Brooks." The name stopped him dead in his tracks. That shit sent chills down his body. He had heard about the shooting at Nancy Brooks' home in Harford County. What he didn't know was that a dead body was the product of that shooting. And now here he stood looking into the grave of the late Sasha Brooks. With two known killers as brothers, the city would bleed daily. He lit a cigarette and sat on the nearest tombstone. He wasn't going to do shit about this one, because whoever disrespected the Brooks family in that manner, deserved death.

***

Kev sped down route 40, Washington Park his destination. Kev was in the zone, he weaved in and out of traffic like a NASCAR driver.

"Damn shorty, slow the fuck down! I'm not trying to get pulled before we get to the Park, lor nigga. You trippin', lor bro," Tez said, dropping the choppa from his lap trying to hold on.

"Nigga, fuck you mean? I want to catch these niggaz."

"Catch who?" Tez was confused. Kev looked at him, face serious as a muthafucker.

"Fuck you mean? The nigga who shot our sister's fucking funeral up!" Kev cried. He was hurt. He couldn't even bury his sister in peace.

"I'm not tripping on catching them niggaz, per se. There are no rules, Ru. Don't get the game fucked up, if we do find out who did this, they will die. That's not what I'm tripping on at this point, Kev. What I do know is you better get ya shit together, because all that crying and emotional shit lor nigga, this not the time for that. I can't lose you because you wanna run around on some emotional shit. You copy, nigga?" Tez said calmly as he loaded the choppa to its capacity. Kev wiped his face. He knew his brother was right. He had been an emotional wreck since he lost Sasha. The hurt he felt inside his body was torturing his soul. Kev blamed himself for his sister's demise. He slowed the car to a reasonable speed. Kev knew he needed to get his emotions in check. What Tez didn't know about his little brother was, Kev was ready to leave the world anyway. Between the drugs he snorted on a daily basis and the loss of all the loved ones close to him, he was losing his mind. He focused his mind on the mission at hand.

"Ru, you sure you ready to do this?" Tez-Mo asked as he read the sign on the way across the bridge into Washington Park.

"On dead homies," Kev responded.

"Say less." Tez looked around, the complex was deserted for the most part. When Tez spotted a woman walking, bags in hand, he smiled.

"Pull in here, bro." Kev did as his brother asked.

"I'll be back, hold my back. Make sure no surprises come my way." Tez wrapped his maroon flag around his face.

"I love you, nigga," Tez said before he got out.

"I love you too, shorty," Kev replied, confused at the terms of endearment. Tez hopped out the car and walked up the block as if he belonged. *They're gone feel this one.* He laughed to himself as he approached the woman on the phone.

Tijuana walked through "The Park," enjoying the breeze of the spring air, she laughed at Drew as he talked shit to her.

"Cuz, where are you? You been gone for a hour with ya goofy ass." He laughed through the other end of the phone.

"Shut ya ass up, you should have went and got this shit, with ya lor lazy ass. I'm the pregnant one by the way, you do know that, right?" Tijuana said playfully.

"I know, sis, that's why you the best ever." Tijuana looked up as she rounded the corner in the attempt to cut through the complex. The figure she saw walking behind her in the neighborhood was surely out of place.

"Drew, come out here. I'm coming through the cut on Hamilton and it's a lor nigga out here walking around with a maroon-colored bandana on his face. That's some gang shit, ain't it?"

"What! Listen, I'm coming now. When I hang up, walk faster to my spot. Sis, as soon as you can see the lobby door, take off. You hear me?" Tijuana instantly got scared. The tone in Drew's voice told her the nigga behind her was probably on bullshit.

"Yeah," she said in a tremble. Drew hung up and immediately grabbed his Glock .17 off the dresser. He didn't have time to get dressed. He slipped his feet into a pair of sneakers and ran out the door.

"Shorty, can I holla at you for a second?" Tez-Mo called out to Tijuana.

Tijuana continued to walk up the street as if she didn't hear him.

"Excuse me, shorty, can I holla at you?" Tez asked one more time. Tijuana walked faster through the cut, trying to make it to a building, any building.

"Bitch, if you don't stop, I will kill you!" Tez-Mo finally exclaimed. Tijuana dropped the bags she had in her hands and took off. Tez-Mo smiled and lifted the AK-47. *It's broad daylight, he wouldn't try no dumb shit,* Tijuana thought as she tried to outrun her attacker. The explosion from the gun made her jump, she ran faster. The gun sounded off again, but this time it felt as if someone had pushed her. Tijuana lost her balance and fell face first to the ground. She tried to get up so she could run again, but found she wasn't able to. Tijuana rolled over and felt around her body for any injuries, when her fingers ran over her stomach, she felt the wet place and panicked. Tijuana couldn't breathe, she was having trouble concentrating. Her body began to numb up, Tijuana cried. "My babies ... Why me, God? Why me?" Tijuana's body jerked from another bullet caving her torso. Tez-Mo stood over her and hit Tijuana in her chest three more times, ending her time on earth.

"Bitch!" Tez-Mo said as he walked away. Tez was done playing with niggaz. If it was up to him, it would be a funeral daily in Washington Park. When Tez rounded the corner, his peripheral vision saw a crowd begin to form. A shot whizzed by his head. *Oh shit*, he thought as he ducked and turned around in the same motion. He saw Drew running his way. Tez raised the AK and squeezed a three-round burst. Drew ducked behind the dumpsters closest to him. Tez stood still for a second, he was ready to send another soul to hell. The screeching of burnt tires pulling behind him took his eye off Drew. Tez-Mo didn't hesitate, he turned and squeezed his choppa. The bullet lodged into the car, he was ready to fire again, but looked into the car and saw Kevin ducked low. When Kev knew Tez recognized who it was, he reached across the seat and opened the passenger side door.

"Get the fuck in, shorty!" Kev yelled from the driver's side window. The shot that hit the car sent Kev back into the car. Drew rose from behind the dumpster and squeezed his Glock at Tez-Mo. Tez raised the AK to his shoulder and shot back. Neither man hit anything but metal. Kev put the car in park and joined his brother's side.

"Let's go end this nigga," Tez demanded.

"No bro, let's fucking go!" Kev pulled on his brother's sleeve. At that opportunity, Drew came from behind of the dumpster and tried to run closer. Before he had the chance to get stationed behind a car, Kev raised his weapon and let that bitch bark, hitting Drew in his shoulder and chest.

Fuck! Drew thought as he kneeled behind the car. He popped his magazine out and the indicator read seven more shells left. He peeked through the window of the car and saw the brothers were advancing to the spot he was at. "Fuck it!" he told himself as he rose from behind the car. He aimed at Kev, the more experienced shooter, and fired. Drew's breathing was labored from the wound to his chest. Kev ducked and kept walking towards Drew. Tez shot, hitting Drew in his arm.

"Arrrggghhhh!" Drew yelled. He rose from behind the car and squeezed the rest of the bullets he had in the direction of Tez-Mo. Drew knew he was about to die, but he was okay with that. As long as he stood for Tijuana, he was cool with that. He was ready for the reaper to take his soul and send him to hell. Drew was going in and out of consciousness. When he came to, he saw his little niggaz Peedi and Rocc running up Hamilton, guns banging. The flame from the guns was constant and comforting. The sight of his brothers gave Drew hope. All he could think about was going to sleep. He was growing tired. He heard no sounds. He could see the guns firing but couldn't hear the shots. Drew closed his eyes and fell into darkness.

Tez-Mo and Kev returned fire as they backed up and hopped back into the car. Kev floored the gas as he turned onto Old Post Road. Tez raised the gun out the window and fired on the two men until he was no longer able.

"Wooooooo!" Tez hollered. His heart was racing from the action. He didn't think it would have gone down like that. He looked over at Kev with pride all in his face and smiled. "Now, that's how you shoot!" Tez laughed as he mimicked Will Smith in *Bad Boys II*.

Kev looked over at his brother and laughed.

"Nigga, you a fucking nut."

"Tell me something we all don't know." Tez laughed sinisterly. "Fuck them crab ass niggaz. Tell them niggaz pick them bodies off the ground." Tez reached into the glove box and pulled out a pre-rolled blunt, something he learned from his little nigga Santana. He sparked the blunt and inhaled deeply, easing his soul. The weed closed in and around his body, easing the tension. He took another pull on the blunt and passed it to his brother.

"I'm good, shorty. Let me get to where we need to be first," Kev said as he kept looking into the rear-view mirror to make sure he wasn't being followed.

"Say less, shorty. Say less." Tez leaned his chair back and closed his eyes.

Chapter 4

Simfany paced back and forth through her living room. The thought of her son being harmed yet again had her on edge. Darla and her son were present so she couldn't talk as freely as she wanted to.

"Ma, sit down," Santana said. The glare she gave him silenced him almost instantly. Darla laughed. She loved the fact that Santana respected his mother so much. It was definitely a turn on.

"What you laughing at, Mommy?" Melquan asked his mother. Simfany stopped and looked at Melquan and winked. The innocence of the child soothed her mood out a little. Not being able to discuss the situation at hand was aggravating her. She smiled at Melquan and spoke.

"Come here, big boy. What you been doing today? How was ya day in school?" Melquan smiled, loving the attention.

"Goooodddddd, Ms. Simfany, and how was ya day, Pretty Lady?" Melquan smiled innocently. Hearing those words softened her heart to the core.

"Awwww, my day has been great. Thank you for asking, handsome." Simfany walked over to Melquan and reached out her arms. "Come here, handsome." Melquan ran into her arms.

"Auntie, you so pretty," he said and kissed her cheek. Simfany smiled big, she looked up and saw Darla's lips scrunched up. She laughed.

"What? I know you ain't jelly?" Simfany joked.

41

"Ain't nobody jealous, with ya beautiful self." Darla rolled her neck playfully.

"Because I was about to say, how you got Santana ass acting...Hmmmph...That shit must be good."

"Ma! Melquan is present. And for the record, with ya nosey self, we haven't done no shit like that—"

"Yet!" Darla jumped in. They all laughed. Melquan looked around in confusion. That made them laugh even harder. The moment was of laughter and smiles, but they all knew nothing was a joke. Someone just had tried to kill Santana, but for the sake of exposing her son to the drama, Darla asked for the conversation to be talked about at a later time. Simfany understood pieces of her decision in bringing him with her. Simfany knew that look Darla wore so often. She was in love. It was something about Santana that kept the hearts of the women he graced. She smiled internally as it seemed history was repeating itself. She could see her and Dracula in Darla and Santana. Simfany rocked back and forth instinctively as she held Melquan. Melquan stirred in her arms, getting comfortable, he put his head on Simfany's shoulder and closed his eyes. After a few minutes of continuous rocking and kissing, Melquan fell asleep. Darla admired Simfany greatly. They locked eyes and the love they both saw was something neither had felt in a long time from someone outside of their immediate family.

"He's knocked," Darla whispered. Simfany looked down. She kissed his head again and walked to her room so she could lay him down. When she returned, they all knew what time it was. Simfany looked at Santana to make sure bringing Darla into the fold was what they both wanted. The look he returned confirmed his approval. Though Darla said nothing about it, she saw the energy pass between the two. Ever since she'd met the pair, she prayed daily that she and her child would share the bond Simfany and Santana held. It was amazing, to say the least.

"So… now, tell me what you did to get here… to this point, Santana?" Simfany asked. Santana looked over to Darla and spoke.

"Ma, listen… the shit you bout to hear, I expect you to keep to yaself. The conversation I wanted to have with you about what I had going on, is this one right here. Now, if for some reason, you feel like it wouldn't be a good idea that you're present, I would ask you to leave." When Darla didn't attempt to move, he continued.

"Alright ... Last week me, Zach and Heem went into someone's house and robbed them for thirty bands and half of a brick. The next day, one of the niggaz Haseem knows pulled up on us and put all three of us on point of what was being said. The consequence of the loss, they put fifteen bands apiece on our heads. The bounty to me was a steep one, so in truth, I prepared my niggaz to go to war. But I see they aren't the war ready type of niggaz. They might squeeze if shit get greasy, but I don't see the aggression. Of course, I'm different in these kinds of situations. Also, when I was out there with you the night Nessy got killed, I seen the nigga Von looking all crazy at me from afar. It was him and that nigga that just got killed the other night in front of his mother's house. So, I can only take it that he feels some way about me killing his brother. So not only do I have that going on, but now I got these full blooded niggaz on my line. Whoever shot at me tonight has me clueless. Soooooo ... any questions other than that? Because that sums everything up in a nutshell."

Simfany was fuming from the notion of her son having so many enemies because he robbed someone. The killings that happened to protect them was one thing, but to go out on straight bullshit is another.

"Let me get this shit straight, these niggaz is chasing you around here trying to kill you because you robbed a nigga for the shit he worked for? I just want to make sure I have all this straight. Did you kill anyone in the process?" She waited on his answer. When he put his head down, she knew that meant no. Even though Simfany had never displayed those types of characteristics, she knew what came with that type of action. She shook her head back and forth in disappointment. Santana was tripping.

"What you want me to do, Ma, keep asking you to fucking take care of me? That shit is prideful enough." Simfany got offended and stood up to her feet.

"First the fuck of all, who are you talking to? I'm your fucking mother, lor nigga. I sacrificed everything for us. I have done shit to excel us both and you asking me, are you supposed to keep asking for money? Yes, you stupid muthafucka. Don't you think it would be better than having to watch every step you take? Don't you think it would be better than bringing kids into your bullshit that will eventually get them killed? But you claim you love these niggaz." Simfany walked up to Santana and looked down on him.

"What you are becoming, you better retract that shit before it get us killed. You wanna keep running around like ya gun is the only gun that has flame? Well, news to you, Santana… it don't. Your bullets ain't the only ones that kill, lor nigga. Get ya shit together. I wanna take you out of this state, but you have been here a while and I know what you are going to contest to. All I want you to think about is this, I'm ya mother, you have help protect me since you became a young man, so you know my life and existence revolves around you. I'm ya biggest supporter, but also ya biggest critic. Know when you drive that car off the cliff, we both going to be in that bitch. Right or wrong—"

"Siempre, Familia." Santana finished Dracula's favorite saying. Simfany walked to her son and kissed his face.

"I love you, baby boy, I just want you to enjoy this thing they call life. I wasn't able to, so you need to. You hear me?" she asked, tears streaming down her face. The scene was breaking Darla's heart. The plea from a mother to son, one thing they all knew though was that going back wasn't an option. It was only up from there.

Santana had two options in order to live that life she wanted. One was to kill anything and everyone moving, or second, he would have to move from the city of Charleston altogether. And Darla knew neither one of those were sound options to Santana. One thing she could gather from his character, he was definitely a king. She knew the little nigga was more than what met the eye. His demons had shown some time through his actions, the fact that he never talked about the shit with Breeze or moved afterwards, let her know he was a savage in his own right. She looked over at an embraced Simfany and Santana. Her eyes watered, she didn't know what she was getting herself into, but the feel of family had never felt like this before. She had loved hard before, even almost losing herself in the process, but she'd never witnessed or been a part of true love before. And watching her man and his mother hold their embrace sent chills up her spine. Darla rose from her seat and walked over to where Santana and Simfany sat and hugged them both.

"I love y'all and I promise, no matter what happens in the long run or short future, I'm here. I'm here for the duration." She kissed Santana on the forehead. Simfany looked up at her and searched her eyes for the truth. Seeing the love written all over Darla's face softened Simfany's crushed heart. She opened her arms to let Darla into their embrace. The three hugged each other tightly. Darla loved the feeling. She knew meeting Simfany that day in Gino's was a blessing, but not in a million years did she think it would amount to this.

"I want hug too." They all looked up. Melquan was standing in the doorway of Simfany's room. His lips were poked out, attitude flaring from being left out. They laughed in unison. That seemed to make him angrier.

"Come here, lor man. Auntie not leave her baby out." That was all he needed to hear, and he ran full speed into the crowd.

"And I'm not a baby, right, Mommy?" He looked into Darla's eyes.

"That's right, baby boy. You a big boy now," Darla assured him. He smiled and looked back at Simfany.

"Tol' you, Auntie Pretty Lady." Simfany smiled and kissed his face.

"Yo son, I love all y'all and all, but a nigga leg just went to sleep. And you muthafuckas are not light. Phat booty muthafuckas." Santana laughed. Simfany and Darla simultaneously smacked Santana in his head.

"Hey!" Melquan shouted. "Don't be hitting Tana, Momma, Auntie Pretty Lady."

"Yeah, what he said." Santana laughed. Simfany and Darla looked at each other for a brief second. They scrunched their faces up and drove straight in and started tickling both Santana and Melquan. They both were ticklish as hell. They squirmed and laughed hard, trying to escape the assault. They had no chance.

"Ahhhhhhh!" Melquan laughed. "Auntie, stoppppppppp!" he laughed uncontrollably. He wiggled his way out of their embrace and ran. Simfany and Darla attacked Santana in his absence.

"Dang, son, you just gone bounce on me?" Santana said through laughs.

"Sorrby, Tana," Melquan said and ran back to the action. They all laughed. The time was one Santana would retrace many times in his mind to find peace. *Damn, this the life I want on a daily*, he thought as he held Darla in his arms. Simfany's phone rang, momentarily stopping them from their wrestling match. She got up and grabbed it from the kitchen counter.

"Hello," Simfany answered. The smile disappeared from her face when she realized the person on the other end of the phone was sniffling from holding back obvious tears. She looked at the number that called her and frowned. The number was that of her friend, and Santana's baby mother, Tijuana.

"Hello? What's wrong, Momma T?" Simfany asked.

"This isn't Tijuana, Simfany, this is Nadia. Nadia Burke, Tijuana's mother." Tijuana's mother sniffled.

"Oh... hey, Ms. Burke, how are you doing? Are you okay?" Simfany asked in concern.

"No baby, I 'm just calling you to let you know that Tijuana was killed—" Ms. Burke broke down, she couldn't finish her statement before Simfany dropped the phone and grabbed her mouth. She couldn't believe what she was being told. She hurried and grabbed the phone off the floor.

"Ms. Burke, are you still there?" Simfany asked urgently.

"Yes, baby." Simfany's heart went out to her. She had lost two children in less than a two-year period.

"What are the streets saying happened?"

"Not much, just that she was caught in the middle of some gang shit these boys had going on out here. I think it stems from the retaliation of my son's murder. The red gang and the blue gang have been trading murders back and forth. Tijuana was killed, and my son's childhood friend is fighting for his life as we speak. I just wanted to let you know what was going on. Sorry I bothered you." Ms. Burke abruptly hung up. Simfany looked over at Santana. He was watching her, and she could tell he sensed the bullshit. She couldn't fight the urge to cry. The tears ran down her face, she not only cried for the lost soul of Tijuana Moore, but she cried for the unborn children she held in her stomach for Santana.

"Ma, what's going on? Why are you crying?" Now all of them were looking at her, lost. It was just a happy moment only minutes before. What news could she have gotten that changed her mode so rapidly?

"Baby, I'm sorry. Tijuana is dead." The words alone sounded off kilter. Those words weren't supposed to be in the same sentence with each other.

"My nigga, what?" He moved Darla and Melquan off his lap and stood. "What the fuck are you talking about, Ma? Please say that is a mistake. Ma, please." Santana cried for the first time since his mother was shot. His baby was dead. He put his head into his hands and cried a deep cry. Simfany walked over to her son and rubbed his back.

"It's going to be okay, baby," Simfany tried to assure him. But in all truth, it wasn't. It seemed as if all the bad shit the world had to offer followed them. No matter how good they treated people, or how loyal they were, trouble and bad karma followed. The bodies that piled up due to his mother's shooting was out of pure love. He never carried ill intent for people who didn't deserve it. Justice, Pee Wee, and Tijuana were now gone. The innocence they held was genuine. Santana let his thoughts run rapid, as all the good memories that he and Tijuana shared he shuffled through his head. Santana wiped his face when he felt Melquan's small hands wrap around him also.

"Tana, are you kay? I wuv you. Don't cry. Mommy told me big boys don't cry." That comment made Santana laugh. *This little boy is a trip, man. Thank you, God, for bringing him into my life*. He knew helping raise Melquan would be life changing. He was such a great person already.

"And ya momma right, Quannie, big boys don't cry. I couldn't help myself this time though. Something happened that hurt my heart. So, can I get one pass?" he asked, smiling and looking into his little eyes.

"Yes sir," Melquan responded and hugged Santana around the neck.

"Thank you, my G. That was greatly needed." Santana hugged him tightly. "I have to talk to Auntie real quick, you hear me?" Melquan nodded his head in agreement. "Thank you."

He walked into the kitchen, only a few feet away from Darla and her son. "What the fuck happened?" Santana's eyes were bloodshot from the tears. He was pissed, hurt and devastated all in the same breath. "How could this happen?"

"Tijuana's mother just called and said someone shot her over some shit that was going on about her brother's murder. The Bloods and the Crips had been trading bodies back and forth. No details were given besides the fact one other person was shot with her. It was her brother's right-hand man," Nadia said. That statement alone had his mind spinning all crazy-like.

"Did she give you the name of the nigga that was shot with her? Because the nigga I was rocking with in Hickey was her brother's only right-hand man." The thought of Drew being killed with Tijuana was breathtaking. Santana rubbed his temple in circular motions. He didn't know what to feel. One thing he was going to do was kill someone in her name for sure. A nigga wouldn't get away with killing neither Tijuana nor Drew. They were his family.

"What you need to do is calm down. Because the thought you think you have in ya head, you need to get rid of. I will not allow you to go back out to Baltimore to seek revenge, not now at least. You know I ask myself what is my purpose on this earth, and what does God have planned for you while you're here. I've always come up empty minded until now. You have an instinct to protect everyone around you, Santana. And I truthfully don't know if that is a gift or a curse for you. You are loyal by a default, son, and I need you to understand you have too much on ya plate to get fogged with this new issue. Survive with the bullshit at hand, then you worry about other shit. Because no matter how you feel, you are my son and what happens in your life is very, very important to me. I know where you stand with people and how you bringing shit but damn, when do you live for you, Santana? When do you stop the bullshit and live ya life? You are only sixteen years old, lor boy. I don't care what you have experienced or went through. You may never see the streets again after this shit catch up to you. Nigga, make some fucking memories. I loved T just as much as you did. I didn't have the kind of relationship that y'all had, but damn was it close. I'm hurting too, son. And in due time, the niggaz that killed our angel will pay. So, calm yaself down and go be with that beautiful woman in there waiting for you to hold her and tell her you are okay." Santana knew arguing with his mother wouldn't be a good idea right now. The look in her eyes told him she was not only talking to him, but she was also talking to herself.

"I love you, Pretty Lady."

"I love you too, baby boy. Now go and get ya mind off all of this bullshit. I got Melquan." Simfany kissed his head and watched him walk back into the living room. She cursed herself for not telling him about the children Tijuana carried for him. At this point, the blow would be so devastating that it would of drove him straight to Maryland on a suicide mission. And Simfany wasn't about to be the cause of that. Plus, Santana had too much going on as usual. She really had created a demon. *This nigga ready to kill at the drop of a dime*, she thought as he sat down next to Darla on the love seat.

"Quannie, come spend some time with ya auntie," Simfany called out to Melquan.

Without a second thought, Melquan ran to Simfany. He loved her so dearly, and damn did she need his innocence. He was the stabilizer of this family right now.

"So, what you trying do tonight? You wanna go play arcade games?"

"Yes ma'am, I wanna. Is Mommy or Tana coming?" he asked curiously.

"Not this time. Dang, I can't spend time with you by myself?" She poked her lips out as if she was hurt.

"No Auntie, I not say that." He hugged her leg, trying to comfort her. Simfany smiled and rubbed his head.

"Go get ya coat, lor man, first person to the car gets a vanilla ice cream." Simfany playfully ran to the coat rack. Melquan ran faster and grabbed his coat, throwing it on all while trying to open the door. Darla fell out. She laughed hard as hell.

"Don't be doing my baby like that, Simf." Simfany winked at her and closed the door behind her. Santana stood in the middle of the room thinking about what had just happened to his future. He needed to get back to Maryland, Tijuana wouldn't die in vain like that. Someone had to pay 'bout that body. Darla cleared her throat jokingly, snapping Santana from his thoughts. He looked at her sinisterly at first, but when he realized who it was, he put a smile on his face.

"Can I ask why you over there looking so evil?" Darla bolted upright.

"One of my people just got killed in the city. Some sad shit, man, shorty wasn't on shit for real. Nothing that coulda got her caught in the middle of a gang war." But he knew her demise fell on him solely. With TTP's illest soldiers killed, a war was left behind. Bodies were dropped and blood spilled, both sides were feeling the loss of another. Santana knew what the possibilities were and he didn't give a fuck when he left. He gave those niggas what they asked for. Subconsciously he didn't know what Tijuana was killed behind, but in his heart he knew it could have been because of what he had done to Hood, Stacks, and Piru. He prayed a silent prayer for Tijuana and sat down next to Darla, taking her in his arms.

"Are you going to be okay?" Darla stared in his face. The sorrow she saw in his face was hurting her. She grabbed his chin and stated firmly, "Santana, I need you to know I'm not a little girl. If I'm going to be yours, I need to know what you are and who you are. I don't want to love you and you leave me. This crazy shit you have going on is cool for the time being, but remember, I have a child and he needs me. I know a lot has happened in your life and I can only imagine what, but baby, you are too young to hurt internally like you do. I see the good man in there, that's why I'm here. Your mother raised you to be a protector, this I clearly see, which isn't a bad thing at all. You just have to know when and who to protect. Now this is my plea for you to handle whatever you need to handle and chill out. You have to be ready to take a break from the bullshit and live. Right? Are you ready to live yet?"

Tears threatened to fall down his face. The shit Darla was saying was close to the shit Simfany was preaching only minutes earlier. Santana knew what he needed to do to live life and be good, but what everyone didn't understand, or grasp was the fact his life was never going to be normal again. He sought vengeance in the shooting of his mother, ending the lives of three people. Two he had grown to love. The bodies left in that after-match were the product of his current Murder warrant, He was a wanted man and he lived and acted as if he had nothing to lose, because to him he didn't. He listened intently to Darla but being the type of nigga she wanted was out of his reach.

"Listen," Santana said, cutting Darla off in the middle of her spilling her heart. "You may want to reevaluate if you wanna be with me or not, Darla. I hear all you have been saying and baby, I swear the day I can slow down and play by those rules, that will be the day I can give my sigh of relief. There is a lot going on here I may not make it out of. I'm also not trying to feel as though I'm dragging Quannie into any of this. I truly do love you, Darla, and have for a while now. This is me and this is what I am, I pray every day that my dealings in these streets don't haunt those around me, but after the death that just took place, I'm not sure anymore if I can honestly keep people out of harm's way. The only thing that can be a true statement is, if something was to happen to you, I could kill in your honor. And that's not a hell of a way to live. So, what I need you to do is think about what you really wanna get into with me. I don't want what's between ya legs that bad, ma. I know that shit gone snatch my soul, but when it does, I want that shit to be pure. You are the daughter my mother may have always needed. So that, coupled with how my feelings run for you, I have to do right by you. You're my baby."

The words sounded strange as Santana said them, the conversation wasn't to the exact T, but it was definitely similar to the conversation he had with Tijuana after they made love for the first time. Santana leaned over and kissed Darla's forehead. Santana lay down on the couch and closed his eyes. The memories of Tijuana flooded his mind. Silent tears ran down his face for his dearly beloved. Darla crawled up his body and kissed his trailing tears. She kissed down his face until their lips met. They kissed passionately when their tongues met, they swirled around each other, and their eyes closed. The feeling was pure bliss. Darla pulled back and looked Santana in his eyes, no words were spoken between the two, she just closed the distance and laid on his chest. His heart was beating erratically. That made her smile, she knew he loved her in more ways than he would ever admit. As Santana rubbed her beautiful hair, she cried silent tears. God had finally sent her, her angel. And no matter what she wasn't going to let him go. Right or wrong ... Siempre Familia, she remembered they had said. Without thought, Darla just spoke.

"Baby?"

"What's good, ma? Santana replied.

"No matter right or wrong." Santana smiled and answered instinctively.

"Siempre Familia." He ran his fingers through her hair until he heard her breathing slow into a slumber.

***

Von sat in the basement and reread the message over and over. An unknown number had texted him with the words ...

Two down, one to go.

Von just sat and pondered on what the message could mean. *Did someone kill two out of the three lil niggaz Torrey put money on*? he thought, he was lost at what the message necessarily indicated. He pulled on his blunt to escape the bullshit the world had to offer at this point. He lost his brother, his mother wasn't the same since Breeze's death, he had to banish Fatty Man from the hood, and his right hand just got killed only nights prior. He pulled on his blunt again and relaxed his mind. He was thinking too much into shit, or was he? He questioned his sanity. Von pulled his Nextel from his pocket and placed a call. The phone was answered on the first ring.

"Yooooo," the voice answered on the other end.

"What's poppin', Fully?" Von greeted his youngest member of his Full-Blooded gang. "I'm blooded. How you, big homie?"

"More or less, I just got a text saying the bounty of two of the little niggaz was carried out. You hear anything about that?" Von asked.

"Nah, I can't confirm that rumor. The last I heard, earlier tonight Freezo and Sleeze had the OT nigga on skates. The nigga he was with was all hit up though. The ambulance rushed the old head Doug spot right after that," the boy informed.

"Ight look, hit Freezo or Sleeze and see who and what they hit. Hit back and let me know what the word is. It's a must that I find out what's up with these bands, if team did work. Loyalty is everything."

"FB till my cold slab," the boy said proudly. Von smiled, he was proud of how far his team had come. The love and loyalty shown within its ranks was not only surprising but amazing. He didn't have the usual issues most gangs had. There were no issues about rank, position or pay. None that he had heard about anyway, he hung up the phone and read the text again. The shit just didn't make sense. Von lit the blunt back up and pulled hard, hoping the weed could fix his problems momentarily. The weed did its job and calmed his nerves, Von opened his phone and began to scroll through the pictures that he had of his brother. The memories were priceless, just if he could relive them. He missed his brother tremendously.

He looked at the pictures that held the whole team, from the beginning to what it was now. He looked on with pride when he scrolled deeper into the gallery and ran across a few pictures of Fatty Man and Breeze together. He scrunched his face up at the picture. "That bitch ass nigga let you die, bruh, that bitch ass nigga let you die." He dropped his head and cried. Von hadn't had the alone time to reflect on himself after the murder. All he wanted was to shed blood, but there was no one until now to take blame. Von grabbed the Hennessy he had handy and popped the top. He took a swig from the bottle, the liquor burned going down, giving his soul a cleansing. Von raised the bottle to his mouth to take another swig, his phone vibrated. He took a drink and then pulled his phone out. He had a message from one his illest killers, FB Sleeze.

Botched Fully ...

Von slammed his phone shut. *What the fuck*, he thought as he opened the text message yet again.

He thought about anyone and everyone that could possibly be responsible for this kind of act. He came up blank. He shook his head back and forth trying to shake off the haze he was in. He stood from his chair and stumbled, high as fuck. He regained his balance and gathered the trash he had accumulated in the last few hours since being in the basement. His phone rang loudly, scaring him. *I thought I put that muthafucka on vibrate*, he thought, confused as hell. When he opened the Nextel to talk, there was no call coming in. He began to look around for where the noise was coming from. His heart sank as he turned around to see Fatty Man leaned up against the staircase with a Glock in his hand. The clip he had inside the gun meant he was on bullshit. Von looked down at his Heckler and Koch on the ground near the chair.

"Nigga, I wish you would," Fatty Man said venomously.

"You wish I would what, Fully?" Von said, trying to reel him in with their gang's signature slang.

"Ain't shit Fully bout me but this Glizzy in my muthafuckin' hand, bruh."

"Say less, tough guy, do what you have to do if that's what you here to do then, my nigga. Fuck you waiting on?" Von said, prideful. If this would be his fate, so be it. Fatty laughed at Von and his antics.

"Soft ass nigga, you not even cut like that. Without that gun on ya hip, you a fucking bitch, my nigga… stop playing with me. I know you. I grew up with you, nigga. Keep faking on that gangsta shit gone get you air lifted out this bitch." Von listened intently, trying to figure out a way to make it out of this fucked-up situation alive. It was as if Fatty could read his thoughts.

"What you thinking about, big bro? That is what you are, right…my big bro?" When Von didn't answer, Fatty continued.

"Nigga, answer me! That's what you are, right… big bro?" Von looked to the ground. Fatty aimed his gun and shot past him, lodging a bullet into the concrete wall behind him. Von ducked, trying to escape the bullet he felt was coming for him.

"Bruh, what the fuck you doing?" Von asked, his voice cracking from fear. Fatty Man laughed.

"My how the tables have turned, you were the same person that had a gun pointed at my face only a week prior. Now it's, what the fuck am I doing? My nigga, you kicked me out a hood that is mine. I grew up here, I was born here, nigga. This my soil to bleed on. You weren't trying to hear what I had to say, it was Remy's truth over mines. Your right-hand man, your brother. Nigga, I grew up in the same home as you, nigga, your mother was my mother. Breeze was my brother, but you were our big brother. The day you told me I had to leave or get left stinking, we were no longer family."

"Fatty... I swear, bruh... it wasn't like—" Von tried to explain.

"Shut the fuck up! I'm not here to hear you cop pleas. That shit you did was treason, my nigga, and in our oath you made, that shit is punishable by death. Right? Isn't that what you taught us?" Von nodded his head. "Nah nigga, speak up."

"Yeah," Von answered simply. Fatty Man laughed.

"You have two options that are nonnegotiable. You let me come back home, or you die on the spot. Which one you gone choose? So, big bro, you gone let me come back to the hood? By the news that been airing, you need another gun present anyway." Von sighed in relief.

"We do, a lot has been going on around here in the last week," Von replied, defeated.

"Bet... Call Sleeze and let him know I'm good around this bitch, because if one of those lil niggaz up them guns on me, I won't hesitate to drown they ass," Fatty Man stated seriously.

"Bruh, I got you. Put that muthafucking gun away. You trippin'. I'm ya brother."

"Oh, we brothers again? Oh okay," Fatty Man said and tucked the gun into the pocket of his Carhart Construction jacket. "You gone call Sleeze, bro. I'm not bout to keep being a fucking outcast around this bitch." Von pulled his phone off his hip and called Sleeze. Sleeze answered on the first ring. Von put him on speaker. He didn't want Fatty to get no crazy ass ideas.

"Fully, what's banging? I called around about the OT nigga and who was present with him when we slid on him, and no bodies were dropped. The fiend nigga got popped in the shoulder, but I think the lil nigga did it, because if Doug bitch ass woulda got touched by what we was banging, his shoulder would be missing instead of wounded. I'll keep you posted on that though."

"Bet. Make sure you do that. But on another note, I'm thinking bout letting Fatty slide back. My momma was just asking bout him. I feel like shit, that was my nigga just as much as it was Breeze's."

"You know I try to stay out of y'all shit, but my nigga, you was wrong for that. Fatty has put on for us since we started banging this shit. Long Live Remy, but bro had his own agendas against Fat Man. So, I think that would be what's needed around here right now. That shit between y'all divided the hood, in all honesty." That was news to Von, he didn't know his soldiers felt some kind of way about Fatty being gone. Shit, Fatty was surprised himself by what he heard.

"So, if you had a vote, what would you vote?" Von asked, knowing what his answer would be.

"That's a dumb question. I love that nigga. Like I said, you was wrong off jump, believing that ratchet ass bitch over a nigga you call your brother. I'm pretty sure every nigga on team would want bruh back into the fold," Sleeze answered honestly.

"Say less, I'm going to try and reach out to bruh and get him home." Von winked at Fatty.

"Big homie, can I be bluntly honest though?" Sleeze asked.

"Shoot, lil bruh."

"Do you think Fatty would want to come back after you did him like that? Because if it was me, bro, I woulda drowned you for doing me so like that." Von laughed.

"I'm going to let that slide but shit, all I can do is extend the hand. Let the nigga know I was wrong. It may or may not work. I don't know really. Only time will tell."

"Say less bro, bang at me if you need anything else. Loyalty is everything."

"FB till my cold slab," Von replied and hung the phone up. The silence in the room was awkward. Fatty Man thought about all the shit they had been through in the past couple of years. The ups the downs, the pros the cons. He also thought about his role in the making of their gang, Full Blooded. There were a lot of good memories, mostly of him and Breeze as children. He smiled at the memories as they flashed through his head. Fatty stuffed his chubby hands into his coat pocket and leaned against the banister in deep thought. Two down, one to go... The message he sent to Von only hours prior played in his head over and over. Killing Nessy and Remy was easy and long overdue, but to kill Von, now that was another story altogether.

The memories of Ms. Rhonda, Von and Breeze's mom, kept his gun tucked away in his Carhart. Ms. Rhonda had taken Fatty in as a young child. She fed him, clothed him, and loved him. She made sure he didn't want for nothing, and to add to it, all the love he received from her and her family was priceless. He gritted his teeth at the turn of events. He felt as if he was not only betraying Breeze for what he was about to do, but he was betraying the only woman he ever loved, his mother Ms. Rhonda. Fatty glared across the room and shook his head in disgust. Von deserved death and Fatty wanted to be the one who drowned him, but he wasn't sure if he was emotionally detached enough to do so. The two men just kept eye contact, no words, gestures or movements. The hate and love between the two was evident.

"You gone keep mugging me or are we going to talk about this shit?" Von broke the silence. Fatty laughed.

"Talk." Von laughed at Fatty's reply. *This nigga a fucking clown, he bet not let me get to this fucking gun*. Von tried his luck and tried picking up the remaining trash off the floor. Without hesitation or a second thought, Fatty stood erect and pulled his gun out his coat pocket.

"Move again, bitch ass nigga. Keep trying me, nigga." Fatty laughed sinisterly. "You think shit sweet, huh? Don't you? You really think niggas is beneath you, huh? You can just say and do whatever Von wanna do without consequence. Sorry to bust that bubble, Fully, this ain't that."

"I never once said or acted as if you or any other nigga was beneath me. What the fuck are you talking bout? I stood with you on any decision you ever made. I don't know what you want me to say, bruh. The streets talk, my nigga, and it said you froze on that drill that ultimately caused the demise of my little brother. The truth of the matter is, I didn't kill you, my nigga. I didn't let or call on anyone else to kill you, my nigga. I love you, bruh, but to keep looking at you reminds me of Breeze and what happened that day." Von spoke his truth.

"Fuck all that, you remind me of Breeze, shit. You had a fucking loaded gun pointed at my face, bruh. Me, my nigga, it was me. We grew up wearing Power Ranger underwear together, nigga. But yet you aimed a gun at my face over hearsay. You don't know what happened out there in the field that day besides one thing, two niggas lost their lives. You let Nessy and Remy get you drowned, Von. Damn, my nigga." *Two down, one to go,* he thought as he aimed his gun at the man he once considered his brother. "I love you, bro, I promise to take care of our lady." Before Von got the chance to protest or plead, Fatty opened fire, hitting Von multiple times in his chest.

Boc ... Boc ... Boc ... Boc ... Boc ...

Von fell back violently as the bullets pierced his flesh.

Fatty calmly walked up to Von and looked at him squirm. He was in a state of shock. Fatty looked him over for a second and spoke his last words. "You should have killed me when you and Remy embarrassed me in front of our men. Oh, and before you go, I did freeze momentarily when Breeze got hit and I'm sorry for it. I promise you... more men will follow you to hell." Fatty smirked as he emptied the rest of his magazine into Von's facial structure.

Chapter 5

Ramos sat at his desk and looked over the files regarding the shooting in New Cathedral Cemetery when his phone rang. He ignored it. The caller hung up after the voicemail picked up. The phone started to ring again, he picked the phone up and answered.

"Ramos."

"My office… now," was all Captain Davis said before hanging up. Ramos looked at his phone, shook his head and put the receiver into its cradle.

"Rude bitch," he whispered under his breath. He grabbed his folder and walked to his superior's office. Ramos raised his hand to knock on the door but thought better of it. He twisted the knob and walked in. The look on Captain Davis's face pleased him. He was pissed. Ramos laughed inside. *Bitch.*

"You don't know how to fucking knock?" Ramos walked in and sat down, ignoring Davis's remarks.

"What am I being summoned for this time?" Ramos asked irritatingly.

"First off, lose the fucking attitude. Am I clear?" Ramos nodded in agreement. Davis rubbed his forehead and continued. "Anyway, I have two things I want to discuss with you," Davis said as he went through the papers stationed on his desk. "Okay, I talked to the commissioner about the evidence you produced and against my better judgment, I helped you get that murder warrant for the juvenile…" Davis looked at the paper in front of him. "...Santana Vasquez lifted, but he is still wanted for questioning. We need to know what he may or may not know about the untimely deaths of his friends. I want to talk to him personally."

"Thank you!"

"Don't thank me. I try my best to follow the law we took an oath to uphold. Secondly, I hear you were at the scene of the cemetery shooting."

"I can explain wh—"

"I can care less, Ramos, let me finish before you get to making excuses. Alright, so as we know, we have a big ass problem on our hands right now. This beef between the Bloods and Crips is bouncing back and forth from Harford County to Baltimore City. We don't know who all the players are, but we do know the girl in the casket that was flipped upside down with bullet holes in it, was the sister of Kevin and Tezier Brooks. But check this, they are the best friends and gang associates with the deceased Tree Top Piru members." The look Ramos gave his captain made Davis smile, he didn't know why, but he did.

"Why the fuck are you looking like that?" Ramos asked inquisitively.

"Because I know all about what you might be about to say and more. I can actually tell you what I have learned if you're interested. On you, or I can shut up and listen to you, your choice." Davis sat back in his chair and screwed his face up.

"By all means, Detective Ramos. Explain away." Ramos got excited to explain what he found out over the past few days.

"The deceased woman turned upside down in her casket was the late Sasha Brooks, the sister of Kevin and Tezier Brooks. That you seem to already know. Now, I have discovered these two men are the head lieutenants of the Tree Top Piru gang led by Hassan 'Hood Ru' Jamir and Jaquan 'Stacks' Taylor. Sasha Brooks was killed at her mother's home while she sat on the porch in conversation with her younger brother Kevin Brooks, who we feel of course was the primary target. A 911 call came in later that night regarding the burning of a vehicle. When he responded to the call, the officer on the scene was informed by the Aberdeen Fire Department, Station I, that a body was found upon arrival."

Ramos opened his file and looked through his paperwork to make sure he was correct with the information that he was giving his superior. "Okay, the body that was found belonged to Tyshawn Fazon, a known member of the infamous Shotgun Crips, a gang heavily populated in the Washington Park sector of Aberdeen. Further investigation into how this could be connected to anything else, I found the deceased was present the night Kane Moore was killed." Captain Davis seemed very intrigued. Ramos noticed. He continued.

"Kane Moore was killed by his childhood friend, Andre 'Dre' Jones, but get this. He killed Moore over another friend, Narvel 'Blaze' Harris. Harris was also a known gang member, only he was affiliated with the Tree Top Piru's. He turned state's evidence against Jones and was later killed. Excuse me, Harris and his mother, Cynthia Harris, were later killed in a gang style shooting at his mother's home. The pair was found dead on arrival with blue flags draped over their faces. When I found that out, I looked at the other shootings that took place close or around the time of the Harris murder and came up empty. But I remembered I had heard or seen a scene that was similar. I looked and looked, coming up empty. Then I remembered where I heard that from." Ramos laughed. "This shit bout to get eerie, Cap. When the responding officer secured the scene of the Vasquez shooting on Edmondson Avenue, he put in his report that he found Simfany Vasquez unresponsive with a blue flag draped over her face." Ramos let the revelation of the connection linger for a minute.

"The connection is eerie but doesn't make any sense, of course. Her son being connected to the Tree Top Piru's threw me for a total loop. So, I began to concentrate more on the Brooks brothers in hopes of finding a connection. I called the Harford County Sherriff's office in Edgewood and spoke to the sheriff in charge of the connected murders." Ramos thumbed through the stack of papers in his folder and produced a paper and handed it to Davis.

"That paper is from a detective by the name of Mandrel Combs. He sent me that fax earlier, updating me on the latest murders that took place in his county. The body that I spoke of earlier... he was found next to the burning car that was just recently linked to the murder of Sasha Brooks. It was the same make and model the perp used to flee the scene of the murder. The Shotgun Crips has claimed her body as their work. Two days ago, Tijuana Moore was fatally gunned down and Andrew Henry left fighting for his life in ICU. The shooters wore burgundy bandannas to conceal their identities. But I'm sure we know who was under them bandannas. The shooting took place only hours after the cemetery shooting, and I don't believe in coincidences. My hunch and gut say one, if not both Brooks brothers, were present for the murder of Moore and the attempted murder of Henry. Oh shit, I almost forgot, Combs also mentioned that Tijuana Moore was the older sister of the late Kane Moore."

Captain Davis coughed in his coffee, hearing that Tijuana and Kane were of the same blood line.

"These kids are killing with no regard for life. I can't believe they are killing each other so gruesomely. Does anyone know how this war began?" Captain Davis asked.

"No," Ramos answered.

"We seem to know majority of the players, but don't seem to have a clue as of why this war started in the first place." Captain Davis leaned back into his chair and rubbed his long gray beard in thought.

"No, no one has the slightest to where this beef between the two gangs came from," Ramos replied.

"Before I begin with what I have, do you have anything else to add?" Ramos shook his head no. Davis always had a way of making him feel less than, or just not a good enough detective. Though he seemed insensitive towards the feelings of others, he knew Ramos wore his emotions on his sleeves regularly and the look on his colleague's face read insecurity. Davis spoke.

"With your investigative work combined with mine, it not only helps but in hope it will save some of the lives of these children. Good work, Ramos," Captain Davis said genuinely.

"I appreciate it, boss," Ramos replied halfheartedly. *Smart ass bitch*, Ramos thought as he put his paperwork back into their rightful folders.

"The biggest connection between all these murders, are the bandannas being left on the victims' faces. As you said earlier, the first flag that was dropped was in our city. Simfany Vasquez was the first, the second noted case was the killings of Narvel and Cynthia Harris." Ramos listened intently now, because he was lost as to where his superior was about to go. "The third and most prolific of the three was the double murder that took place in our city. The double homicide of twins Duke and—"

"Don Murphy," Ramos said, finishing Davis's comment for him. He was speechless. Chills ran through his body. *That's why all these people are dying*, Ramos thought.

"Yes, Duke and Don Murphy were shot callers for the Shotgun Crips. Born and raised in Washington Park in the early 80s. In the early 2000s, they migrated to Baltimore City as young adults, making Belair Road their second home, bringing their gang ties with them. Nonetheless, the pair were killed in Chapel Hill, found tied up and gagged, with multiple gunshot wounds. What confused the investigators were the sentiments of the case. Flags were also draped across their faces, only these flags were burgundy colored. And like you, I don't believe in coincidences. Since the deaths of the twins, the beef between the Bloods and Crips has worsened. But that case was a more recent case indicating their murders weren't the spark of this war. I do believe their deaths intensified this shit. I want you to look into the other victim that was shot with Moore. See what kind of connection he has to any other person directly or indirectly attached to these murders. But other than that, good work, Ramos. Lawson would be proud that you took his dying declaration to heart."

"Thanks, Cap." Ramos gathered his papers and got up.

"Question, Ramos. Off the record of course, do you think the Vasquez kid killed them two kids on Monument Street?" Ramos chose his words carefully.

"No, no chance. He's a child and no matter how evil or demonic a child can get, they make mistakes. No costly mistakes were made in that Monument case, none that we can find. Either he had help or he didn't do it. And by the CCTV in Windsor Valley on the morning of the murders, it was humanly impossible for him to be the perp. So, I'm putting all my chips on the latter. Good day, Cap." Captain Davis nodded at him. Ramos walked out with a smile on his face and never broke his stride, he needed to talk to Andrew Henry. The day was turning out better than he expected it to. He got the murder warrant lifted off of Santana and was able to put some pieces together that needed to fit in order to move on. Ramos hopped into his car and pulled off with Harford Memorial in mind.

***

Santana pulled up to the corner of Lewis and Beauregard in the rented Crown Victoria Darla purchased for him hours prior. He didn't know who fired the shots at him the other night, so he took precautions and slid through the hood in a different whip. Santana surveyed his surroundings, he wanted to see what if anything was different than what he already knew about the street. The traffic was as always.

There was no way the shooters knew he was going to be there. He knew for sure they weren't following him, because they would have ended him when he pulled into his favorite spot on Dixie Street and rolled a blunt, before pulling up to meet Doug. He shook his head, the games these bitch ass niggas play. He looked in his rear-view mirror, the bags that sat under his eyes told him a lot. He wasn't getting any sleep. Somebody needed to fall for that attempt on his life.

Santana eyed the house Doug lived in. The traffic wasn't suspicious. Fiends being fiends. What he did find unusual was the fact that he didn't see anyone but fiends pull up to the home. He thought he would at least see a nigga that sold some kind of drugs pull up, so when he didn't, Santana went into his head and began to overthink. He pulled the Glock .27 from his hip and checked the magazine. He had a new clip that held 22 at its capacity. He had 20 in his clip and one in the head. Ironically, Piru was the person that taught him to never fill his clip to the capacity, because if fired in rapid successions, it would give the gun reasons to jam. And one thing he didn't want to do is be caught in the middle of some shit with his gun jamming. Santana knew that would cost him his life. He placed the gun back into his coat pocket, flipped his hoodie on his head and exited the car.

Santana got out and walked up the side of the first house he came up to. He waited in the dark to see if anyone was following him, watching him, or just outright being nosy. He didn't see any windows being occupied, or any movement from any homes on the street. The street was deserted. When Santana realized no one had seen him or paid him any attention, he came out of the shadows and walked up the street to Doug's house. Santana gripped his Glock .27 tightly as he approached the residence. Before walking up the stairs to knock on the door, he looked up and down the street. He walked up the steps and knocked on the door, no one answered. He knocked again, and then put his ear to the door. He heard nothing. He knocked again. He knew someone was in the house, he saw the traffic only minutes earlier. He put his ear to the door yet again, he was getting frustrated. Santana pulled his head from the door when he heard the echo of footsteps approaching. Santana straightened up and put his finger around the trigger, ready to send a nigga to hell. The door opened to a smiling Doug.

"Oh, I wasn't expecting you. Come in," Doug said as he stepped aside to give Santana access. Santana laughed to himself. *This nigga high as shit.*

"I see you feeling good, but how that shoulder holding?" Santana asked as he stepped past Doug into the foyer. The smell of crack smoke invaded his nose. *What the fuck ... these niggaz gone die off the smoke alone.* Santana coughed the smoke out his lungs and covered his mouth with his hand. Santana walked from the foyer into the living room, the smell of smoke wasn't as evident. He looked around and to his surprise, the home was very clean and tidy. The smoke was there, but without that, the activities that took place would be blind to the naked eye. Doug saw the curiosity and shock on Santana's face and laughed. Doug winced at the pain that shot through his body.

"Fuck!" Doug cussed. Santana turned suddenly, but calmed down when he realized there was no danger.

"Son, you good?" Santana walked over to Doug to render aid if needed. Doug looked at Santana with the, *nigga, do it look like I'm good eyes.*

"My bad my G, dumb ass question," Santana said sincerely.

"Why are you here tonight, young blood?" Doug asked as he sat down on the couch and slightly rubbed his shoulder.

"I want answers. I need to know who tried to kill us the other night. I'm still clueless on who tried to back me down. Have you heard anything?" Doug looked around for a second, contemplating if he wanted to offer the information he knew.

"I'm not trying to get involved in your bullshit young blood. I have already been shot behind this. The people that are after you are dangerous. The men—"

"Listen, my nigga, the men you speak of have already placed threats on my life and I don't take that shit lightly." Santana laughed. "Son, they popped you in the process." Santana breathed deeply, trying to process his next move. "I have nothing to lose but my life, you heard? So please stop playing with me and tell me what the fuck I want to know." Santana trained his gun on Doug awaiting a response. Doug looked down the barrel of the gun and began to laugh an eerie laugh.

"Bitch ass nigga, what's so fucking funny?" Santana asked through gritted teeth.

"You!" Doug said firmly, standing his ground.

"And why the fuck is that?" Santana asked as he pictured his Glock exploding Doug's facial features. Doug looked at Santana yet again and stood. If he was going to die, he would die on his feet as a man.

"Look, young blood, if you 're going to use that gun, then stop playing with it. That shit don't run no fear through my heart. Like you, the only thing I have to lose is my life. So, are you going to end all my misery or keep pointing that damn gun at me in my shit?" Santana had no plans on killing Doug, he was acting out of pure emotion. Something he told himself he would stop doing. Santana lowered his gun and returned it to his coat pocket. He took a seat and rubbed his temple. He was frustrated to the max. He had niggas that wanted to kill him for more than one reason. His list of enemies was beginning to pile up. Maybe it was time for him to relocate as his mother said they should. *Fuck outta here.* He had never run from an issue before and just because he was no longer on offense, he wasn't down for running now.

"I need to know, old head. I need to know who shot at me. My life depends on your knowledge. I'm not going to keep asking questions you should have given me answers to.

I understand what you feel about these men as you call them, but they aren't the only lames that's crazy, dangerous or deadly. I get that—"

"Duly noted. But you keep on continuing to say bullshit. I'm not afraid of no man that walks on this earth, young blood. I may have succumbed to smoking crack, what people look down upon. but I am functional. This shit I do is a hobby. I party because I can, not because I have to. I live my life on my fucking terms, so don't play me with that bullshit. Let me also explain something to you. I will explain one time and one time only. I am an ex-Marine, so I was trained to kill. I don't give a fuck about none of those boys. You need to be the one worried about them, your ass can't shoot a lick and your anxiety goes to the roof in combat. I saw that firsthand. I see you're used to being the aggressor. I say that to say this, when you felt as if you were caught dead to rights, you panicked. You surprised me, you didn't run. But I feel if I wasn't present, you would have. Does that make you soft or anything of that nature? No, but it makes you unprepared and vulnerable."

"What are you talking bout? Ain't shit vulnerable about me, I bang this bitch at all costs. I don't fear nothing but God, my nigga!" Doug looked around to make sure they were still in the room alone.

"Who is that spiel for? Your own mental state or are you truly trying to convince somebody to believe that you 're a helluva shooter. I can be wrong, but I just don't see it. A lot of you young men are like that though, look at what happened the other night, for example. These little niggas ran up with them assault rifles and didn't do shit but fuck my damn car up."

"They banged your shoulder up too," Santana interjected. Doug eyed Santana for a second. "No pun intended, of course." Santana smiled.

"No! Your bullet was what hit me in my shoulder. I knew it the night it happened, but if you didn't shoot back, they woulda probably walked us down. So, I took the lesser of the evil." Santana looked dumbfounded, the revelation was embarrassing. His face turned beet red. It was Doug's turn to laugh now. "You good, I see your face all blood shot and shit. You saved us that night and I thank you for it. Plus, it wasn't the first time I took a bullet for the greater good. Now about the people that are on your tail, it's some guy that goes by the name Big T. He put money on your head because of some kind of robbery you and your friends committed. Now this is where the shit get tricky, the bounty is for anyone who catches you lacking. But the word is, you specifically are being hunted by a gang that goes by the name Full Blooded." Santana looked lost, he had never heard of the gang prior to the conversation that was being held between the two.

"The look on your face tells me you don't have a clue who the fuck I'm talking about. Okay, the man that you killed at the Shop N Go was the brother of one of the founders, his name is Von. The hit is personal from what I hear. They want your head on a platter like yesterday. They offered us some drugs if we were willing to set you up and though I don't owe any loyalty to you, I still can't agree to do no shit like that." Santana instinctively rose to his feet and put his hand on the gun that rested in his Carhart. He looked around, nothing seemed out of order.

"My G, what type games you playing? Where them niggaz at?" Santana asked anxiously.

"Young blood, this not that. I have not called no one and I will not be calling anyone. This beef has nothing to do with me technically, but I was brought into this by their actions. They tried to kill you while you were with me, if they had the chance, they would have left both of us stinking there that night. Those little niggas had no kind of regard for my life, why should I help them in any way shape or form? Though I won't be running around killing no one of course, I will commit to helping you calm yourself in time of war. Being able to control yourself under pressure is key, and actually being able to hit a target will be damning to their offense. At this time, that's all I can offer. If you're looking for more information than what I have already given, little homie, you're out of luck. Take this for what it's worth, just because they missed the first time, don't mean they will miss again. There is one that you will have to look out for, his name is FB Sleeze. He is the ruthless one of the bunch. That little nigga will shoot on sight, no matter the time or day. His gun is definitely one you will have to be careful about. Truthfully, after you're taught how to move in combat and under pressure, no one will be able to match your gun. It won't make you invincible of course, but you will have an advantage."

Santana smiled, he was hype. He felt like his aim was already on point, but being taught how to use his Glock with precision couldn't hurt none.

"I hear you, when we gone start this training? Because I swear my niggas need this shit, bad. They aren't experienced at all with guns." Doug didn't say nothing, but he knew that his look was of frustration. Santana was momentarily lost but understood almost instantly. He addressed the issue at hand.

"You will be teaching my niggas also, right?" Santana asked inquisitively.

"I'm not going to say no because of the circumstances that y'all are in together as a whole. Don't get me wrong, it ran across my mind because to be dedicated is one thing, to baby sit is another. But I got y'all once my shoulder heals good enough to move around frequently. Can you manage to stay alive until then?" Doug waited on Santana's reply. The question was a serious one. Santana's smile left when he realized that Doug wasn't playing.

"Of course. I will be able to survive until you are ready to train me and mine."

"No offense."

"None taken."

"Remember, breathe and don't panic. You'll be okay. I haven't heard much about anyone else but that doesn't mean they aren't coming either. You know what you need to do to stay alive. I'll call when I'm ready. Ight?" Santana nodded his head in approval. Doug stretched his hand out and clapped Santana up. "Now get ya young ass out here so I can get my damn smoke on. You got some for me anyway?" Santana went into his back pocket and pulled out the small sandwich bag that contained a white powdery substance. Doug's eyes grew as his eyes fell upon the sandwich bag in Santana's hand. Damn, old head thirsty as shit, Santana thought as he handed the bag over to Doug.

"Now don't do all that at one time. This can be payment for helping me and my niggas get our shit together. You know, help keeping us alive and shit." Doug smiled, revealing his brown stained teeth. *Eeewwww*, Santana thought as he held back his laugh and nodded his head in departure.

"Do your thing, old head, I use to not like your old ass. But you cool people though."

Santana joked as walked to the front door of Doug's house. He unlocked the door and stepped out, looking both ways before entering the night.

"Aye, young blood?" Doug called after Santana.

"What's good?" Santana turned around.

"I still don't like your young ass!" They both laughed, Santana stuck his middle finger up and walked into the night, clutching his Glizzy.

Santana drove around in deep thought as he let the past few weeks play vividly through his head. Full Blooded meant nothing to him. He had never heard of the self-proclaimed gangsters. *FB Sleeze .... FB Sleeze* ... the name meant nothing, but the circumstance did. He was aware of the rumors, the rumors that niggas were supposed to get their lick back for the death of Breeze. Days, weeks, and even months had slid past. He paid no attention to the hype. He was thugging and ready for the action if it slid his way. So, to hear months later that the same niggas that was too bitch to kill just off the sake of a lost comrade, were now sending shots over another nigga's loss possessions through him for a loop. The thought didn't warrant any panic, but it did make him feel slightly uneasy. He knew he would manage. It was a must that he kept his cool for the sake of the team, because if they saw him sweat, it would cause doubt. And he knew all too well if doubt was found, being tricked out of their position would eventually be inevitable. And he was damn sure not trying to go that route for no reason at all.

Santana let his mind shift through the bullshit as he maneuvered through the nightly traffic on his way back to Darla's house. He came to a stop at Glenwood and 6th Avenue. Darla lived only a few houses up from Candy's, a popular pool hall spot located on the intersection of Glenwood and Grant Street. The evening air hindered people from frequenting Candy's as they usually did on a daily basis. Santana put the Crown Vic back into drive and spun the block. He tried his best to not become a creature of habit, he knew somewhere along the way his paranoia would eventually save his life. He was familiar with the scenery, but not comfortable enough to stop and park without precaution. Santana casually circled the block, all the while surveying the nightly activity before he felt satisfied to park.

"Man, I have to leave this life alone, I'm paranoid as a bitch," he told himself as he looked for a spot to park closer to Darla's home. He had heard of many good men losing their lives over being careless and complacent. When he finally pulled into a reasonable parking spot in front of Darla's home, he turned the car off and hopped out. Santana looked down the street and it was surprisingly empty. It looked like a ghost town. He shrugged it off and walked up to the door to put his key into the lock but was met by Darla in a short blue silky robe.

"Hey, sexy man," Darla said as she leaned in and kissed Santana's lips.

"What's up, Beauty? Have you heard anything else on what I asked you earlier?" Santana asked as he squeezed Darla tightly into an embrace. Her jasmine fragrance drove him wild every single time he inhaled it. He licked her neck. "Damn ma, you smell good enough to eat. Damn, why you be doing me like…" Darla grabbed Santana's dick through his jeans. She rubbed him through his pants, up and down until she felt him grow in her palm.

"Ma chill, you don't have to—" Santana tried to assure Darla, but his words were cut short when she bit her lip and dropped to her knees.

"Hold on, ma, let me close the door," Santana said, pushing the door closed and making sure he latched the locks into place. When he turned back around Darla was still patiently waiting on her man to please him.

"Come here, daddy," Darla said seductively. Darla leaned into Santana and pulled him closer. She undid his Rocawear jeans, all the while taking his gun off his hip and setting it on the table closest to them. She knew him all too well, not having his gun in close proximity would have ended the mood altogether. Darla was learning Santana slowly but surely. He wasn't difficult, he was just somewhat different. He was a man. Darla wasted no time, she pulled Santana's boxers to his knees and gripped his dick. She massaged him back and forth, up and down. She did this momentarily before kiss and licking the head of his dick. Santana's body responded, Darla had him where she wanted him. He looked down at Darla and grew warm inside. He didn't know if it was his body reacting from the love he possessed for her, or the way she gripped his manhood, but he felt as if he was falling in love all over again. Any thought he had up into that point disappeared as Darla took his dick into her mouth. *God damn, ma*, he thought as she sucked him slow and deep. Darla looked Santana in his eyes as she rubbed his ball sack gently and sucked his soul from his body. Santana titled his head back and relaxed for the first time in days.

Chapter 6

Drew stirred, shooting a sharp pain through his body. The bullets that threatened to end his life only a week prior were removed, but the pain left behind was excruciating. Tears ran down his face as he moved around, trying to find solace in his position. "Man, fuck!" Drew screamed out in frustration. Drew ravaged around in his covers, looking for the button that connected him to his pain medication. When his hand finally clasped over the button, he pressed it twice, trying to release a double dosage of morphine into his IV drip. It was the only thing keeping him sane at this point. The pain in itself was unbearable, from his wounds to his heart. Not being able to save and protect Tijuana like he should have killed his soul. Killed his soul slowly. But he couldn't blame anyone but himself. He knew he was responsible for what played out. He just didn't want to admit that, but he knew he was the reason the beef was still relevant.

Killing Sasha had sparked a whole new chain of events. *Inhale, exhale*, he thought as his breathing labored. I'm in this fucking hospital bed fucked up. "I done lost all my family. Who the fuck do I have left? I had nothing to lose." Drew tried to justify things as the morphine slowly made its way into his system. "Kane, Tijuana, Duke, Don, momma ... why? How?" Drew closed his eyes. He hoped maybe the hurt could disappear like the sunlight once his eyes were closed. Drew squeezed his eyes shut as the faces of his loved ones flashed before his eyes. He smiled and opened his eyes back up.

"I tried, momma, I tried," Drew spoke out loud as if Tijuana could hear him.

"Baby boy, there is no need to cry and stress over what's done." Drew jumped at the sound of the voice. Simfany walked from behind the curtain wiping the water off her hands. Drew looked around and saw what appeared to be a Coach pocketbook and clothing store bags scattered all about the hospital room. It was obvious to him that she didn't just come, she had been there for a while. Simfany walked to the bed and hugged Drew as carefully as she possibly could. Drew was genuinely confused. He has never seen the woman before.

"No disrespect, ma'am, but you are in the wrong room. I don't know you. I've never seen you before, shorty." Drew coughed, shooting pain through his chest like needle rods. Drew tried to close his eyes and labor his breathing. The morphine helped some, but even then, breathing in itself was painful as fuck. Simfany laughed, she was used to that kind of reaction from her son's friends. When Drew opened his eyes, Simfany was beside him in the chair closest to his bed.

"Who are you? And what can I help you with? Because I'm confused on why a beautiful woman like yourself is holding vigil for a nigga you don't know." Simfany's smile faded, she was beginning to realize that Drew was being serious. He really didn't know who she was, that was kind of alarming to her. She was staring at one of Santana's favorite people in the world and he had no inkling of who she was.

"My name is Simfany. I'm Santana's—"

"Mother...of course. I see why lor yo never showed us pictures of you. You are very pretty, Ms. Vasquez. Sorry if I offended you. My mind got me fucked up right now, I should still have been able to put two and two together." Drew laughed lightly. "I don't know why I didn't think of that when you made yourself at home." Drew coughed, crumbling his body in pain. Simfany looked on sympathetically, she knew the feeling all too well.

"Fuck, Simf, this shit fucking hurts. How did you get through this shit?" Drew asked.

"Remaining calm. In all honesty, I looked at hurting daily to be a blessing. That shit could have been worse. You and Tijuana could have been killed that day." Drew didn't reply. He just looked at the ceiling as murder ran across his mind.

"Do you know who did this to y'all, and do you know why?" Simfany asked.

"No, I don't know why this shit happened," Drew lied.

"Oh, okay. Say less." Simfany rose to her feet and started to collect the bags scattered around the room.

"These bags belong to you over here; there's clothes, some money, toiletries, hygiene, and a gun. This should be enough for you to chill for a while. Be safe and stay off the radar. Here is Santana's number. Use it," Simfany said as she wrote Santana's number down on a piece of paper and put it on the stand next to his bed.

"You leaving, shorty?" he asked curiously.

"Yes, sirrrrr!"

"Are you coming back?"

"Nope, there is no reason for me to be here. I did my part. I made sure you was good. And to my knowledge you are alive and kicking. Santana don't even know I'm here. I came down here to visit Ms. Burke, figured I could stop by and make sure all was well ya way also. Ms. Burke gave me all the information I needed. She also wanted me to let you know she will love you forever for trying to save her daughter. But I have to go, I'll let Santana know you're okay. You have his number, call him, I'm sure he would like to hear from you." Simfany gathered her bags and began to leave.

"Thank you, I'll make this right when I get back to myself," was all Drew could muster from his lips.

"No need to thank me, I did this because of my son. The vibes I get from you are different from the vibes my son spoke about every time we talked. You know I play in that field too, right? I'm not the police, I never told on a soul in my life. So, don't you ever fucking try to carry me as such!" Simfany said, meaning every word she spoke.

"Huh? What made you say that?" Drew asked, caught by surprise.

"I asked you who did this to you for a reason and you blatantly lied to my face. I don't play those kind of games, my nigga. So, you have a good day, lor nigga. Be safe." Simfany walked away. Drew sighed, this woman is fucking crazy. He cursed himself as he called after her.

"Simfany! Shorty, sit down please." Simfany stopped in the doorway of the room, she turned and looked at Drew. She turned and walked out the room. "Simfany, come back and sit the fuck down!" Drew yelled. "Ahhhhhhh, fuck." Drew covered his face with his blanket. The pain was one he hadn't felt since he woke up with bullet holes all over his body. Simfany stopped in her tracks and thought about if she walked out the door, what that could mean? Would Santana forgive her? She had enough secrets, that alone weighed on her soul. She didn't want to add any other things to her list of bullshit, so she turned around and walked back into Drew's hospital room.

"Peep this, lor nigga, we gone act like that stunt you pulled earlier didn't happen. With that being said, let me know what the fuck is going on out here." Simfany sat her bags back down and got comfortable.

"This ya platform, Simf, what do you want to know?" Drew asked.

"Everything! Fuck you mean, if me and Tana gone blitz this shit full speed, we need to know who and what we dealing with. What's the origin, you know, shit like that?" Simfany asked out of pure curiosity. Drew looked at her like she was crazy. Santana never told him his mother was with the bullshit. Shit, Santana never told him anything about his mother, period.

"I can't say exactly where it all started, but Tez and Kevin got on their bullshit around the same time Hood, Piru and Stacks got killed. Them niggas didn't know who played parts in the deaths of their comrades, so they killed any and everyone they felt had reason to want them dead. They killed for the hell of it. They killed niggas from other Blood sets, Crip sets and even killed a few of their own homies in search of the truth. No one claimed the bodies of the twins, so we were all clueless until I recently found out about the bandannas being dropped on their faces. And I had only heard that being done twice in my life, and both of those flags held relevance to one another. What would make this any different? When you got shot, all me and Santana had was Tijuana and each other. As you may or may not know, lor yo a secretive kind of nigga ... when he wants to be.

"So ironically, I didn't find out about your shooting in detail until after my left-hand nigga got killed. Shorty was Tijuana's little brother. His name was Kane. Good nigga, if you ask me. I'm guessing when Santana seen the pain written on my soul he opened up. Those three years we spent together, man... did we go through a lot. My bad Simf, I didn't mean to get off topic. Santana told me about the Piru niggaz he wanted to down and why. That's my lor man, so we made plans to visit shorty and his peoples. Then one day, Tijuana came in looking all down and shit, so of course I asked her what her problem was. I thought this nigga she was fucking with in the jail did some bullshit, but it wasn't that. She explained to me how she prayed every night on Blaze's demise. I was confused as hell because the rumors we had circulating in the jail, said the nigga Blaze was among the ghosts. She would later tell me about how not only Blaze, but his mother, was also gunned down. And at the scene, flags were dropped on their bodies, confirming the kill for their respectable gangs.

"Damn, I see you pay good attention to what's going on out there on the streets," Simfany said, admiring Drew's attentiveness for retaliation.

"In this line of work, I had to learn to pay attention fast to detail and habit. Even if that shit had nothing to do with me or mine. Some say it can be called nosy, I say it can be called staying sharp. Because the truth of the matter was, I went from acting like I was the reaper, to actually becoming him. I had to stay focused, or I was going to die trying to honor my brother's legacies. Plus, I told myself I wasn't doing no more jail time." Simafny's eyes misted. The thought of a child so young willing to give his life up like that broke her heart, but she couldn't judge because she truly understood. Simfany wiped her eye as the lone tear fell. Drew continued.

"I did get a little smarter though, I learned the virtue of patience from Santana. So, with the evidence I gathered through word of mouth and the actions of others, I sent a missile to the original last living members from Hood's line up. Do you know Tez-Mo and Kevin?" Drew's words began to slur. The morphine began to kick in. Drew closed his eyes and felt the room slightly spin.

"Never heard of them before. Not that I can remember at least. Santana never brought them around or even mentioned them to me. Not on any occasion. But then again, I might have seen them briefly. The day they came kicking shit in looking for Santana with that murder warrant. We was able to get away in time and landed over at the spot where Stacks and a few of his soldiers stayed. They may have been present. Even if you described them to me, I wouldn't know who they were, once again I'm slippin'." Simfany looked over to Drew when he didn't shoot no smartass remarks back her way.

"Are you okay, you looking crazy over there. Do I need to get a doctor or nurse?" Simfany rose to her feet and walked to his bedside.

"Nah, I'm good, shorty, just the meds kicking in. I think I hit that bitch once too many times. I'm fried chicken over here, you hear me?" Drew laughed, trying to make light of the situation. "There isn't nothing wrong with my mental though, shorty, so no worries. We good, I promise."

Simfany smiled a slight smile and replied, "I feel you."

"Well, a few weeks ago, I got the drop on Kev and followed him. He rode around for a little while until he came to this suburban part of the county I had never been to. Belair. I had been to the courts and shit like that, but never in the living areas. So, the area was new for me. I had to stay on point, plus, I wasn't sure if lor yo had made me or not. I almost pulled away because of how I had to follow him. There were no cars in between us, just me and him on these back roads of Belair. To be truthful, the only reason I didn't pull away, was for the sole fact that the lor nigga didn't have a clue we were beefing. Until now. Word on the street is that shorty is into different shit now then he was back then, so I played him with precaution. All we continued to do was drive deeper and deeper until we hit Loch Raven. I was for sure this nigga had made me now, so I was prepared to pull off, that was until this nigga pulled up to the curb of his mother's house. That I found out later. Lor yo parked his whip and hopped out, his arrogance of his murdering skills kept him from paying attention to his surroundings, His awareness could have saved a life that day," Drew stated solemnly.

"Damn, you flamed the nigga in broad daylight? You have to stop acting off of emotion. You better hope no one seen you shoot that boy. Was it worth your life?" Simfany knew she had her nerve because she was the pot calling the kettle black. Do as I say, not as I do she thought to herself as she continued. "You said it yourself it was no real beef between y'all, and before I continue, if I had the opportunity to snatch the lor nigga soul, I might have also. But I woulda followed him at a different time and on different terms. Is that the reason you're laid in this hospital bed and my bitch is being fitted for a casket?" Drew looked away in shame. At the time he felt justified for his actions, but after just hearing Simfany's view of things, his heart broke a little more. Simfany could see the hurt running through Drew as he tried to avoid eye contact.

"We don't have time for that. What's done is done. She is gone, sweetheart. Now is when we talk that talk. Before we indulge in that, is there anything else you have to advise me of? I'm not trying to go into nothing blindsided." Simfany uncrossed her legs and rose from her seat. Drew watched Simfany and wondered what she had up her sleeve. Santana had never told him in detail about his mother, and to him it was crazy the first time they would meet would be on these terms. He watched as she went and grabbed a lighter and cigarette from her pocketbook. She walked to the window and pulled the latch that opened the window slightly. *This bitch is crazy, I know she not about to smoke in a hospital*, and just as the thought left his head, Simfany leaned into the window and lit her cigarette. She pulled deeply inhaled, exhaling almost immediately. She turned from her position and looked at Drew.

"Why are you so quiet? You usually this timid? Or am I just a handful? I hear I'm a handful often." She laughed, then inhaled the nicotine yet again. Drew laughed to himself because she was right, the awe had him acting like a sucker.

"For real, I'm just watching you, in all honesty. Why are you here? I hear the questions you're asking and the shit you're talking bout. It all sounds good, but one thing Santana didn't describe you to be, was a savage. So—"

"And he shouldn't have, what I do is my business. How me and mine get down should only remain within the players of our team. You feel me, shorty? My nigga… don't do this shit for clout, this should be done solely for survival or out of love, nothing more, nothing less. You can feel how you want about this shit. Also, for the record, I'm here for the sake of Santana and the soul of Tijuana." Simfany took another pull on her cigarette. She had the room smelling badly from cigarette smoke. But it was obvious she didn't really give a fuck about that.

"I thought you said Tana didn't know you were here." She shook her head, flicked her cigarette into the darkness and closed the window. She shook the chill from her bones and stretched.

"He don't. I came on his behalf so he wouldn't need to. Well, let me rephrase that, I came so he wouldn't have to at this moment. Your damn friend has *a lot* going on right now." Drew looked at Simfany lustfully, she was so thick. *I know her pussy good*, Drew thought as he watched Simfany shake the sleep from her body. Drew snapped out of his temporary lustful state of mind when Simfany cleared her throat, trying to get his attention. She laughed lightly and continued. "So instead of his emotional ass coming down here, trying to kill the whole state over Tijuana, I came to handle what I could while I was here making the arrangement for T's homegoing. You follow?"

"Absolutely."

"So wha—"

"Simfany, I killed their sister that day I followed Kevin," Drew just blurted out. Simfany's eyes grew big. She was genuinely surprised. She wasn't ready for that.

"Ummmmmmm, you took the lamb from them, their baby, their most prized possession. Now the actions these men took make sense. I was told Tijuana wasn't targeted, how true that is, I have no clue. But to my knowledge, she was just literally at the wrong place at the wrong time, the only person walking the hood that day, thankfully. Who knows what would have happened if they pulled into a packed complex?"

"Does Ms. Burke know that? I'm pretty sure she blamed me for Tijuana's death."

"I'm not going to say she blames you for the death of her daughter, because no one knows you are the cause. But people do know you risked your life to save hers. You did good. At least you tried. We can't bring T back, but damn, I respect you willing to die for my girl. Ms. Burke thinks the act was random. You are okay, your secret is safe with me. Was the shit with girlie an accident or was it intentional?" Simfany asked, disgusted in her own right. The number-one rule in the streets was women and children were to be left alone. So, she was frustrated with Drew's prior action, but she wasn't willing to dwell on the loss. She moved on.

"To be honest, Simf, it was both. I say that because as I ran up, I seen shorty on the porch with the lor nigga and really didn't aim away. He was my target, and my attention was definitely focused on him, she just happened to catch the shells. How? I have no fucking clue. I swear, Simf, Sasha wasn't supposed to take them shots." Drew stared into space. She could tell killing Sasha took a toll on his mental. Drew couldn't stop the tears if he wanted to. He had a lot of shit weighing on his head. He not only took someone's sister from them, he was also the cause of losing his own. Simfany walked over to Drew and put her forehead to his and looked in his eyes.

"Hold no regret for what you do. Just be ready to reap what you sow. Because karma, baby boy, has a way of showing itself in times of comfort and happiness. Never forget! The reaper takes no days off. Not for you, not for me, not for no one." She leaned in and kissed his lips softly before returning to her seat.

"Wipe your eyes please." Drew did as was told. Simfany shook her head from side to side. Drew was a demon, that she could tell, but he was still a child, just like Santana. What Simfany saw was a killer fighting his inner child.

"So, what are the name of the niggaz that killed Tijuana?" Simfany got up, grabbed her pocketbook, then grabbed her remaining shopping bags.

"Kevin and Tezier Brooks," Drew replied.

"The names they go by on the street, Drew." Simfany rolled her eyes. Drew laughed.

"Oh, my bad. They call them Tez-Mo and Kev. What do I need to do? I got some solid niggaz, shorty, we can use."

"Nah, I'm good. No need to change my movements. In time, this will work itself out. I promise. Anyway, I will holla at you before I leave the state. You good? You need anything or have any more information you can give?"

"Nah, that's all."

"Ok, be careful and remain calm, this too shall pass. I will need you back to a hundred percent sooner than later. Love you, lor nigga. Again, thank you for trying to save my girl. That shit means a lot to me. I promise... that shit meant a lot." Simfany turned away from Drew as her eyes misted. *You bet not fucking cry...* she thought. She used her free hand to wave goodbye. Though she didn't look back, Drew waved back. Simfany stopped at the door frame and turned back towards Drew. The pair locked eyes temporarily.

"One more question," Simfany said.

"Shoot."

"If you didn't intentionally try to end that little girl's life, why did y'all go shoot up the funeral?"

"Huh? What are you talking about?" The look on Drew's face was genuine. He had no clue what Simfany was talking about.

"The day Tez killed Tijuana and shot you, was also the day they tried to bury their little sister, but unfortunately the service was shot up. The shooters flipped the casket on its side, spilling the little girl into the grave."

"How do you know this shit?" Drew asked curiously. For only being in town for a few days, she knew a lot of what was going on. "And how do you know the information is real?"

"How I get that is none of your concern. As long as I get the answers we need. But in this case, read the newspaper.

It's in the chair beside you. Ms. Burke had a few copies, so I helped myself to one of them. In this field, baby, you always make sure you're a few steps ahead, because if you're not..." Simfany sighed. "...because if you're not, you may not be amongst the living for long. I'll be in touch," Simfany said as she walked out the hospital room.

Drew leaned over and grabbed the newspaper off the chair. "How the fuck do these people know the details of these killings?" Drew opened *The Baltimore Sun* to see what all the police and public knew. He went page to page, trying to find the article Simfany was speaking of. After looking twice, he realized Simfany had never seen anything in the newspaper. The streets were paying their dues to the young queen.

Chapter 7

"Wake up, bitch ass nigga!" the man said, nudging Haseem as he slept. Haseem didn't budge. Frustrated, the man punched Haseem in the side of his head.

"Aaaaaarrrgghhh!" Haseem yelled and grabbed his face. "What the fuck!" Haseem opened his eyes and his heart sank. He was face-to-face with death.

"Bitch ass nigga, get the fuck up!" Haseem stared at the gun in his face, still in shock. The man punched him again.

"Alright, alright." Haseem rose slowly from the couch. He followed every move the gun made. Haseem looked on in terror.

"Nigga, what the fuck are you doing? And how the fuck you get into my house?" Baby yelled as she walked out the back room in nothing but a robe.

"Bitch, shut the fuck up!" the man replied.

"I got ya bitch, Rasheed, take that fucking gun out of his face." Rasheed didn't budge at his baby mother's words.

"Now!" Baby exclaimed. Rasheed laughed and reverted his attention back on Haseem.

"Lil nigga, you lucky I'm feeling festive in this bitch today, but know this lil bruh, if I catch you in my baby mother's house again at any point in ya life, I will smoke you. Without her, we have no problems. I ain't ya enemy, stay out my baby momma spot. You can go," Rasheed stated with authority, putting his gun back on his hip. You don't have to tell me twice, Haseem thought to himself as he hurriedly grabbed for all his things.

"You get the fuck out too, Rasheed, this some bullshit. You've known that nigga since he was a damn kid. You know damn well I'm not fucking that little boy. Get the fuck out!" Baby screamed at the top of her lungs. Haseem lightly listened to them as he reached in the couch in search of his gun.

"Yeah ight, keep playing with me, bruh. And I promise they gone find ya dusty ass floating in the Kanawha River."

"Fuck ever. Leave befor—" Baby sighed. "Just leave, please." Rasheed looked at Baby with evident hate in his eyes. Haseem was no stranger to Rasheed and Baby's antics. They were a special bunch, that was for sure. Haseem shook his head at what just happened, he was just so close to death it was disturbing. Haseem felt the cold steel of his gun, he grabbed ahold of the handle and looked up to see what Baby and Rasheed were doing. He froze and let the gun go. All eyes were on him. Fuck against his better judgment he pulled his hand from out the couch cushion, leaving his gun that Santana brought him behind. Haseem's heart sank at the thought of being naked without his strap. Haseem sighed and grabbed the rest of his shit and left, leaving his only ally behind.

***

The phone rang, waking Santana from his slumber. He opened one eye and looked at the clock. It was 9:45 in the morning. *Where the fuck has the day gone?* He looked down and rubbed Darla's head as she lay peacefully on his chest. Santana lifted his phone and looked at the calling number. Santana grabbed his phone of the nightstand and looked at the caller ID. He didn't recognize the number, so he ignored it. Almost immediately the phone began to ring again. It was a Maryland number calling, that he knew for sure. Santana answered.

"Yooooo... what's poppin'? Who this?" Santana asked.

"What's crackin, lor bro?" Drew said into the phone.

"Drew?" Santana sat up in bed, waking Darla. Drew laughed at the excitement in his best friend's voice.

"Yeah bro, what's good with you, yo?" Drew asked, trying to play cool like always, though he was just as excited as Santana to hear his friend's voice.

"Oh shit, how the fuck..." Santana was lost for words. "Son, how the fuck...man, fuck all that. how you holding, my G?"

"Huh?" Drew was confused.

"I said, how ya mean ass been? I heard about Ty, but that's another subject for a later date."

"So you don't know?" Drew questioned Santana.

"Son, what you talking bout, know what?" Santana asked with confusion written all over his face.

"When Tijuana was killed, I was almost killed too, trying to save her. And lor bro, when I tell you them blood niggas fucked me up, bro, them lor blood niggas almost sent me up that way. Don't get me wrong, I'm not paralyzed or no shit like that, but how them shells hit me, I have to teach my body how to move properly again. Your mom just left a few hours ago. She was going to be the one to tell you about the damage. I assumed you knew I was in the hospital at least."

"My G, it's a blessing you're still here, ya heard! In a split second, all this shit as we know it can be over. Oh, trust me. I know the vibes," Santana said sincerely. He knew how hot those shells felt.

"Yeah, I heard you were on bullshit down there. You have to chill... you know what you have holding over ya head." Drew reminded Santana of his notoriety.

"I understand my G, ya words aren't falling on deaf ears. But hear this, on my dead homies, son, when I handle my issues out here, we will handle what needs to be handled for the sake of you and Tijuana."

"Say less," was all Drew had to say. He was ready to either kill or be killed, that was for certain. His last move ended him in a hospital bed and Tijuana in a pine box. Drew knew he had to come correct this time.

"I love you, my nigga, you now know how to reach me. So…call bruh, call anytime. No matter the circumstances. You hear me, bro?"

"I hear you, bro." Drew mimicked Santana's growing down south accent.

"Ha… ha… ha… ha, real fucking funny," Santana said, mad as hell. He hated when Drew made fun of how he talked. "But for real, son, all jokes aside. I will come to you now if you need me to," Santana assured him.

"No need, I'm alive and strapped thanks to Mom Dukes. You have done enough for me already, lor bro. I appreciate the love for sure, shorty. And you know what's crazy, Tana, the irony of it all, you didn't even know I got hit. But when ya moms came down to pay her respects about T, she heard about what happened and showed up. You spoke about me enough that she felt like she knew me too. She showed up for me, my nigga and on Kane, I appreciate y'all like a muthafucka! I will never forget this," Drew's voice cracked. Besides the niggas he grew up on his block with, he had no one. His mother was gone, the twins were dead, as well as Kane and Tijuana. In the matter of a few years, Drew had lost everyone he genuinely loved.

"You're my brother, nigga… win, lose or draw, right?" Santana said, trying to make an attempt at lifting Drew's spirit.

"Facts, facts!" Santana couldn't hear him or see him of course, but if he knew his nigga, he knew bro was smiling ear-to-ear. The bond the two had was crazy. Drew was a real nigga through and through. *Damn, bro was really willing to die about Tijuana ... real nigga shit*, Santana thought as they momentarily sat in silence.

"We gone talk, don't trip. We will have time to talk in person. Real soon. You hear me?"

"Say less, lor yo, Mom Dukes knows where she can find me. And I promise to call if needed."

"For anything!" Santana said seriously. "Love you, bro. No homo."

"Love you too, lor yo. And stop saying that gay ass shit. Nigga, I'm not gay." Drew hated when Santana said that dumb ass no homo shit.

"Whatever, nigga." Santana hung the phone up and rubbed Darla's head, slightly playing in her hair.

"Ummmmm," Darla moaned. Santana scratched her scalp as he played in her hair. Darla looked up at Santana seductively. She moved her head off his chest and began kissing her way down his stomach. Santana braced himself. He knew that look in her eye. She was ready for some action. Darla reached into Santana's basketball shorts and pulled out his semi-erect dick. She looked up at him, then back down at his dick in her hand.

"I love you, daddy," she moaned before she swallowed him an inch at a time. Santana closed his eyes and fucked Darla's face, guiding her head up and down with the handful of hair he took only seconds earlier.

"Damn, ma!" Santana looked as his dick disappeared and reappeared wet as fuck. Darla was blowing his mind, literally. Darla slowed, taking back control of her sexual tryst. She let his dick slip out of her mouth, as she rose to position herself better. Santana bit his lip watching Darla in amazement. She lifted one leg and straddled him. Her pussy was soaking wet. The heat between the two was an inferno. Darla grabbed Santana's dick and guided him slowly into her. She moaned, "Ummmpphhh." Adjusting her position to her comfort, Darla grabbed at her stomach and slid up and down on Santana.

"Fuck! Yeah... ma, right there," Santana said as he gripped a handful of Darla's ass cheeks and deep stroked her. *Damn, this bitch pussy fire*, Santana thought as Darla bounced up and down to a rhythm in her head. Darla was going crazy. Santana closed his eyes and curled his toes. He pulled Darla into him with all his might and released his cum into her fast and deep. Darla felt Santana drain inside her, she rode him slowly for a few more moments before getting up, she wanted to catch every ounce of sperm that spewed from him.

"I love you, Tana," Darla said and leaned over on his chest from exhaustion.

"Siempre ma," Santana responded by kissing her forehead, lips and nose. "We forever, ma."

"Siempre, baby. Siempre," Darla repeated back to him.

***

Santana woke up from his slumber. *My fucking head is pounding*, Santana thought as he rubbed both sides of his temples. As if on cue, his phone started to vibrate. He picked it up and ignored the call, until he saw who the caller was. "What's poppin', son?" Santana answered.

"What's good, bruh? Me, you and Zach have to get together sometime today. It's a must we all sit down and talk."

"Heem, you good?"

"Yeah, I'm good."

"You sound spooked about something. You sure you straight?" Santana asked out of care and concern for his comrade.

"Yeah, I'm good. Just meet us at Zach's house at 8:00," Haseem stated, then hung up.

Santana looked at the phone and called back, but Haseem sent him to voicemail. Santana tossed his phone to the side and looked at the digital clock that sat on his bedstand. It was

6:50 at night. "Damn, I was knocked out." Santana stretched, knocking the sleep from his body the best way possible. He had only an hour to be at Zach's, so he got up and got to business.

***

Santana pulled up to Zach's house at 8:05 pm. He prided himself on being punctual, so he tried to be there on time, though he was slightly late. He looked in his rearview mirror out of habit and grabbed his gun. He cocked the gun back, ejecting a shell from its place at the top. He left the shell where it fell, he made a mental note to get it later. Santana turned the Crown Vic off and surveyed his surroundings for a second longer. After the feeling of self-satisfaction, he put his gun into his coat pocket and exited the car. Santana walked the path to Zach's house warily. He didn't know who was plotting to end him, he reminded himself constantly he was in a foreign city that was not his own. So, the games that were being played were on their terms not his, so he stayed ahead or tried to at all times. Once his body was consumed by the darkness of the night, he breathed a sigh of relief. He knew in his heart he was bitching, but he didn't care. Santana was aware of the danger that lurked, and he'd be damned if he was going to feel how hot them bullets could get again. Santana knocked on the door, then twisted the handle. The door opened.

He made a mental note to address that situation immediately with Zach. *These country niggas out here trippin'*, he thought as he locked the door behind him. Santana didn't play that ,"I love thy neighbor" shit. The door needed to be locked at all times, especially now. The house looked as if it was empty. Santana started up the steps and noticed Moca wasn't waiting vigil for Zach tonight. He knew either they were beefing, or that was a telltale sign of him being home. Santana laughed for a second at the irony of the situation and walked up the remaining stairs to Zach's room. The door was closed but as he approached, he could hear the TV playing one of the latest Julez Santana songs. "Money over bitches, that's the motto I follow / take that to the grave, I'll swallow eight hollows."

Zach and Haseem looked up, saw Santana walk in and went back to what had their initial attention.

"What the fuck is that?" Santana asked in a flat uneasy tone.

"It's these pills my nigga gave me while I was in NC. My problem is I don't know what they are," Zach responded, uncertain as hell. "With the fact that I don't know what these are, I'm not try—"

"Man, I keep trying to tell this goofy ass nigga he probably got E pills. It's either that or Xanax's, bro," Haseem said, holding one of them in the air as he examined it. Santana took his coat off and sat it in Zach's Chair. He picked the Xbox 360 controller off the bed and turned the music off. Both Zach and Haseem looked up.

"Nigga, what the fuck?" they said in unison.

"What the fuck is, I almost died the other night and you muthafuckas acting like shit sweet." He was vexed. *These stupid ass niggas out here playing.* Santana sighed and plopped down on the bed. He was beginning to get fed up with the bullshit.

"So, what have you niggas been into, because in my spare time I've been getting shot at. How about you, Zach, what the fuck you been into? Haseem?"

"I been getting to this money and fucking these hoes," Zach dapped hands with Haseem.

Santana looked at his homies and smiled. He was glad he was the only one going through the bullshit.

"What you smiling about, bruh?" Haseem asked.

"At you two stupid niggas, I'm happy y'all not going through the nonsense I am. But all in the same breath, my nigga, this nigga Ty not playing. I haven't seen y'all in a minute. I called both you niggas' phones, no call backs. Bro, we have to do better, or one of us is going to be caught lacking. I don't know about you, but I refuse to be the nigga that has to be buried out this bitch. I already let a nigga pierce skin. If it wasn't for you, my nigga, I would have been a memory on dat east. That nigga want blood. That nigga is sending killers, kids, friends, and family to end us." Santana got up off the bed. He was pissed. Zach just sat there silently. He knew he had been slipping.

"Now hold on, bruh, who is to say I'm not taking this shit seriously?" Haseem asked.

"Nigga, you not!"

"Yeah, the fuck I am. I'm just not running around this bitch uptight like you," Haseem said venomously. Santana laughed.

"Say less… When you looking down the barrel of a gun, or boxed in with nowhere to go, I want you to feel the same way, bitch ass nigga. Do ya thing, handle your business as you see fit. I'm out this bitch." Santana began to walk out the room but stopped and turned back around to address his friends one more time.

"Zach, don't let this money get you smoked. Be smarter than this nigga over here. And by the way, Haseem, that sale you sent me to, was the day those niggas tried to smoke me. They knew I was going to be there, at that time, at that spot." Santana walked out the room, closing the door behind him. As he walked down the steps, he heard the scraping of Moca's nails come toward him. She stood at the top of the landing and peered down at him.

"Take care of our boy, momma," Santana said to her as he walked back into the night with the feeling of being all on his own yet again.

Chapter 8

Fatty Man sat at Breeze's grave and sipped on his bottle of Hennessy. The guilt that ran through him was tremendous. He knew Breeze could have still been alive if he had just shot his gun. Fatty knew he was raw when it came to laying down his murder game. Seeing Santana there that day immobilized him, he wasn't into killing innocent souls. While, on the other hand, Breeze gave no fucks. Watching Santana fall from being shot fucked his head up, at first glance, he thought he was dealing with a child.

"I'm sorry, bruh, I didn't know. I didn't know this could happen." A tear rolled down Fatty Man's cheek. The tear was not for Breeze alone, it was for Von and Remy also. Fatty knew that as they grew, the love shifted around a little, but he didn't think that it would come down to having to kill the niggas he was raised with. As he sat at Breeze's grave, he laughed, cried and talked to himself, hoping Breeze could hear him. Fatty took another swig of the intoxicating liquid, and it burned his chest just the way he liked it. *Nigga, you a demon, stop feeling sorry for yourself. These niggas made their beds, now they have to rot in them*, Fatty thought blatantly. He felt what he did to Remy and Von was justified, they tried to banish him from a hood that he made niggas respect. It was his gun that kept the out-of-town niggas off their block. Just the thought alone boiled his blood.

Zzzzzzzz zzzzzzzzz zzzzzzz.

Fatty's phone vibrated in his pocket. He pulled his phone from his pocket and opened it. The caller ID said "Private."

"Who the fuck is calling me so early in the morning?" Fatty Man asked agitatedly.

"It's me, Fully." Fatty calmed down at the sound of Sleeze' s voice.

"Nigga, why the fuck you calling me so early?" Fatty Man asked, frustrated that he was being bothered at this time of the morning. Since his return to Charleston, Sleeze had been his go-to man. Shit, truth be told, if it wasn't for Sleeze, it was no telling how many more people Fatty would have had to kill in order to gain access back to his hometown.

"My bad, Fully, but this fat ass nigga asking for a meeting with us about the lil' situation he got going on." Sleeze explained, hoping Fatty could read through the lines. He didn't have the patience to get into the logistics of things.

"You speaking bout the lil' OT nigga?" Fatty asked to make sure they were talking about the same situation.

"Yeah, I guess them niggas stripped one of bruh's spots or—" Sleeze tried to explain, but Fatty interjected.

"I'm hip ... When do this nigga wanna sit down and have this conversation?" Fatty looked at his watch, it was 8:10 in the morning.

"Shit bruh, I can slide ya way now. He said we can pull up on him at any time. And I'm mobile. What you trying to do and who we taking with us?"

"We not taking no one. I don't feel threatened by the nigga, so the two of us should be just fine. Ummm, come and grab me around..." Fatty thought as he looked at his watch yet again. "Look give me until nine, then come get me. Or you can just come kick it with me for a few minutes. I'm at Breeze's gravesite, drinking and bullshitting with the homie."

"Bet, I'm on my way, Fully. What you drinking on?"

"Some of that Hen Dog." Sleeze laughed at Fatty.

"Nigga, ya old ass is burnt the fuck out," Sleeze joked, trying to lighten up the mood. The gesture definitely didn't go unnoticed by Fatty. Fatty was going through a lot mentally. He hadn't seen Breeze at all until now, and he would be damned if he just up and left bro hanging to go talk about some shit that could be discussed at any time.

"Say less, bruh, I'm on my way."

"Alright bet, bring a thirty with you, I got da .26 on me, a little precautious gesture just in case this fat ass nigga on some bullshit," Fatty said in a matter-of-fact tone.

"Got you, Fully," Sleeze replied.

"Forever Blooded, bruh," Fatty said before ending the call.

"Forever Blooded, big bro," Fatty heard Sleeze respond back as he closed his phone.

Spring was on its last month, making way for the summer. The weather was beginning to break and produced sunny day after sunny day. The breeze that rolled off Fatty Man's skin sent a chill through his body. He closed his eyes and breathed deeply. The fresh morning air was relaxing. The cold air filled his lungs for a second, Fatty exhaled. He repeated that a few more times before he began speaking to the dead.

"Damn, lil bro, I hope you can forgive me for the shit I had to do to Von and Remy. It's like ever since you died, bruh, everyone's love for me changed. Which in all honesty, they had a valid reason. Those niggas would still be alive if they expressed themselves differently. Breeze, they tried to ban me from the hood over this. What the fuck I look like, nigga, my gun dangerous and this they knew." The thought alone made him snicker. "I just don't know what they thought was gonna happen. Neither Remy nor Von was surprised to see me when I came back, they did me like that in front of niggas on purpose. Von put a gun in my face, and Nessy complying with Remy was the reason. So, in order for me to return and live, I sent them all to you." Fatty spoke as if Breeze could truly hear his words. Before he could finish his conversation with his right-hand, he saw Sleeze's Chevy Caprice pulling up the hill. Damn, this nigga must have been close. Fatty thought. He took another sip from his Hennessy bottle and finished what he needed to get off his chest.

"With that being said, lil bruh, I hope in the hearts of all hearts you can forgive a king for protecting his castle. I love you, gang. Until I lay the little nigga down that did this, I won't be able to sleep properly." Fatty rose from the ground as Sleeze parked his car. Fatty dusted the dirt off his clothes and waited on Sleeze to join him. Fatty looked at Sleeze wearily, he couldn't get over the fact that this nigga put all those damn tattoos all over his face. Sleeze was a dark skinned short stocky nigga that stood at five-five, with the heart of an ape and the attitude of a lion. Fatty had to admit the little nigga was raw as fuck. He smiled as Sleeze approached him with a grin on his face. "This lil nigga always up to something," Fatty said to himself.

"Ahh, what's poppin', bro!" Sleeze said with genuine excitement. Fatty laughed at his comrade.

"You already know what's up with me, trying to make peace with my brother," Fatty stated flatly. Sleeze may not have caught the double entendre in his words, but he definitely was there to make peace with all he had done. Now that was over, he was ready to get down to business. Before he could ask, Sleeze pulled the thirty-round clip for Fatty Man's Glock out of his pocket.

"Always on time, I see. How many you put in this bitch?" Fatty looked at the indicator at the same time he asked.

"Twenty-seven ... like you said, just in case. That shit doesn't need to jam if we need it to back niggas off of us. What time are you trying to go meet this nigga Ty?" Sleeze said as he lit a cigarette.

"We can meet that nigga now if you want. I spoke my peace already. You want the rest of this Henny?" Fatty held the bottle out for Sleeze to grab if he wanted it.

"Nah, I'm good, bro. I need to be on point for this meeting," Sleeze stated as he took one more pull on his cigarette before he flicked it across the cemetery. Fatty shrugged and walked to Breeze's grave and turned the bottle upside down and poured it into his grave.

"This for all the fallen, I love you, fool. Keep watch over me, bruh, I'm going to need it." Fatty Man put his hand over his heart and walked away with Sleeze in tow.

"Now, we get down to business. Also, I want you to tell me how the fuck did you miss the little nigga the night you caught him at that cluck's house," Fatty said as he walked to his car that sat side by side with Sleeze's. Sleeze stopped in his tracks and looked at Fatty Man as he walked in front of him. *How the fuck does he know that?* Sleeze thought as he racked his memory. He knew he wasn't the one who told him about the shooting, and the majority of their gang was wary of Fatty's appearance after Von and Remy's deaths, so he knew they wouldn't have said anything either. He loved Fatty more than he loved the rest of his team and in all truth, he couldn't blame him if he was responsible for Von or Remy's demise, they deserved it in his book.

Regardless of his feelings on the matter, he needed to know what he was dealing with, so he made a mental note to watch Fatty closely. Sleeze would be damned if he let a nigga rock him to sleep. It killed him to even let his paranoia manifest those demonic thoughts about a nigga he considered to be his brother. But his instincts were his key to survival and in the game he played, no one was to be trusted. Cliché, but factual... Sleeze was praying mentally that he was wrong.

"Riding or you following, bruh?" he looked over at Fatty Man and asked before he opened his door to hop in his car.

"I'll follow!" Fatty yelled over the slight breeze. Sleeze hopped in his car, but before he had the chance to pull away, Fatty Man waved him down trying to get his attention. Sleeze pulled away as if he didn't see Fatty waving.

Only if Sleeze knew that ignoring Fatty Man's gesture saved his life, he would be thanking God or whoever he prayed to at night. Fatty watched as Sleeze led the way to their meeting. He gripped tightly on the Glock that rested on his lap. He was vexed. "That's what the fuck I get with my yappy ass mouth. Fuck!" Fatty Man pounded his fist off the steering column. Not only could that have been a death wish, but it was also could have exposed the hand he was trying to play. Fatty Man closed his eyes and sighed. He came close, he came very close to exposing to Sleeze that he was the one that killed Von. Fatty took his fist from around the Glock and placed it in the divider. Damn, was he mad.

Killing Sleeze had never been in his plans, but when he just opened his mouth and asked him about the night he shot at Santana, he made a choice to end him. No one was supposed to know about the shooting besides the two shooters, and the person who sent the missile, and he knew that. So, when Fatty Man mentioned the night Santana got shot at, it was only three people who could have discussed that situation or details with him, Freezo, Sleeze or Von. And Fatty knew Sleeze would automatically clear himself because of obvious reasons. They never conversed about anything even close to pertaining to a situation like that. So, all Fatty could think to do at that time was kill. *Kill, kill, kill, kill, kill.* He knew he had already stooped to the lowest point in his life, he could no longer look in the mirror and see the standup nigga he once was. So, he didn't even feel anything no more. He didn't care. Fatty turned the music up and followed Sleeze to their designated meeting spot.

***

"Heem, I'm trying to talk about last night. Because—" Haseem cut Zach off mid-sentence.

"Man, fuck that nigga, bruh. He think he better than niggas. We ain't did shit but be good to that nigga. And you know like I know, we don't fuck with OT niggas on this home front, yet we embraced his ass," Haseem vaguely expressed.

"Bruh, calm down! Both of you niggas are wrong as fuck. I don't even know why you're tripping. As a matter of fact, explain that to me please, why are you tripping?" Zach said, trying to understand what the fuck his niggas got going on in the shadows.

"What?" Haseem seemed confused by the question.

"I said, why the fuck are you tripping for? Because yeah, Santana is mad. He has a right to be mad. Now if he wasn't mad, I could say fuck that nigga, because he didn't care. But that's not the case right now. He wants us to survive this shit, Heem. The Puerto Rican nigga is right, we need to start taking this shit more seriously," Zach spoke his peace, hoping to talk some kind of sense into Haseem's thick ass head.

"Well, since you want to take his side, fuck you too!" Haseem started grabbing his things that were scattered all around Zach's room. Zach didn't move an inch or try to stop him from leaving. He was even starting to see the money was becoming a problem for Haseem.

"So, you telling me you're just going to up and leave because we as a team disagreed about something?" Zach asked, arms stretched.

"Bruh, miss me with that shit. You didn't say shit to that nigga when he left last night, so don't try to say nothing to me. You know, Zach, that's the shit I be hating about you. I swear, I hate this nigga Rodney be right. But damn, my nigga, when a new nigga come around, you start acting different to the niggas that you played in trees with and spent your whole life around," Haseem said coldly.

"Oh yeah, so that's how you and your bitch ass cousin feel? So, when did niggas start kicking each other's back in? Because the last time I did check, I never said one bad thing about either one of you bitch ass niggas, and you niggas is the most flaw niggas around this fucking neighborhood. And just food for thought, the same OT nigga that you niggas are so hung up on, Santana... that nigga caught Big Will in Value City's parking lot and sent shots at that nigga in broad daylight. All because he shot Rodney in his stomach, the same OT nigga that coulda kept that half-brick from that lick, that same OT nigga that had your back and made sure you had food and clothes when you got released from Tiger Morton. Bitch, you ungrateful. You don't have to do this gay shit you doing, hoping a nigga ask you to stay, get the fuck out. How bout this, get ya shit and get the fuck out. Fuck you and fuck Rodney, both you niggas are bum ass niggas. I don't understand how I even fuck with y'all niggas for real, because I swear in my gut, I can feel the hate. But it is okay, because y'all niggas won't ever be able to prosper from that kind of shit. And by the way, did you set our nigga up to get slaughtered?"

Zach looked into Haseem's face in search of the truth. Zach crossed his fingers and prayed Haseem wouldn't stoop that low in the name of money. Haseem just stared at him. Haseem could see the disappointment on his face as the silence grew.

"Do you think I did?" Haseem asked in return.

"I don't know, I seem to not know you as I once did. Between the shit your cousin puts in your ear and the shit that you have learned since being locked away, you have changed. Some of which is great, but some shit I can rather go without. Please don't confuse the fact that I love you Heem, but it sounds like you could have played a role in the situation that just took place with Tana. Am I wrong? Tell me I'm wrong and I'll believe you. Am I wrong, Heem?" Zach asked, looking at his friend from across the room. Haseem put his head down and shook his head.

"I didn't set bro up, Zach. Please, I need you to believe me."

"Then explain because right now, bruh, I'm not sure what to think about you." Zach folded his arms across his chest.

"I was with one of my east side niggas when Doug called me about trying to get him together. I wasn't able to do it, so I called you and when you said you were OT, I called Tana."

"Hold up, didn't you tell us that you were also going to be out of town?" Zach asked in a as a matter fact tone of voice. Haseem looked up at Zach and just continued to stare. He looked as if he had suddenly stayed up for days on end. His eyes were bloodshot from all the arguing and frustration he was enduring. Haseem had never been through any shit like this in his life.

Zach could tell he was tired of feeling like he was being interrogated, but it had to be done. Zach wanted answers. "So bruh, can you at least explain what the hell is going on? I'm not feeling like you can be trusted right now. I do need you to know that money that is on us includes you. And if for some reason you think they will let you slide for your part in this… good luck." At this point Zach was just throwing shit out there in hopes that what he felt was totally off from the truth.

"Look…" Haseem cleared his throat then started to explain himself. "Ok look, I don't have a clue what you have running through your head. I don't know what Santana has running through his head, but one thing I can and will tell you is that you muthafuckas are tripping! You know for sure you are my brother over everything in this life. That shit you said about me and Rodney was some bullshit, but I can understand, bruh. I know I can be overbearing, but to compare me to Rodney, oooooooohhhh that's low, my nigga." Haseem laughed, then Zach followed suit.

"Yeah, my bad for that one, bruh. I was just in my feelings about the bullshit that has been going on. If you're saying you didn't send a nigga to Doug's, what happened because whether you want to believe it or not, someone knew Santana was going to be there at Doug's around that time of night." Zach fished more. He wanted so badly to believe Haseem, but none of the shit was adding up to nothing.

"Bro, I was with these hoes in Kanawha City at this one nigga's spot." Haseem looked in the air, trying to retract his memory for the name or names of the people he was with that night. "I can't remember dude's name, but the nigga from Missouri. You know who I'm talking about?"

"The black ass nigga with the dreads from St. Louis?" Zach asked.

"Yup, that's him. Anyway, he had Freezo, Slime, Stunt and a few others over his spot in Kanawha City. The call came through, you already know the sequence of events. I didn't stay there that night, I had Baby come and get me from dude's house. I knew I was toooo high to be around a group of people I didn't know, especially with Ty having that chicken on my head. You know me and Freezo was in The Mort together, but he fucks with them FB niggas tough. And with the rumor that's going around about them and Santana, I try to stay clear of them niggas by any means. I went to Baby's house that night." Haseem left the part out about Rasheed pulling his strap on him. He was too embarrassed to admit to his friend that he let a nigga slide with that kind of disrespect. He had a plan for Rasheed, but he knew it would take time to handle. Haseem rubbed his hand over his hair, he was stressed to the max. He could see in Zach's face he was having a hard time believing him. Haseem was lost for words at this point, he hated explaining himself. Even to his best friend.

"Did Freezo or any of those other niggas overhear your conversation with Santana? Bruh, you have to admit none of this shit is making sense at all, Heem. Okay, let me ask you this, if you was in Santana's shoes at this moment, what would you do and how would you feel?" Zach asked prudently. Haseem looked up and shrugged. He knew he would be pissed and feel a certain kind of way if the roles were reversed.

"Nigga, you know how I would feel. I would want a nigga's head, for real. I'm not blaming that nigga for feeling no kind of way. I got shit going on with me too, bruh, what the fuck! I ain't been banged on or no shit like that, but I got my own demons I'm dealing with too, nigga."

"Like what, bruh?" Zach asked with an expression of disbelief written all over his face.

"You know what, nigga, fuck you and fuck that bitch ass nigga!" Haseem said frustratingly. Zach looked over at Haseem and laughed. He found Haseem funny as hell, he couldn't care less if Haseem had an attitude, he just watched as Haseem gathered his things from around his room. Once Haseem finally had everything in his hands, he walked by Zach and out the room. Zach ran his hands over his face. He was livid, stressed, and slightly confounded. At this point, all he could do is guard his wellbeing better, because Santana was right, he and Haseem were lacking tremendously. He was only sixteen and dying so young wasn't in his plans nor his cards. Not if he could help it at least.

Grrrrrr.

Zach heard Moca's nails scrape across the wooden floors rapidly. He stopped and listened, trying to hear what Moca was getting herself into. Zach chuckled at the thought of Moca fighting with her shadow again.

Bark ... Bark ... Bark ... Bark ... Bark ...

"Aye girl, stop!" Zach yelled. Zach heard her growl again. *What the fuck*, Zach thought as he rose to his feet. Mocca had her moments, but this seemed to be different altogether. She had never reacted like this. Something was wrong. Zach's hands trembled as he grabbed his gun off his hip to go see what the fuck had his dog in such an uproar.

"Moca, come here, momma!" Zach yelled out for her. Moca barked again.

"Moca!" Zach called again. Before he had the chance to turn the corner, Haseem appeared, shaken.

"Nigga, what the fuck?" Zach looked at his friend questionably.

"Bruh, get ya muthafucking dog. She tripping, she won't let me off the steps." Haseem explained. Zach looked past him into pure darkness. The only light on in the whole house was his. His mother and father both were gone. His mother was at work, while his father went to North Carolina to take care of his grandparents. So, the only people in the home were him and Haseem. Haseem looked down toward Zach's side and saw he had his gun drawn ready for action.

"Why the gun?" Haseem asked curiously.

"Do I really have to explain that?" Zach looked at Haseem as if he was the dumbest nigga in the world. He sighed, then explained what he felt should be obvious. "You walked out my room minutes ago. Then my dog started tripping shortly after. Why wouldn't I have a gun out, you sound silly as fuck right now, bro. I thought you were gone, and I didn't know what was going on downstairs. All I knew was my baby started going crazy. I wasn't bout to walk through this dark muthafucking house empty-handed. Furthermore, why are you still here, my nigga? You being weird, bruh."

"Yeah… ight nigga, get me pass this stupid ass dog and I'll be gone," Haseem replied, making sure to put an extreme emphasis on gone. Zach just looked at Haseem and put the gun up. They both were being petty and he knew it, but he didn't care.

"What the fuck did you do to her?" he asked, mugging Haseem. When Haseem paused, he walked past him and called Moca to him yet again. "Come here, now!" Moca didn't waste any time as she ran up the stairs to her owner's side. She walked past Haseem and sat at Zach's feet, waiting for her next command. Haseem looked at Moca and then at Zach.

"Stupid ass bitch," Haseem said as he turned to leave and walked down the stairs, leaving the insult in the air for both Zach and Moca to grab.

"Watch ya mouth, my nigga," Zach replied.

"You heard what I said," Haseem countered without looking back.

"Nah, nigga… you heard what I said." Zach stood his ground. Haseem stopped at the bottom of the steps and looked up at Zach. He had no words, but if looks could kill, they would be fitting Zach for a casket.

"Lock the door behind you too, big dog," Zach flatly stated.

"Opp ass nigga!" Haseem replied coldly. The words that left Haseem's mouth, sent a chill down Zach's spine.

"Oh okay, eat a dick and die, nigga. In that order," Zach replied back just as venomously.

Haseem bit his bottom lip before he said anything else that could ruin their relationship completely. He opened the door and walked out, slamming it behind him.

"Fuck!" Zach yelled at the top of his lungs. He didn't know what the fuck was happening or transpiring between him and Haseem, but it was taking a toll on him already. In all the years they had known each other, the pair had never had a spat like this before. It seemed like ever since Haseem came home from doing that juvie bid, they weren't the same. And now with the newly added pressure, it helped none. He reached into his pocket and pulled his phone out. He dialed Haseem's number from memory. Zach knew he was trippin, he and Haseem needed to sit down and talk this shit out. Zach took a seat on the top step and waited on Haseem to answer his phone. Moca nudged him as he held his phone to his ear, she could sense her master was saddened.

"It's going to be okay, momma, Heem just mad right now," Zach said, rubbing around her ears. The call went to voicemail. Zach hung up and tried again. This time he was sent straight to Haseem' s messaging system.

"You reached Heem, you know what to do."

Beep ...

Zach called back, knowing his friend would not be answering. The line rang once before the voicemail picked up yet again.

"You reached Heem, you know what to do."

Beep ...

Instead of calling back again, he left Haseem a message. "Bruh, come back. We are better than this shit, you acting crazy, my nigga. I was outta pocket, my bad. Be safe and hit me back," Zach said, making his best attempt at apologizing for his part in the bullshit. Even though he swore to himself he wouldn't, he tried calling again, getting the same result. "Whenever you wanna stop acting like a female… call me, nigga," Zach said into his phone.

That was the last time he would make the attempt to right his wrong. He wasn't about to kiss nobody's ass, Haseem's or Santana's. Zach put his phone back into his pocket.

"Why are they making this thing so complicated? Huh, mommas? Huh, mommas? Huh mommas?" Zach laughed as Moca squirmed around from him rubbing and tickling her. Zach rubbed Moca a few more times before planting a kiss on the top of her head.

Chapter 9

While the streets gathered their information, so did Detective Williams. Though he closed the case that involved N.O. and Breeze, he left no stone unturned, and the streets told the story best. Justin Torres, better known to him now as Santana, was not as much of an innocent victim as he once thought. He knew it was more to the story, so he continued to follow his gut and investigate, but before he had the chance to indulge in the rumors circulating around Santana, Nessy Garland was murdered, followed by her on again off again boyfriend, La'Remy Woodson. The murders not only left him in a state of awe but threatened to cripple the city of Charleston as a whole. So, as he stared at the file of the late Devon Saunders on his desk, he stood conflicted. Because what he once thought he knew regarding the murders of Nessy Garland and La'Remy Woodson, now changed drastically. Not only were there two people of the same circle killed, but there was also now a third. The Full Blooded Gang. Detective Williams was not only at a loss for words, but he was completely mystified on what was taking place in his own backyard.

"Danny, what do you make of this shit?" he asked his partner, Detective Daniel Schooner, while dropping the file on his desk to read.

"I have no fucking clue. I read the file earlier myself. None of our C.I.'s have information regarding these cases. There are no rumors being passed around, no one has claimed the bodies. There isn't enough to even speculate, no outstanding beefs with anyone besides with Cameron 'N.O.' Dukes and you see how that ended. All dead ends, Rodriguez and Carter are working this case, and the roadblocks seem to be endless. No one seems to genuinely know what transpired, no one can say nothing besides the fact that Bre'Shawn, Devon and La'Remy were all a part of the same gang. Whereas the Nessy girl fits into none of this shit, another dead end. According to her peers, she wasn't a part of any gang, nor had ties to gang activity. Well, you know besides loving the one guy, La'Remy. That is our only connection, which doesn't make sense because she was killed alone at her own home. But..." Detective Schooner paused.

"What Rodriguez did find out recently was Garland played heavily in the rumor mill. Before her death she talked about her presence on the day of the double homicide in front of Shop N Go. To what extent, I have no clue. You would either have to talk to Carter or Rodriguez to find out anything further. And I highly doubt they could explain anything more, because if so, they wouldn't be asking for our help." Williams listened intently. This shit was honestly blowing his mind. He had been on the force for twenty years and had never seen an accumulative number of cases without evidence or meaning. In the matter of eight months, five people were killed and all somehow connected through one way or the other. And yet still no answers could be given.

"What about the rumor mill? Lies can sometimes lead to the truth. Any—" Detective Schooner cut his partner's words short.

"There is no information, Brian. When I mean none, I'm serious when I say that. It's none. The only possible lead we can go off of is the girl. And the only fact that we have for her is she has a big mouth. So, unless she told someone something before she passed, we're back to square one."

"Square one we go," Detective Williams said disappointedly. He rubbed his temple, a habit he had consumed as a child,

"Well, I'll see you later. I need a god damn break. How the fuck do we have three murders and nobody's heard or seen shit. A muthafucka and his crew is running around killing people and we have no way of stopping it. That shit just sounds stupid." Detective Williams admitted as he rose from his seat and grabbed his jacket. He was slightly disgruntled to say the least. He needed an ear to express his frustration. Detective Williams pulled his phone out his pocket and called the one person he knew would listen intently and let him vent. The caller answered on the second ring.

"Hello," Kat's angelic voice answered.

"Good evening, beauty. How has your day been?" Williams asked into his phone, all smiles.

"I'm doing okay, baaaby, making these plates to feed my daughter and grandbaby. How is your day at work going? Anything interesting?" Kat asked.

"I'm glad you asked. I'm frustrated like hell. All these unsolved murders are fucking my head up. There are no leads, no witnesses coming forward, just pure dead ends. Charleston is too small to be experiencing shit in this magnitude. Three unsolved murders, man, now that shit is crazy. But enough about me, what has your day consisted of?"

"Taking care of Niyah while Raven works, I don't have anything special that goes on here... well, besides you and you never come here. So... no shade of course." Kat laughed, knowing she was taking playful shots at him. She had been begging for him to show his face more, but he continued to ignore her request. Detective Williams was having fun with Kat and right now that's all it was, she knew it just as well as he did. That still didn't stop her from wanting more in return. What he didn't know was that she was trying to get her mind off of Santana, the person he thought was her blood nephew. Kat was a sexual person, she wanted that instant gratitude from whoever she was dealing with, like most woman in life. She wanted to be loved, cherish, and fucked well. Detective Williams did okay in the lovemaking department, but he wasn't Santana. The young nigga had a skill that would be hard to match.

"See there you go. I told you what type of problems I can have if the department finds out we have been having a relationship," Detective Williams tried to explain for the umpteenth time.

"Brian, you continue to say that, but have yet to tell me how fucking me could get you in trouble at your workplace. I'm lost, have been lost and frankly I'm getting exhausted from chasing you around Charleston. So, please explain to me what the issues are, so I can leave this part of our relationship alone. So, please get to explaining," Kat stated with irritation clearly in her voice.

"I can't," Detective Williams simply said.

"Well, 'Mr. I Can't,' I'm sorry but this little sexcapade we have going on will have to come to an end. I can respect the fact you have to hide me for reasons of work, all I'm asking is for you to tell me why and you can't even do that? Yeah, I'm good on you. At this point I feel like you are hiding something. So, thank you for all the amazing nights we shared, but until you are man enough and willing to at least explain why I must be a secret, this shit is coming to an end." Kat tried not once, not twice, but several times to mend the issues plaguing their relationship.

Williams sighed into the phone. He knew if he didn't give some kind of response to her liking, she would leave, and in all honesty, he didn't want that. He hadn't told her, but he was falling head over heels for her. The pussy was fire, he loved the way she conducted herself as a woman and just her vibe alone was intoxicating. It was a choice that needed to be made, either compromise his case or follow his heart. In his head he weighed the pros and cons. The pros of being with Kat definitely outweighed the stress and bullshit of his job. Against his better judgment, he thought with his dick instead of his brain.

"Alright, if I tell you this, I swear you better not speak this to nobody. This shit could end my career." Detective Williams put a little more on it than he had to. The investigation he was doing on Santana was solely for his own agenda.

"Boy, ain't nobody going to speak on your cases, what the hell?" Kat replied smiling.

"Okay, well messing with you would be a conflict of interest, reason being is because I'm still investigating the murders of Cameron Dukes and Bre'Shawn Saunders. So, I just—" Kat instantly got mad but suppressed most of her anger. The only other person that could be involved with that case was Santana. And she would be damn if she allowed him to send Santana to jail. She loved Santana in many ways that no one could understand.

"So, hold up… you telling me you're investigating my nephew still? Justice has nothing to do with what happened that day at Shop N Go, and you told me that yourself. Am I right or did you not say that the case was closed?" she asked intently.

"I'm saying, well… yeah, it technically is closed. But since finding out about his dealings in the street, I reopened it. Also, the streets aren't calling your nephew Justice, they call him Santana. and if I can recall the day at the hospital, you also called him that at the nurses' station. Please don't be upset, I am a detective, Kat. I just want to make sure we don't have a killer on the streets. Of course, not saying that's what your nephew is. I just want to be able to sleep soundly at night. So there, that's why I don't want to be seen publicly with you just in case my hunch is right. So, please keep this to yourself. If he is straight, there is nothing to worry about. Right?"

"Right. I understand. Was that all? I thought it was some serious shit you had to say. My nephew goes by the name Santana, has been since he was a baby. And if that's all you're looking into, then we are good. We have no issue at all for real. You just make sure you slide through tonight and beat this pussy down like I like it. How about that? Can you do that for momma tonight? I want you to eat this pussy like I like, you know all wet and sloppy-like. Muah... te amo, papi." Kat purred into the phone. The thought of making love to Kat later that night had his dick standing at attention. He was excited.

"I love you too, momma. Let me get back in here and take care of the bullshit on my desk and I will call you later on tonight. Is that okay with you? And please... Kat, don't repeat what I said to you. If you truly love me, you will make sure I'm straight. So, we good?" Detective Williams asked solemnly.

"Papi, we good. I promise. You just make sure you call me tonight with that good ass dick of yours. Talk to you later," Kat replied.

"Okay beauty, I'll call you as soon as I get off of work."

"Bye."

"Bye honey," Kat replied and hung up the phone.

Detective Williams put his phone up and walked back into the police department. He now had something to look forward to once he was relieved of his duties.

***

Kat ended her call with Detective Williams and sat down on her sofa. The blow he just delivered knocked the air out of her. The police were still investigating Santana. *What the fuck*, she thought trying to control her nerves. Her hands were trembling uncontrollably. Kat was visibly shaken.

"Ma!" Raven called from the top floor. Kat ignored her daughter momentarily, she was trying to figure out a way to help Santana get from under the rock that seemed to be trapping him.

"Ma!" Raven called again. When she didn't get a response the second time, she sighed and then stormed down the stairs in search of her mother. When Raven turned the corner and looked into the living room, she saw her mother was deep in thought. Raven just watched Kat for a second, she could tell that her mother was extremely disturbed by something. Raven turned to go back upstairs but thought better of it. Raven didn't know what was really going on, but she be damned if she wasn't about to find out.

"Mommy, are you okay? You look crazy as hell right now. What's wrong?" Raven sat down next to Kat on the sofa. Kat looked over and smiled at Raven. Her baby was always on her team, no matter what, and she loved her for that.

"I'm good, just got some shit on my mind that Brian told me," Kat replied, not really getting into detail.

"Do you want to talk about it, or is it none of my business?" Raven laid her head on Kat's shoulder. Kat kissed the side of her forehead and ran her hand down her silky hair.

"This nigga just told me he was investigating Santana for his part in the murders that took place in front of Shop N Go." Raven lifted her head off of Kat's shoulder, with a look of dismay.

"What? Why?" Raven asked with concern written all over her face. Raven now understood the look her mother had only minutes earlier.

"I have no clue, Raven, and stop yelling before you wake Niyah up. All I can tell you is what he told me."

"Which is?" Raven asked, growing impatient.

"He basically stated that he wasn't trying to leave no stones unturned. A lot has been going on around Santana apparently and he wants to make sure that he is living by the way of the law. Well that's what I got from it at least. He thinks your cousin is running around killing people." Kat laughed trying to explain what Detective Williams had told her. She just couldn't see Santana being nobody's killer. She knew he was bad as hell, but being murderous is something other in itself. But only if she knew what type of person Santana grew into.

"First off, let's get this shit straight, that fine ass nigga is not my cousin. Secondly, I would have heard if that nigga was… Hold up! I did hear about a rumor going around about Santana and those two niggas he be with. They were supposed to hit a nigga named Ty for some money and dope. How true, I don't know, but as far as the other shit, I highly doubt he on that type of shit yet," Raven explained.

"And who the fuck is Ty?" Kat asked confused as hell. She had known about the first lick he hit because she was the one that found the half of brick that was hidden in the cigarette cartons. But the name Ty didn't ring any bells. She was lost, she ransacked her brain trying to match the name to a face, but she continued to come up blank.

"Ma, you know who I'm talking bout, he a big fat nigga. He stay jeweled up. All I know about him is that he is ugly as fuck, fat and paid. A lot of my friends be fucking with him. He not stingy with his bread, if you know what I mean," Raven explained to Kat who Ty was to the best of her ability.

"Yeah, you have to be talking about Torrey. He the only nigga paid like that around here. How much did you say Tana and his friends hit him for?" Kat fished. She already knew Santana robbed Torrey because he had told her himself. She wanted to know if Ty was a different person altogether, or if he and Torrey were one and the same. She prayed they were the same person.

"It's a lot of rumors, but the shit they speaking about is kind of outlandish. I can be nosy and find out if you want me to, but I'm pretty sure none of the shit I hear will be factual. I would just ask Santana myself if I was you. As a matter of fact, I haven't seen his sexy ass in a minute. Does he not live here anymore?" Raven asked in a matter-of-fact style of manner.

"He don't, he been staying with Montez little friend, Zach."

"That makes sense, but why?" Raven was totally lost on the fact Santana left.

"Because he told Simfany that we live unsafe. He explained to her how we keep the door open at all times of the day and night. I really can't fault him, because coming from where he is from, that shit is a no-no. So, I agreed as long as Simfany agreed." Kat shrugged. Raven understood but her face displayed something else. She was pissed. She twisted her face up and snarled her lips.

"I'm from Courtlandt too, and?" Raven said as she twisted her neck like a hood rat. Kat laughed. Her daughter was something else.

"Girl, you got problems." Kat laughed.

"I'm just saying, I was looking forward to seeing his sexy ass running around here."

Raven pouted. *Damn, this little nigga got an effect on us Torres women. Bitch, if you just knew what that dick was hitting on*, Kat thought lustfully.

"I don't know, baby, he living grown and Simfany don't care, so I don't either." Niyah started crying in the distance. "Go get her," Kat said. Raven got up.

"You okay though?" Raven asked, looking down on her mother.

"Yeah, I'm good. If you wanna see him while he here, I'm bout to call him over here and let him know what's going on," Kat informed Raven.

"Depends on when he show up. I have to be up early to go to work. If I'm not awake, just let him know that I love him and that we miss him." Raven leaned down and kissed her mother on the forehead.

"Got you, beauty… and thank you for your care and concern, love."

"Always Ma, always. Good night," Raven said, stopping at the corner of the entryway.

"Good night," Kat replied back. The floors creaked, indicating Niyah was up and moving around.

"Let me go get this girl before she get to tripping, thinking no one is here." Raven rolled her eyes and disappeared around the corner.

"Niyah momma, here I come pretty." Kat could hear Raven call out as she ascended the stairs. Kat smiled to herself. She loved how great Raven was with Niyah. Kat let the thought pass as she grabbed her phone off the coffee table and pressed 2 on her dial pad. That was Santana's number on her speed dial list. The phone rang twice and then immediately went to voicemail.

"I know this muthafucka didn't just send me to voicemail?" she said to herself out loud.

Kat laughed at the irony of the situation. Instead of calling back, she texted him.

Send me to voicemail again, little nigga, and we are going to have a problem. Answer ya damn phone. NOW!

Her phone beeped before she had the chance to call back. Santana had texted her back.

LOL ... Call back beautiful I was busy.

Kat rolled her eyes as she read the message. The chill bumps that appeared on across her skin told her enough, she had it bad over the little nigga. A simple word drove her insides crazy. Santana calling her beautiful lit her face up. She was smiling from ear to ear, slightly warming her insides. She knew she had to get herself together and placed the call. Santana answered on the first ring.

"Hello?" Santana answered nonchalantly. Kat could hear him smiling through the phone.

"Oh, so you think you're funny, huh?" Santana busted out laughing.

'What you talking bout, ma?" Santana played dumb.

"Whatever boy, what are you doing at the moment? Are you still busy?" Kat asked, changing her tone to let him know she was no longer joking.

"Nah, not no more. I was temporarily, but I'm free. Why, what's good? You okay?"

Santana answered her question with his own. *This nigga,* Kat thought.

"I'm fine. I need to talk to you regarding this detective nigga I've been seeing," Kat replied.

"You talking about Big Willie, no homo?" he laughed hysterically.

"Why are you so silly?" Kat asked, not being able to contain herself from laughing also.

She tried to regain her composure.

"Now is not the time, Tana, I'm serious. When can you make your way through here?"

"I can come through now if it's that important," Santana answered.

"Please," was all Kat said back in reply.

"Bet, I'm only around the comer on Dixie. I can be there in about five minutes," Santana assured her.

"Okay, the door will be open, just walk in."

"Y'all just don't learn." Kat sucked her teeth at his smart-ass remark.

"Boy, shut up and come on," she said and hung up, not giving him a chance to reply.

***

Santana looked at his phone, it returned to the home screen where he had a picture of Tijuana set as his screensaver. Kat had hung up on him. *This lady is crazy, man,* he thought as he pulled on his Dutch Master. He was parked in his favorite spot in the whole city. It was located in a deep cut on Dixie Street that overlooked the road. It was one way in, one way out. It was his place of solace, a place for him to be comfortable, a place for him to think and get his mind right. He loved the hideaway spot, he knew it was impossible that he was the only person that occupied the space.

Santana took another pull from the Dutch, filling his lungs to its capacity and held in the smoke until he coughed. The mid-grade weed had him high as a kite floating to the sky. He needed it, between the death of Tijuana and the currents issues he was having with his friends, taking the time to himself was damn near mandatory. After a few more minutes of sitting and thinking, Santana stubbed the remainder of the blunt out and put his rental in drive. After looking both ways, he pulled out of the cut and sped recklessly to Jackson Street.

Less than five minutes later, he pulled up to the front of Kat's house. It took him a little longer than expected to pull up, his paranoia had kept him from just pulling onto Kat's block. To others, it may seem silly or even cowardice, but to him it was life preserving. He wasn't into playing with his life. Santana grabbed his gun off his lap and tucked it away into his Flight Jacket. The April air was slightly warm with a nightly chill. Santana got out the car, looking both up and down the street. He was ready for the bullshit if it presented itself, he made sure from now on, he would try to be ready at all times. He at least tried to convince himself of that. He walked to the door and turned the knob, the door opened. Santana walked inside and closed the door behind him. Securing the door, he latched the chain and turned the dead bolt. *What the fuck do they have a dead bolt for if they never lock the door? These people are fucking confused*, Santana thought as he made his way around the house. He walked into the kitchen in search of Kat, but the kitchen was also empty. Santana went to walk out the kitchen, but a thought hit his mind, so he turned and walked to the refrigerator. He opened it to see what was inside. The refrigerator's capacity was okay, but it could be better. He made a mental note to fill it up the next day. Santana closed the door back and pulled his phone out of his pocket. He searched for Kat's number, and when he found it, he texted her.

I'm here, where are you? His phone vibrated instantly in return.

In my room, I'm on my way down. Took you long enough, didn't it... Kat texted back.

Bet... I'll be in the living room, bring a blunt and make sure you wear them shorts I like, Santana replied jokingly. He knew she would find humor in his text.

Lol... Okay

Santana walked back to the front of the house and took a seat in the living room, making himself at home. He took his Flight Jacket off and removed his Barkley's. His feet hurt from all the traveling he had been doing for the last few days. It seemed like he couldn't find any time to rest, even when he was at home with Darla. Darla had that nigga working overtime, literally. But he couldn't complain because Santana loved every minute of it. Santana reached into his jacket pocket and pulled out the Ziploc bag that he used to store his weed. He emptied a few blunts' worth out onto the coffee table, then sealed the bag back. While Santana waited on Kat to appear, he crushed the weed down to the best of his ability. Santana subconsciously stopped when he heard the floor begin to creak. He knew it was Kat on her way down. Fuck if the walls could talk, the floor snitched every time.

Santana laughed to himself. He had the craziest thoughts. He was always told it was okay to talk to yourself, as long as you didn't answer yourself back, you were good. He was baked out of his mind. He looked at the weed and sighed. He didn't even know why he was crushing the weed up. He didn't want to get any higher, but he knew Kat loved to smoke, so he compromised. As the thought left his head, Kat entered the room. Santana looked up and his dick instantly got hard from the sight he saw. *What the fuck*, he thought damn near drooling on himself. Kat walked by him gracefully and sat down in the love seat across from him. Kat had on skintight Juicy Couture boy shorts that left nothing to the imagination, with a matching silk halter top. Her hair was silky and wet as if she had just stepped out of the shower. He looked at her for a second in awe, closed his mouth and went back to crushing the weed down. Santana was truly lost for words.

"Did you bring the blunts with you?" he asked, breaking the silence.

"Yes sir," Kat answered, throwing the box of Dutch Masters on the couch beside him.

"So, what's good, ma? What was so important that couldn't have waited until tomorrow?" Santana asked, trying not to make eye contact.

"Well, since you want to get straight to it..." Kat explained in detail everything she and Detective Williams spoke about earlier that evening. Santana sat and listened intently while he rolled up.

"That's all he said?" Santana asked inquisitively.

"Pretty much. I don't think he wanted to seem like he was accusing you of anything yet, but it sounds like whatever rumors are circulating about you has his antennas on high alert."

"You wanna hit this?" Santana asked as he lit the blunt in his mouth.

"Do I? I would love to," Kat replied seductively. Santana's cheeks turned red from blushing. He wasn't sure if she was even talking about the blunt anymore. He couldn't keep his dick from standing at attention, he was turned on to the max. The sight of Kat alone made chills run through his soul, but her having those little ass boy shorts on, now that shit had him on ten. Santana pulled on the blunt a few times before reaching the blunt out for her to grab. Kat was too far from him to reach it, so he knew one of them had to get up. And he knew it definitely wasn't going to be him, his dick was way too hard to leave the position he was in. Kat uncrossed her legs and got up. Her shorts had risen higher into her crotch from the way she was seated. Santana couldn't help but stare at Kat's fat pussy print. He bit his bottom lip subconsciously. Kat looked at Santana and smiled, his eyes screamed lust. She walked over and grabbed the blunt, then walked back to the sofa and began to puff away. The sexual tension in the room was high. Santana didn't know what to say, and Kat looked at Santana try his best not to make eye contact. *This little nigga is something else*, she thought as she pulled on the blunt. They sat there in silence for a second before Kat finally broke the silence.

"So, Mr. Vasquez, what have you been up to? Haven't seen or heard from you in a few weeks. Why?" Kat pulled on the blunt again, the weed was doing its job. She was growing mellower by the second.

"Trying to stay alive. This nigga Ty done put them goons on me over that lick me and the homies hit," Santana replied.

"Raven was telling me something about that earlier. She mentioned this Ty nigga, but I was unfamiliar. I wasn't aware you robbed somebody else. Santana, you—" Santana interjected.

"Nah, you know we not on no shit like that. It's the same nigga. It's the dude Torrey, I guess they call him Ty too. Fuck that nigga, I'm not even trying to blow my high thinking about that silly ass shit right now."

"That's cool, here." Kat reached the blunt out for Santana to grab. Santana looked at her but didn't move.

"Nigga, I'm not bringing this shit to ya lazy ass, you got me fucked up." Kat hit the blunt again. *Fuck it*, Santana thought and got up from the couch. Kat looked down at Santana's hard on, it was hard for her not to notice the bulge poking from his jeans. Kat licked her lips, by habit she bit her bottom lip when she was turned on. Kat pulled the blunt back, forcing Santana to stop closer to her. Santana knew Kat was on bullshit, but he didn't care, Kat was too intoxicating.

"Give me the blunt, ma," Santana said as he grabbed for her hand. Kat moved the blunt above her head and out of reach for Santana to grab.

"Ma, stop playing." He walked closer, trying to grab the blunt from her. Kat wasted no time in reaching out and grabbing Santana's dick through his jeans. He closed his eyes and his dick jumped in response.

"Can I have... please?" Kat begged, rubbing his bulge up and down through his jeans.

"Same time, same time. I don't trust you," Santana said playfully, reaching for the blunt yet again.

"My pleasure," Kat purred, handing the blunt over. Santana pulled on the blunt, it was out.

"See, look what you did," Santana said playfully.

"I'll make up for it," she replied lustfully. Kat pulled Santana closer, unbuckling his belt all in the same motion. Santana watched in awe at her crave him. It only took a few seconds for Kat to free Santana's dick from his jeans. Kat looked Santana in his eyes as she slowly beat his dick back and forth.

"Damn ma, that shit feel good as fuck," he growled. The only reply Kat had to that was a sensual lick around the head of his dick. The precum that oozed from his penis sent her over the edge. She took him into her mouth slowly, getting her throat and mouth adjusted to his size. Kat seductively licked Santana's shaft from the bottom back to the top, all while looking in his eyes. Kat went to work. The blunt was long gone and the back of her head had replaced it.

"Yeah, eat that dick, ma. Eat that shit. Fuck! Tell me you love me!" Santana said, growling in pure ecstasy.

"Te... amo...papi," Kat managed to say around Santana's dick. That shit drove him wild. Santana gripped Kat's wet hair and pushed deep into her mouth. Kat didn't miss a beat, she sucked him harder each time Santana's dick touched the back of her throat. She was trying to swallow him whole. Kat grabbed Santana's hand, placing it on her inner parts. She continued to eat him hungrily. Santana rubbed Kat's pussy up and down through her boy shorts. *God damn her pussy wet*, Santana thought, finding her clit and giving all his attention to that spot. Santana went to pull away, he wanted to stick his dick in her, but she locked her mouth on to him and sped up. Kat sucked and slurped faster around the head of his mans. Santana's touch alone hypnotized her soul.

Kat could feel Santana's nut building up through his dick, she picked up her pace and slightly massaged his ball sack. Santana closed his eyes. He was in heaven, he tried to hold on longer, but he just couldn't. He pulled Kat's head deeper onto his shaft, squirting his cum deep down her throat. Kat was a pro, and she swallowed every single drop he had to offer. The floor above creaked, but Kat didn't care. She continued to suck Santana's soul through his body. Kat looked up as she slowly jerked his dick up and down, making sure she got all the cum from out of his dick. When she was satisfied, she slowly pulled him out of her mouth, savoring the taste of him. Santana looked behind him, no one was there, but he wanted to make sure of it. The stairs creaked again, whoever it was roaming the house was now making their way down the stairs.

Kat looked Santana in his eyes and licked the head of his dick once more before finally letting him go. Santana hurriedly pulled his pants up and buckled his belt, just in time as Niyah came wandering around the corner, rubbing her eyes.

"Namm ... I hungry." Niyah looked past Santana whining.

"Okay, momma, Nanna got you." Kat got up from the couch to assist her granddaughter.

"Oops, Nanny, you had accident." Niyah's innocent mind pointed at Kat's wet crotch. Kat looked down and covered herself when she realized the wetness from her coochie was evident.

"Come on, Nanna gone give you something to eat so you can go back to sleep." Kat turned Niyah around so they could walk to the kitchen. When Niyah made eye contact with Santana she smiled and started yelling.

"Mommy... Mommy... Tana here, Mommy." Niyah broke from Kat's grip and took off up the stairs to wake her mother. Kat sighed. She knew her night was over with Santana. He walked over and pecked her on the lips.

"I'll make it up to you, ma. I promise," Santana reassured her. He could tell by her demeanor that her feelings were hurt. Kat said nothing, she was seconds away from tears filling her eyes. She walked over to Santana and sucked on his neck, then licked around his earlobe before speaking.

"I love you, Santana, don't make me have to wait this long again, please. You're the one who begged for this, not me. Now you got it, so stop playing with me." The floor creaked rapidly under Niyah's little feet. Niyah was on a mission. Santana grabbed Kat's pussy and rubbed up and down, a low moan escaped her lips.

"Who's pussy is this?" Santana whispered.

"Ummmmm... papi, yours," Kat replied sexually. He was driving her wild, and she truly loved every minute of it. Santana stopped rubbing her pussy through the fabric and started to ease his way past the hemline of her shorts. Kat's eyes went straight to the entrance of the room. She knew Niyah would be back soon, either with Raven in tow or by her lonesome. But one thing was for sure, Niyah was coming back. Santana skillfully moved inside her boy shorts and found her clit. Using his thumb and forefinger, he rubbed her clit gently, coating his hands with her slippery juices.

"Oh my God!" Kat moaned, pulling Santana closer. She licked sloppily around his neck, she couldn't handle it anymore, she wanted to cry real tears. "Stop doing this to me." Kat gripped onto Santana tighter as she felt the waves of a climax coming. Santana rubbed Kat's clit faster and faster, getting her further lost into him.

"San...tan...na...plea...se...daddy...I...looovvveee... youuuuu. Awww, fuck."

Santana tried to cover her mouth to the best of his ability, but it was no use, she was getting louder and louder. Kat's pussy started to swell under his touch, Santana licked on Kat's neck. He wanted badly to kiss her, but after cumming in her mouth he knew it was a no-no. Santana turned around to the sound of Niyah running down the stairs. Santana slowly pulled his hands out of her shorts, gently rubbing everything on the way back up. His hands were soaking wet with Kat's juices. He licked his fingers hungrily because he loved how Kat tasted. They stared at each other for a second, Kat smiled and walked away. It was just in time, Niyah walked around the corner with a sleepy Raven in tow. Kat looked back at Santana and the energy was real live undeniable. They were fire together. Kat mouthed, "I love you," to Santana before she disappeared up the steps.

***

Fatty Man and Sleeze finally pulled up to the Lil Page apartments. Fatty Man sat in his car a second longer as he thought about all that had transpired in the last few months. The niggas he loved most in the world had turned their backs on him. After so long, he reevaluated the whole situation, and he asked himself every time, what would you had done if it was Breeze, Von, or Sleeze that froze on a drill? He asked himself, often coming up blank every time. He didn't know what he would do, because he could have saved Breeze. He knew a shot in the air was all that was needed, and Breeze would have run off, he fucked up. Living with that guilt was tough, but Fatty Man tried his best to forget it, it was ruining him. All he seemed to consume in his mind now is killing the people closest to him. He looked up at the sky, it was dark. *Where did the day go*, Fatty thought. Fatty felt like he was just sitting in the graveyard talking to Breeze only hours ago. His intentions on meeting with Torrey that morning was short-lived.

He had to sleep and get his mind together. A lot was going on and he felt he wasn't sharp enough due to his lack of sleep. He looked over as Sleeze shut his car off and hopped out. Fatty tried to make the malice thoughts disappear, but he couldn't dig deep enough to do so. Fatty momentarily shook it off and put his game face on. He turned his car off and grabbed the Glock .26 off the passenger seat and got out.

"You ready?" Sleeze asked, tapping his hip.

"Always," Fatty Man replied. "Lead the way." Sleeze walked through Lil Page with Fatty Man close behind him. They walked until they got to the building they were looking for. Fatty laughed to himself when he saw it was a man standing outside playing bodyguard. *What the fuck these niggas on, now they Nino from Tha Carter*. This shit had Fatty weak, he had never seen anything so stupid in his life. *Yeah, this can't be real.*

"What's good, bruh, you got business down here?" the man guarding the front of the building said. Fatty Man just stared at him, Sleeze saw where the conversation was going, so he spoke up.

"Yeah, we here to see the nigga Ty," Sleeze replied annoyingly. The man caught the sarcasm in Sleeze's voice, but let it slide.

"Hold on I'll be back," the guard informed.

"Hold on, I'll be back." Fatty Man mocked the nigga guarding the building. Sleeze busted out laughing.

"Bruh, you a fool."

"No, that nigga the fool, acting like that. This some movie shit nigga. Like niggas really can't gun him down and barge into they shit. Yeah, okay. I know the fat ass nigga got some bread, but if he got niggas acting like this, what the fuck he need with us for?" Fatty Man inquired.

"Facts… when you right, you right," was all Sleeze could say. Because he knew it was the truth. The man stood at the top of the stairs and waved them in. They walked up the stairs in silence, no words needed to be said, it was game time.

"Ty would see you now," the guard said as he opened the door to let the pair into the apartment. When Fatty Man walked in, the first thing he noticed were the naked women. It seemed like he had them in groups. One group was bagging up money, while another group bagged what looked like cocaine. One of the chicks he recognized from high school. He nodded in acknowledgement, she nodded back with a smile. Fatty continued to let his eyes wander around the small apartment. It was plush to say the least. The furniture was up to date, with the latest home appliances. Torrey watched as Fatty Man and Sleeze surveyed his domain.

"Please sit, make yourself at home. Mi casa es su casa." Fatty Man stood in his place, taking a seat wasn't an option. It was no reason to be comfortable. All Fatty Man wanted to know was why he was being summoned, nothing more, nothing less.

"My nigga, I asked you to sit, it's rude to have a conversation of this latitude on your feet," Torrey explained.

"I get it, bro, but I'm not trying to be comfortable when I'm already uncomfortable. What the fuck are we here for, Ty?" Fatty waved his hands around as he talked, he was beginning to get mad. The look of confusion filled Torrey's face. Fatty could tell he was lost.

"Look, you can call me Torrey. Ty is some stupid shit these stupid ass niggas made up. More or less I have you here, because as the whole city may know by now, three lil' niggas took some shit from me and I want them dead in exchange. Need I say any more?" Torrey smiled when he seen the smirk pop up on Fatty's face.

"What's the bounty on each of these niggas?" Fatty asked.

"Fifteen apiece," Torrey answered, rubbing his hands together. "Am I speaking ya language or what?" Sleeze whistled at the price. That was news to him, Von told him it was five apiece for each body. *Scandalous ass nigga*, Sleeze thought after hearing the price being offered.

"Though it's none of my business, how many niggas been in this same seat hearing this same spiel?" Fatty needed to know what he was going up against.

"Not many, bruh, but there is enough. So far, no one has succeeded in getting this done. I'm tired of playing games with these little niggas. Them lil niggas out there spreading my money around and fucking hoes on my expense, and nigga, I don't play like that. So, can you get this shit done or not? Talk to me, I talk back."

"Who are the lil niggas you speak of?" Fatty played dumb.

"Look bro, stop playing with my emotions, you know what's going on. The whole damn city knows what's going on. So, do you want this easy bread or not?"

"I do, dead ass. The only nigga I knew you had on the menu was the young OT nigga. But other than that, I'm clueless on what the fuck you talking about. I've also been on my own hiatus, who are the other two?" Torrey looked at Sleeze, then looked at Fatty Man. Torrey sensed the question was a real one.

"It's the little light-skinned nigga Zach from the east and lil Haseem. You know who I'm talking about? These little niggas are kids for real. But they entered into this here grown man business, you feel me? So, what's it going to be?"

"I got you on the two light-skinned niggas, but I'm not taking no bounty up on Haseem, bruh. That's my nigga's people. I won't be the one to break bruh heart in that fashion," Fatty Man explained making sure it wasn't a misunderstanding as to where he stood regarding Haseem. "The hood not gone sit well with you putting money on Heem's head. I just want you to keep that in mind big dog," Fatty added.

"Well, if somebody has any problems, send them my muthafucking way!" Torrey replied coldly.

"Just have my chicken together when I put wings on these little niggas backs," Sleeze said confidently.

"That's the energy I like," Torrey said, rubbing his hands together.

"Watch the news, bruh," were the last words said before he and Sleeze exited the apartment.

Chapter 10

Simfany sat in the rented black Chevy Cobalt, watching the crowd of the men that hugged the block. The taste of revenge that seemed to consume her soul gave her patience she never knew existed inside of her. The death of Tijuana hit differently, she not only grew to love her as a sister, but the girl was family. Simfany felt she owed Tijuana the world for looking after Santana while he was booked. So, sliding for her name was mandatory. Her only problem was she had no clue what Tez-Mo or Kev looked like. Drew did his best to describe the brothers, but the description wasn't good enough for her to react upon. The only other answer she came up with to solve her problem was to stalk "The Commons" and wait until the pair showed their faces.

It was day three of her lying in wait. Simfany was beginning to get impatient. She wanted blood, and Simfany was at the point where she was damn near willing to do anything to shed some. Her emotions were running wild, they were beginning to get the best of her. Not once had she stumbled upon this kind of problem before. She was beside herself. Simfany prided herself on staying away from dealing in emotion, because she knew the consequence could only amount to jail or ultimately death. *Where the fuck are you, nigga?* Simfany thought as she watched the crowd of men have the time of their lives.

Each minute she wasted waiting on the brothers was time she could be making sure Santana was straight in his endeavors. The constant thought alone almost made Simfany pack up and run back to West Virginia. The cat and mouse game she was playing in Maryland was taking its toll, but instead of giving up entirely, she got smarter and enlisted help. Simfany had to admit that the territory was unfamiliar, and she needed help. She called Drew and asked him to lend his assistance. Drew, of course, agreed and sent his favorite left-hand man Peedi. Peedi was a hot-headed young nigga that took pride in stripping niggas' souls from their bodies. He was definitely the kind of person Simfany needed at the moment, plus he was knowledgeable of all the happenings going on in and around Harford County. So far, Simfany had deemed his presence useful. Simfany loved his demeanor, he was all about completing their mission. Peedi was also salty over the way Tijuana got gunned down, so when he was asked to join Simfany's side, he didn't hesitate. Now they both sat in silence, a block away from a TTP's most known trap house.

"Do you know any of these niggas out there?" Simfany asked, not taking her eyes off of the circle of men.

"Yeah, I know a few of them niggas. I did juvie time with all of those clown ass Blood niggas. You see the one that got the flag tied around his head, he they big dawg. His name is Resse. If you really trying to find out where them niggas are holed up at, he the nigga to ask," Peedi replied with his hands tightly gripped around the SKS assault rifle he had laid across his lap.

"I've been out here off and on for three days and still haven't seen anybody remotely close to the description Drew gave me," Simfany stated with obvious frustration.

"No disrespect, shorty, but what the fuck we waiting on? Let's start making these niggas chase us." Simfany thought about what Peedi was saying, she wasn't into killing innocent people. Simfany looked over at Peedi, and his demeanor screamed murder. He was ready for whatever. Simfany turned back to the crowd and sat silently. *Bitch, them niggas would kill you if they was ordered to*, Simfany's thoughts ran wild.

"Fuck it, get down, I'm bout to get one of those niggas over here." Simfany looked over at Peedi and briefly explained her plan. Peedi just looked at her, he said nothing in reply, he just slid down the seat, taking himself out of eyesight. After he got as comfortable as he would ever be in that position, Peedi nodded his head, giving her the go-ahead to begin. Simfany rolled the window down and turned on the overhead light, making the inside of the car visible. Simfany opened her door and got out, taking a breath of the night's dewy air. Simfany bent over into the car and began to act like she was looking for something in particular. Simfany tapped the horn, purposely trying to gain some kind of attention from the men on the corner. She bent down and looked under her arm, trying to see if she grabbed anyone's attention yet. She did. And her luck, it was the worst one, so Simfany thought about it a little longer and pondered on whether she should go through with the plan or not.

This for my bitch, fuck these niggas. I love you, momma. Rest easy, Simfany thought to as she saw Reese making his way up the block. She could hear the men behind him clowning him and cheering him on, only if he knew she thought. Simfany bent back down into the car and turned the overhead light back off, making the inside impossible to see unless you were up on the vehicle. Simfany wore all-red leggings that left nothing to the imagination, a Biggie Smalls Rest in Peace t-shirt, and some black and red retro Jordan 11's. She was a sight to see, but damn, was she a gift and a curse.

"This nigga about to be here, be ready if I need you," Simfany said, looking at Peedi with pleading eyes. Simfany was somewhat scared, she already had a hard time trusting people, now she was being forced to trust a nigga she had never met until now, with her life. Her eyes must have said it all because Peedi's face softened for a second when he replied.

"Shorty, you bad as fuck for real and you my brother's people, so I got you. Please don't worry when it comes to this, this is what I do," Peedi assured her yet again, that she was in good hands.

"Thank you," Simfany whispered as she grabbed her Glock 17 off the seat and tucked it into her waistband just in time. Reese pulled up on her casually and began spitting game.

"What's poppin, shorty? What's ya name?" Reese asked with authority laced all in his voice.

"You want my name, why should I give you my name, sir?" Simfany asked seductively.

"Because a nigga wanna show ya sexy ass a good time, but first I must have a name to do so. So, what do you say? Can a nigga please have your name? And your number?"

"Okay, well since you put it that way, my name is Simfany Vasquez, but the majority of my friends call me Simf. My number is 443-555-7236. Hit me," Simfany replied as she slid the Glock off her hip.

"Say less, ma, what do you hav—"

Boc ...

Simfany lifted her gun and shot Reese in his chest. Reese grabbed his chest in pure panic.

"Where the fuck is Tez-Mo and Kev? You tell me, I'll let you live. Where the fuck are they?" Simfany said as she swung her gun and hit Reese in his face, gashing it wide open. Reese held his face.

"Where the fuck are they, lor nigga?" Simfany asked again. Reese said nothing and continued to hold his chest. His breathing was labored. Peedi hopped out the car and stood by Simfany's side.

"Here they come, shorty," Peedi said calmly. Simfany looked up the street and then looked down at Reese's crumbled body. She raised her gun and squeezed the trigger.

Boc... Boc... Boc... Boc... Boc... Boc...

Reese was no longer amongst the living. Simfany ran to the car, Peedi started letting the choppa off as men started to run up the street. After they realized what type of gun he had, they began splitting up. Peedi squeezed at anyone he could place his eyes on. Peedi ran for cover behind the car.

"Get in the car!" Simfany yelled. Peedi rose from behind the car and let off a three-round burst.

Fssshhhh...

The men returned fire, Peedi ducked again and waited for the gunfire to quit and quickly popped up. *Got ya bitch ass*, he thought as he spotted a shooter stop and aim at Simfany. Peedi fired.

Blattttt... blatttt... blatttt... fssshhhh...

The shooter didn't stand a chance, he crumbled.

"Nigga, get in the fucking car before I leave your stupid ass!" Simfany yelled as she leaned over and opened the passenger side door. Peedi hopped in the car. Simfany put the car in reverse and stepped on the gas. Three shooters came out of nowhere and ambushed them. Bullets peppered the car.

"Oh, shit!" Simfany exclaimed as she ducked. Peedi lifted the assault rifle out the window and began firing back.

Fssshhhh... fssshhhh... blattt... blatttt...

When Simfany heard the gunshots subside, she rose and looked out the back window. "Oh my God!" She smashed on the brake as hard as possible. Peedi put his arm across Simfany's chest trying to stop her from plowing forward into the steering wheel. Once the car stopped, she took a deep breath, she was panicking. She looked back, the car she almost hit was only a few inches away. She had gotten lucky again. She must have really had angels that watched over her on a daily. *Thank you, God*, she thought as she closed her eyes and silently prayed. Peedi still had his hand across her chest. She looked at him, he removed his hand quickly, but not before brushing his fingers across her hard nipples. The gunfire that erupted sent Simfany back in survival mode, she put the car in drive and cut up the street, the right way.

Peedi looked back and saw three of the shooters standing in the middle of the street, returning fire. Peedi didn't budge. He knew they were too far out for the bullets to hit anything. Peedi turned back around and looked at Simfany. He could see the fear and anger written all over her face, she was pissed. He didn't know if she was pissed at him, or if she was pissed because she was scared. Peedi didn't know, but he knew he wouldn't bring the topic up if it she didn't address it first.

"You good?" Simfany asked, running through a deserted red light.

"I'm good, shorty. Didn't think you had it in you to drop lor dude like that. I was definitely rooting for you, damn, was I was in a fucked-up spot." Peedi laughed. Simfany looked over at Peedi and rolled her eyes.

"You almost got us killed, Peedi," Simfany said solemnly. Peedi sighed. He said nothing because the truth of the matter was, she was right. Shit could have gone south real fast.

"My bad, shorty. I have no excuses. I just wanted to make sure you were okay," Peedi said, trying to explain his reasoning for his stupidity.

"Fuck it, as long as we both good, then all is well. I have to take you back to where you came from." Simfany smiled, trying to lighten the mood a little.

"Again shorty, I'm sorry."

"I said you good, we good. My only advice is to get the fuck on the next time. But on a more serious note, thank you for saving my life, shit almost got ugly for us. Though your fault, no pun intended." She laughed. Peedi didn't, he just looked at her with lust in his eyes. Simfany put her eyes back on the road. She knew that look from anywhere. Simfany let it go and continued her drive back to Washington Park.

Simfany pulled into "The Park" fifteen minutes later. Peedi leaned over and hugged Simfany, taking her a bit by surprise. He embraced her, catching a whiff of her Polo Girl perfume. Peedi let Simfany go and looked her over one more before departing. *Damn... shorty bad, I need her*, Peedi thought lustfully. Before Peedi had a chance to say anything, Simfany shot down his dreams.

"Look, lor boy, I see how you over there looking at me, not gone happen. I'm a firm believer of keeping business and pleasure separate. You sexy, but aye... rules are rules, right?"

"I can respect it, hit me whenever you need me, shorty. Be safe and make sure you do something with that whip." Peedi went to get out, but stopped with one foot out and one foot in. "So, if we didn't go on this mission together, would I have had a shot?" Peedi asked, wanting to know.

"No, because what you did back there is what even made me consider rules. You did ya thing tonight. My only advice is don't stop trying, and by the way, how old are you anyway?" Simfany was curious about that herself since he got into her car.

"Twenty-four," Peedi replied. She wasn't expecting that answer. He was a grown ass man. *Shit, I might have to bend the rules for this nigga.* She laughed at her thoughts. Simfany joked but she knew it probably wouldn't happen. "You make sure you stay low and out the way. I got your number if I need you again."

"Bye sexy," Peedi sang to Simfany as he tucked the SKS into his jacket and got out.

"Bye boy." Simfany smiled again. She liked Peedi, he was cool. Peedi nodded at her before walking off. Simfany stayed posted until she saw him enter his building safely. Simfany felt vindicated for what she had done, but still she held a spot of disappointment in the pit of her stomach. Simfany pulled off, hoping the message she and Peedi sent was loud and clear. Just thinking about it was making her pussy wet. Killing Reese wasn't in her plans at all, but killing the opposition always justified her actions. It is what it is, she chalked it up and pulled out. She thought about Peedi momentarily, the young nigga had her curious. Simfany bit her bottom lip and smiled. *Curiosity killed the cat*, she thought as she exited Washington Park and headed home, the night was a rough one and she was in need of a good shower and some sleep.

***

Tez-Mo and Kevin pulled up to their main trap house located in Harford Commons. When they pulled up to park, they noticed the block was packed with people and police officers. *What the fuck is going on,* Tez thought as he parked and got out. Tez-Mo could hear women wailing, men crying and being ignorant. The scene brought back memories from the day Stacks and Pim were killed, the people, the police, the crying and the anger. He didn't know exactly was going on, but his common sense told him someone was severely hurt or dead. The presence of the police told him more than enough. He looked around until he found one of his homies, Tez walked up to him and asked the obvious.

"Who got caught lacking?" His soldier had a look of dismay written all over his face.

"Reese and Twan." As soon as Tez-Mo heard Resse's name, he began looking for Kevin. Resse and Kevin had been best friends since they both were toddlers. Reese's mom, Ms. Wendy and Momma Brooks were best friends growing up, so the two were more so raised around each other their whole lives. Kevin was the only reason Reese even fathomed the thought of being Piru. Reese wanted to follow Kev, though they were technically the same age, Reese looked up to Kevin.

"So, you telling me Reese is gone, gone forever?" His little homie nodded in agreement.

"Fuck!" Tez-Mo screamed, grabbing the attention of the people around him. The year was proving to be a crucial one, they had lost Sasha and Reese within only months of each other, and he didn't know what he could do to stop the madness besides causing it. Tez-Mo searched the crowd, he couldn't find his brother nowhere. *This right here is going to send this lor nigga over the edge,* Tez-Mo thought as he walked off in search of his brother. Tez-Mo was lost for words, he was tired of experiencing the losing side of this shit. He pulled the pint of E&J out of his pocket and took a swig. He loved the way the liquor burned away the stress, the E&J was strong, but soothing all in the same breath.

A thought hit him as he stayed planted in place. *Find Ms. Wendy.* Tez-Mo finished off what he had left in his bottle and threw it to the ground. He used the back of his sleeve to wipe the alcohol off his mouth. Tez-Mo rubbed around on his hip to make sure that he was still well guarded if need be. When he felt the comfort of the Colt .45 he had on his hip, he walked to the yellow police tape. He figured if a loved one was killed, the family would be hugging the crime scene. Tez-Mo only took a few steps before it became clear that he was right, he looked up and saw Kev consoling Reese's mother. He sighed and walked up.

"Hey beautiful, you okay?" Tez-Mo didn't know what to say. He knew the loss was very significant. Words weren't enough at this time, but he still tried. Ms. Wendy looked up at him with tear-stricken eyes. His heart broke for her, but she had to understand that in the life they lived there were consequences and unfortunately this was one of them.

"Tezier, do I look o ... fucking kay?" Ms. Wendy replied coldly.

"I'm sorr—" Tez-Mo tried to say, before he was interrupted by Ms. Wendy.

"Nah, don't be sorry, you and the rest of these niggas need to go out there and find out who did this shit to my baby. I used to hear you tell that nigga you love him, now take your fucking ass out there and prove it. You're the oldest, how the fuck could you let this happen?" Wendy tucked her head back into Kev's chest and sobbed. Kev rubbed her back, at the same time assuring her the deed wouldn't go unpunished. Tez-Mo made his mind up at that moment, he needed to leave. He was way too insensitive to what was going on around him. Losing Sasha took Tez-Mo's compassion. He was ready to leave, there was nothing else that he could do, but sit and watch people act a fool.

"If you need anything, you know I'm a call away. I'm sorry this had to happen to you, you or Reese didn't deserve this. When I find out who did this, I'll—" Tez-Mo stopped in midsentence. There were too many ears around.

"Look, I'll have Mom call you. Make sure you come over so you can see Diamond, she has been asking about you and Reese." Tez-Mo wiped the tear from his eye, just thinking about his niece. She had lost her mother and now her father, within months of each other. Talking to Diamond he knew would prove to be the hardest. Diamond was at the age of understanding what was going on around her, and knowing that, it made the talk no easier. Ms. Wendy said nothing in return, she just continued to sob, asking God why. Tez-Mo rubbed his head and looked up. Kev was staring at him. Tez-Mo shook his head from side to side. Kev knew after losing Sasha, it was going to be hard for them to feel anything for anyone else. "What the fuck," Kev mouthed to him. Tez-Mo just shrugged. He had no answers. Kev nodded for him to come and hug Ms. Wendy. Tez-Mo had no problem with doing that, he stepped closer and embraced both Kev and Ms. Wendy.

"I love you, Momma, I promise to rectify this shit. Please come over and make sure your granddaughter is going to be okay." Tez-Mo kissed her forehead. There was nothing else that needed to be said.

"I'm out, bro, I can't do this. Seeing Ms. Wendy all fucked up like this and hearing these lame ass niggas talking like they killers got me in my body a lor bit, bro. So, hit me when you ready to leave. As a matter of fact, here... take these keys and I'll grab a cab home. I don't want to leave you out here stranded. You strapped?" Kev nodded his head and tapped his waist.

"Bet, say no more. I love you, my nigga. Stay *050* and call me when you on your way out of here. See if these stupid ass niggas know anything. I love—" Tez-Mo's words drowned out when Kev looked up and locked eyes with his first love, Gloria. *What is she doing here?* Kev thought, following her through the crowd of mourners.

"Nigga, are you listening?" Tez-Mo said and snapped his fingers in Kev's face. "Kevin!" Hearing Tez-Mo yell his name so loudly brought him out of his trance.

"Yeah nigga, I'm listening. You loud as hell, I was just in thoughts about some other shit. My mind is all over the place," Kev explained, trying his best to avert suspicion. He didn't want Tez-Mo to see Gloria.

"Bro, I got you. You just make sure you make it home safely. I can call one of my hoes to come and get you, she lives right around the corner. Do you want me to?" Kev asked. Ms. Wendy pulled her head away from Kev's chest and wiped her eyes.

"Y'all heard what I said," Ms. Wendy stated coldly and walked away. Both Tez-Mo and Kev looked at her as if she was losing her mind. Kev pointed at her as she walked past the crime tape to speak with an officer. Tez-Mo shrugged.

"Look, bro this is your people, so make sure you handle your business. Call shorty and tell her to slide through. I'm gone go chill in the trap until she comes. Is the shorty that is coming your main or side?" Kev smiled for the first time that night, his brother was a fool.

"Nah Tez, shorty just a bad ass jump-off. If she let you slay her, do your thing, just don't be trying to kick my back in to do it with ya hoe ass." They both busted out laughing, because Tez-Mo was terrible for doing the wildest shit to fuck hoes. Tez-Mo stuck his middle finger up at his brother.

"I ain't never did you like that, you lor bitch. Now for that, I'm gone fuck the shit out of shorty. And depending on how bad she is, I might eat that pussy all sloppy like from the back." Kev snarled his face up.

"Eeeewwwww. You's a nasty nigga. If that's what you're into, do your thing, my nigga."

Kev laughed as he slapped Tez-Mo up, showing that no matter what, it was all love.

"But all jokes aside, bro, I can't just stay here. The atmosphere is—"

"Nigga, I already know. You don't have to explain. You just make sure you don't get into nothing without me by ya side. For real, big bro. Go and chill tonight, get some pussy, smoke, do something. Just stay out the way for the night. *Po 9* will be on a lot of bullshit. They got two bodies stretched out with no explanation. You still want me to call shorty for you, or are you just gone have sis come and grab you?" Kev asked as he lit his cigarette. Tez-Mo looked into the air for a second, he was thinking. He didn't know if he wanted to try something new or just go home to his bitch. *Home is where the heart is*. Tez-Mo smiled as he thought of the corny ass saying. He laughed, but he knew it was the truth.

"Nah bruh, I'm just gone call Wanda's ass to come and get me. I appreciate you though, shorty. It's about time I face the music anyway." Tez-Mo slurred his words.

"You calling her now?" Kev asked curiously. He looked behind him, making sure to keep Gloria in his eyesight. He needed to speak to her, but he knew if Tez-Mo was there, the conversation would go left. Gloria hated Tez-Mo with a passion, but how could he blame her? Tez-Mo had done some bullshit, and that bullshit later was the demise of their relationship. Kev was patient, hopefully Gloria would still be present when all the smoke cleared.

"Yeah, I just texted her. She around the corner in Beacon Terrace. She'll be here in a second," Tez-Mo answered sloppily. He sat down on the edge of the curb. He was dizzy as hell and felt nauseous. Tez-Mo wiped the sweat from his brow and rubbed his stomach from side to side. The liquor was wearing on him.

"I'm gone have one of the lor homies sit with you until she pulls up. That's straight, shorty? You sure you good?" Kev asked, taking a deep pull on his cigarette.

"Yeah, I'm good, bro. Go take care of Ms. Wendy right now, she is going to need it. I love you, bro, call me if you need me for anything. You know Wanda bout to be on bullshit, so… but if you call I'm there," Tez-Mo said, eyes closed. Kev looked down at his brother.

"What the fuck is this nigga high off of?" Kevin asked himself. This nigga always got something to say about me but can 't even handle his own shit. Kev shook his head from side to side. Whatever he was on worked fast, Tez-Mo was just alert and on point not even twenty minutes prior. Kevin sighed as he stood vigil over his older brother. Kevin searched the crowd again for Gloria, this time coming up empty. Gloria was gone. Fuck! He had missed his shot at being able to talk to Gloria because of Tez-Mo's drunkenness. Seeing Gloria made him think about his life before all the mayhem, before the gang shit, before all the notoriety, before the fear and money, before the bodies.

When Kevin was with her, he was pure. Gloria had brought the good out of everyone she graced with her presence. A lone tear threatened to roll down his face, just the thought alone of what he had lost fucked him up internally. The headlights from an approaching car brought Kevin out of his somber mood. He lifted his hands to cover his eyes from the beam of the lights. Usually, he would be on bullshit, trying to figure out who and why someone was pulling up onto their block, but he knew the circumstances were different at the moment.

The driver pulled up to the curb as close as allowed and honked the horn. Kev looked on, trying to figure out who the driver was, he had never seen the SUV before. He had no clue who the driver could be. He looked on, hand on his hip ready for whatever the driver had in store. The driver honked the horn again, when Kev didn't move forward, the window began to roll down. Kevin looked down at Tez-Mo, and though he was kind of out of it, he was on point more than he gave him credit for. As Kevin looked into the car he smiled, God was on his side today. Gloria's beautiful Puerto Rican features looked back at him.

"Are you going to get in or what?" Gloria asked nonchalantly. Kevin looked down at Tez-Mo, then back at Gloria. He had a choice that needed to be made, but his choice would be the most obvious. He wasn't willing to leave his brother in his current state.

"I have to make sure my brother mak—" Tez-Mo grabbed his leg.

"Go bro, I already did enough, go talk to shorty. Try to right my wrong. I promise on Sash, I'm good, bro. Plus, Wanda will be here in a minute. You better go, shorty, before you miss it." Tez-Mo nodded his head towards the car and looked away. Tez-Mo suddenly felt bad for all the harm he had caused throughout his life. *I need to stop fucking with these drugs, man*, Tez thought as his mood changed somberly. Kevin looked at his brother, then looked back at Gloria. Gloria was saying something but to him it was all a white noise.

"Aye, you getting in or not?" she asked through the halfway rolled window. Kevin sat there momentarily stuck. He was at a loss for words. He had never pictured this day coming to fruition ever again. He just knew for sure Gloria would hate him and Tez-Mo for the rest of his life, for what they did. The only thing that ran through his head as he opened the door was the last memory of seeing Gloria.

"Kevin, are you coming?" Tez-Mo asked his younger brother.

"Bro, Mom wants us home at ten. She not gone be happy if—" Kevin responded, trying to remind his brother of their nightly curfew.

"Nigga, you can go home at ten. Hood wants me to handle a situation for him. Are you coming or not? You keep acting like you want this shit, but when it's time to put work in you be bitchin', lor nigga!" Tez-Mo exclaimed coldly, spit flying from his mouth. Kevin didn't say anything, he showed no emotion. He knew his brother was mad, but he really didn't give a fuck. He had never killed anyone and in all honesty, he wasn't really looking forward to the act. But that was the greater good in him talking, because deep down, he wanted to be able to add a body to his belt. It seemed like the people around you showed more respect when they knew you could end their existence. Kevin was at his crossroads, he knew a decision had to be made, and made fast. Kevin thought long and hard because this was a big one to make, he knew whatever he decided would change his life forever.

Snap! Snap!

Kevin came out of his thoughts at the sound of Tez-Mo snapping his fingers in front of his face.

"Nigga, wake the fuck up! Are you coming or not?" Tez-Mo asked, loading the mini choppa.

"Who and what the fuck we bout to do?" Kevin inquired.

"Lor bro, you asking too many questions, you rocking? Damn, all this twenty-one-question ass shit you on. I told that nigga Hood you wasn't—"

"I'm coming," was all Kevin said in reply. "Just let me hit girlie and let her know I'm going to be late." Tez-Mo looked up at his little brother and shook his head from side to side.

"What?" Kevin asked, looking up from his phone.

"That Puerto Rican bitch got your ass sprung. You gotta be adopted." Tez-Mo joked. Though Kevin didn't want to laugh at his brother's stupidity, he really had no choice. Tez-Mo was a dang clown.

"Shut up, my nigga. You just pissed these hoes don 't fuck with ya ugly ass." Kevin joked back. Tez-Mo stopped laughing almost immediately, he didn't find none of what Kevin said funny, not one bit. Tez-Mo knew he was a fly nigga, at the age of eighteen all he cared about was getting money, running through hoes, and making a name for himself in the streets. He didn't have time for love or any other distractions for that matter. Kevin seen the serene look fall over his brother's face. It was weird, because in all truth, the only time he'd seen his brother at peace was right before he went on a mission. Love seemed to be out of the cards for Tez-Mo. Tez-Mo said nothing else before looking to the ground. He dropped the conversation altogether. He didn't have time for the arguing, whatsoever.

"You done?" Tez looked up, eyebrow raised. Kevin ignored his brother and placed the call to his first love. The phone rang a few times before it was picked up and answered.

"Hello." The sound of his girlfriend's accent got him every time, his heart warmed.

"Como estas, mami," Kevin greeted Gloria in her native tongue.

"Hey sexy," Gloria replied.

"What's poppin', beauty?"

"Where are you? I've been waiting for an hour now," Gloria said with a hint of frustration in her voice.

"Aye, my bad yo, dealing with this nigga Tez done held me up. I'm not sure I'm going to be able to make it tonight, this nigga—"

"Are you freaking serious, Kevin?" Gloria asked, seriously disappointed. "You always have excuses when it comes to me. Man, whatever. Hit me when I can take priority in your life."

"Don't act like that—" Gloria abruptly hung the phone up. Kevin looked at his phone and shook his head. *You fucking up*, Kevin thought as he put his phone back into his pocket.

Tez-Mo put his helmet on and grabbed for his keys. Not knowing what Tez-Mo had in store, Kevin followed suit. He ran into the back room and grabbed one of Tez-Mo's spare helmets and put it on, dropping his book bag onto the couch on his way out. Kevin made his way out the house to where his brother was waiting for him. Tez-Mo leaned against his new Honda CR 500. The dirt bike was bulky, to his liking.

"You driving, hop on the front," Tez-Mo instructed. The sight of relief washed over Kevin's face, Tez-Mo took note of the gesture, placing it in the back of his mental. He was going to have to have a talk with Kevin regarding his actions. Second guessing was almost for sure to either get them killed or caught. But he would revisit that conversation for another day. Kevin took his position on the front of the dirt bike. Tez-Mo climbed on the back, strapping the mini choppa around his body.

"Where we going?" Kev asked. He was a known monster on bikes. *That's why this nigga wants me to slide with him,* he thought as he hopped on to the bike and revved the engine. Kevin didn't show it, but his heart was beating out of his chest. He was scared as a muthafucka. Kevin ignored all the signs of danger and popped the clutch.

"Candle Wood!" Tez-Mo yelled through his helmet. Kevin nodded and sped off, with Candle Wood Court being his next destination.

Kevin pulled into Windsor Valley. "Slow down, keep ya eyes open for a navy-blue Acura Legend," Tez-Mo yelled, gripping the choppa across his chest. Kevin nodded, slowly riding down Meadowood Drive looking both ways for the navy-blue Acura Legend. Not seeing a car of that description, he made a left, turning down the hill to the Candle Wood sector of the complex. The atmosphere alone in this section was different than all the others. What transpired daily in the court made the section for sure the most dangerous of them all. Gang violence plagued the row houses that occupied the small space. Women were scantily dressed, while fiends lurked for their next fix. The lure of the nightlife was constantly present.

Tez-Mo tapped Kev and pointed towards the corner of the court. Candle Wood Court was one way in, one way out. And damn, did that prove to be deadly at times. As Kevin entered the courtyard, he surveyed his surroundings. Candle Wood Court was set up like a box, with one long drive that led to the complex's main road. Kevin looked in the direction Tez-Mo pointed and saw the car they were looking for. The navy-blue Acura Legend was double parked outside of someone's residence, with the blinkers flashing. Kevin slowly circled the car to see if anyone was in it. When Tez-Mo double tapped his back indicating their mark was present, he rode a little, acting as if he was looking for a spot to park his bike.

"Stop at the driver's side window on the way back through!" Tez-Mo said, yelling demands, hoping Kevin could hear him through his helmet and loud music. Kevin didn't need to look back or respond, he just nodded in agreement. Kevin's hands trembled as he made the turn of his life. He wasn't so sure if he was ready to be involved in something so tragic. *Fuck it, I'm already here*, Kevin thought as he slowly rode up to the driver's side window. The occupants inside had no clue that danger lurked. Kevin pulled up swiftly and stopped on the driver's side of the vehicle. Without hesitation, Tez-Mo lifted his mini choppa and sprayed into the car. Kevin watched horrifically as the bullets tore into the flesh of the man behind the wheel. When he heard the shrieking sound of a woman screaming, he reached into his hip to silence her. But before he got the chance to squeeze the trigger, the scream halted altogether.

"Go! Nigga, go!" Tez-Mo exclaimed excitedly, hitting Kevin on the back numerous times.

Kevin looked into the eyes of the woman and couldn't believe who he saw. It was Gloria. He was confused and though he had a helmet concealing his identity, the energy was too strong for the two to ignore. They locked their eyes for what seemed like an eternity. The look she gave him killed his soul. Not being able to handle the stare any longer, he put his gun back on his hip and pulled off angrily, popping a wheelie all the way out of the court.

Kevin sat down and closed the door behind him. Gloria's fragrance was the same as the last time that he could remember. Her beauty was flawless, and she still had that glow about herself. He could tell by her look alone she was doing good for herself, and deep down, he was happy she still knew what happiness was. Kevin just sat still looking out the window, he was at an extreme loss for words. Kevin swiped at his beard a few times before resting his hands back on his lap. Gloria put her back against the window and smiled as she looked at her ex. The gesture she knew all too well to be one of his tell-tale signs of being in an uncomfortable environment. Gloria contemplated her words carefully. The silence in the car was deafening. A tear slowly slid down Gloria's face as she watched Kevin. The person she saw, wasn't the same person she once loved. His demeanor was different, she could tell that for sure. Gloria wiped her eyes and broke the silence.

"How you been, papi?" Kevin looked over at Gloria. *Man, what the fuck is her aim*? he continued to ask himself. She had been gone for so long that popping up on the day two of his soldiers got killed was weird. He looked into her angelic face and didn't see any blemishes. She was perfect. Gloria was the spitting image of Selena, the only difference between the two was Gloria was so much thicker than the late Spanish beauty.

"I'm good, what brought you around here?" Kevin asked suspiciously.

"You want me be honest?" Gloria asked. The look he gave her spoke volumes. He wasn't trying to play her game. Gloria rolled her eyes, visually frustrated.

"I came back to see you, Kevin."

"Why?" Gloria shifted in her seat and looked out the window.

"Why do you have to be so fucking mean? You know what, get out!" Kevin looked over at Gloria before finally reaching for the handle.

"I'll leave, tell me why you came back. For real, shorty, why did you come back after all these years?"

"Because I've missed you, Kevin, okay? I fucking missed you!" The tears that cascaded down her face broke Kevin's heart into pieces.

"I just don't understand though, shorty, why leave? That shit killed me inside. I am what I am now because of your rash decision." Gloria wiped her eyes angrily.

"Rash? What the fuck do you mean? What was I supposed to do, Kevin? You and your brother killed my cousin in front of me. Let me ask you something, you contemplated on killing me, didn't you?" Gloria asked, hurt reflecting through her eyes. Kevin stared blankly at her. He knew she was still hurt over the day that snatched her closest family member's soul.

"I was until I saw who was in the passenger seat," Kevin answered bluntly.

"Then, why didn't you? You killed my cousin, scarring me forever. What if I told, then what?" Kevin had replayed his consequences over and over many times back then. He definitely expected her too but prayed the love she once had would override that decision.

"I know you, Gloria, what do you want me to say? I didn't know who we was supposed to hit that night, okay? All I knew was the make and model of the car, the rest was left up to God. I'm sor—"

"Bitch ass nigga, God though? Left it up to God? You held our lives in your hand that night. You were God for that moment. Thankfully, I was spared, but I continue to ask myself, was I really? Like fucking honestly, was I? I lost all of my family behind you. I lost my whole fucking world behind you and your brother's fucking senseless act of violence."

"I'm sorry." Kevin ducked his head and apologized. He really didn't have much that he could say, what already happened, happened.

"Not good enough, Kevin," Gloria said sadly.

"Then what do you want? Why are you here?" Kevin asked again, feeling himself getting annoyed.

"I came to make sure you were okay. I heard about what happened to Sash—" Kevin interjected immediately.

"Keep my sister's name out ya mouth. If that's why you came back, leave." Kevin opened the door finally. He wasn't trying to revisit the shit that happened. It was bad enough that every chance he got, he drowned in his sorrow for his role in her death.

"Kevin, if you get out this car, I'm done forever," Gloria calmly stated.

"I wish you the best, shorty," Kevin said as he put one foot out the car. Gloria started the car and pulled off, dragging Kevin's foot along the pavement.

"Yo! What the fuck!" Kevin yelled, pulling his foot back into the car and closing the door.

"You got me fucked up. You promised me till death and I'm here to claim stake. Are we still forever, Kevin?" Gloria asked, looking over momentarily as she paid attention to the road.

"Are you serious or are you on bullshit? I don't have time for oppy ass vibes. I'm not the same nigga you knew when I was sixteen. I have killed and robbed for nothing. I have done a lot, shorty. Is that the nigga you want to help raise your children?"

"Yes. I need you back. I really miss you, please don't make me beg," Gloria pleaded.

Kevin looked at Gloria for sincerity. The tears that welled in her eyes showed him everything he needed to see.

"Come here." Kevin reached for her arm. Gloria intertwined her fingers with his and smiled.

"I need you to stop at the Shell on Hanson so I can grab some Dutch's and some food."

"Okay," Gloria replied, whipping her SUV skillfully through the streets. As Gloria pulled into the gas station her phone rang. Gloria looked at the caller ID and answered.

"I'll be back," Kevin mouthed to her before exiting the car and running into the gas station. Gloria went back to her call.

"I got him. Where do you want me to pull up at?" Gloria asked her caller excitedly.

"Take that nigga to Joppatowne, you know where they built the new Sheetz?"

"'Yeah."

"Take him there and suck his dick real good and I got the rest."

"I'm not sucking this nigga's—" Kevin opened the door to the gas station and walked out, halting her conversation. Gloria hung up. Kevin opened the passenger side door and hopped in.

"Who was that, shorty?" Kevin asked, eating a jumbo-sized hot dog.

"Nigga, chew with ya mouth closed. I was talking to my abuela. She is sick, which was another reason I am back. Why, you don't trust me no more?" Gloria raised her eyebrow in disappointment. *Damn, I'm good.* She laughed to herself.

"Yeah, I'm straight. Let me see your phone." Without hesitation, Gloria handed him her phone. She had no idea what he was looking for, because it was nothing to find. She made sure of that before even pulling up in Harford Commons. Kevin grabbed her phone and looked at the last number Gloria had contact with.

"Okay, I see you don't trust me," Gloria said, visibly offended.

"It's been a long six years, shorty. In this stage of life no one is to be trusted. No disrespect intended, of course. Just being precautious, it's what comes with my life," Kevin replied in a matter-of-fact tone of voice. He handed Gloria her phone back, satisfied with his search. Gloria's heartbeat was erratic as hell. It felt like her heart was going to burst at any second from anxiety. Gloria put the car in drive and pulled into traffic, wanting to end this once and for all.

Peedi looked at his phone as he sat next to Rocc.

"What she say, shorty?" Rocc asked.

"The lor nigga went for the bullshit." They both laughed sinisterly.

"Goofy ass Blood niggas, man, I tell you. So, what's the plan," R asked.

"I'm bout to call shorty and let her know what's going on. We need her to perform one more time tonight." The look on Roe's face was priceless, he was pissed.

"No disrespect intended, cuz, but what the fuck are you doing? Them niggas killed Kane's sister. Don't you think them confirm kills belong on this soil?" Peedi knew deep down he made a point, but if Drew trusted the broad, then so did he. And once his mind was made up, there was nothing else to discuss, this Rocc knew all too well.

"I do, but lor nigga, that command came from Drew. Shorty apparently is like family to both him and T. Her involvement is crazy, cuz, all I can do is respect this as it comes. Don't worry though, shorty. We gone get our shot. But right now, shit is closer to Joppatowne then we are and having me continue to explain shit to you is wasting time. So, may I?" Peedi replied sarcastically reaching for his phone. *Damn, I hope shorty still up*, Peedi thought as he dialed Simfany's number from memory. Luckily for them, Simfany answered on the second ring.

"What's up, Peedi?" Simfany answered drunkenly.

"The lor nigga went for it, shorty."

"What? Where?" she exclaimed, excitement registering in her voice. *God damn, I love this bitch,* Peedi thought, her gangster was impeccable and her beauty, now that was a whole other topic. He let his thoughts fade, getting back to the mission at hand.

"Shorty on her way to that spot we spoke about near Sheetz. How far are you from there?" Simfany grew silent. "Shorty, you still there?" Peedi asked, looking at his phone to see if the call dropped. His phone still indicated Simfany was still on the line.

"Having second thoughts, beauty? I can understand if—" Simfany cut him off midsentence.

"Second thoughts? Hell nah, I'm gone body that bitch ass nigga for what he did to Drew and T. My silence was for many reasons, one being the chick y'all used to set the lor nigga up with. Secondly, I'm drunk as fuck, but don't worry I can still handle me, I can promise you that. I'm leaving now, one more thing, what do you want me to do with the Spanish bitch?" Simfany asked soberly. Peedi looked over at Rocc, he was playing the newest *NBA Live.* He knew his next decision could either make or break them. Peedi went with his gut instinct.

"Send shorty with him."

"Say less. Love you," Simfany slurred.

"Be safe," Peedi replied, overlooking Simfany's term of endearment. He knew she was drunk as hell and didn't mean it, so instead of pressing it, he let it slide.

"Always."

"Alright, call me when you confirm," Simfany said nothing further and hung up. Peedi looked over at Rocc yet again cursing himself. He felt bad but the order he gave Simfany would save them all the legal troubles in the long run. Gloria knew too much, she had to go. She was a liability. *It's too many bitches out here, lor bro,* Peedi thought, trying to justify his callous actions. Rocc looked up and smiled, Peedi smiled back.

"What you smiling for, lor nigga?" Peedi laughed slightly.

"Just thinking, I told you shorty would get it done." Rocc beamed with pride.

"You were right. I salute, quit that game. I'm bout to bust ya ass. You over there getting worked by that weak ass computer," Peedi laughed, trying to revert his attention away from Kevin and Gloria.

"Grab the sticks then, cuz," Rocc said, quitting the game. Peedi picked up the controller off the table and picked his team. Though Peedi moved his hands and tapped buttons, his mind was elsewhere. Peedi just hoped Simfany would be fine, he tried his best to erase his anxiety. He played the game skillfully, waiting on his phone to ring.

Ring ... Ring ... Ring ...

Chapter 11

Haseem looked at his phone for the umpteenth time, both Zach and Santana were trying to reach him. He knew they were worried, but he wasn't in the mood to talk to either one of his friends. Between Santana assuming the role of big dog, and Zach basically dick riding his every word, he needed a break. He loved his niggas for sure, just at the moment, too much shit was going on that he needed to step back from. Everybody seemed to be having problems, some greater than others. But with Haseem being equipped with his own life and death situations, the only person he could care about was himself.

Ring ... Ring ... Ring ... Ring ...

Haseem looked at his phone frustratingly. This time the caller was different, it was FB Freezo. Haseem thought about answering but thought better of it. He sent Freezo to his voice mailing system. *What the fuck this nigga want?* Haseem thought as he aimlessly walked down Ruffner Avenue with no destination in mind. The night was wet and dewy, warm but slightly cooled. The dark sky was beautiful, the purplish hue that masked the sky illuminated the dark clouds. Haseem missed his nightly walks. It was really a daily remedy he had gotten used to once he was released from the Tiger Morton Detention Center. It seemed corny to many people, but looking at years in solitude made him appreciate the simple things in life that brought peace. That was before all the present stress he had accumulated since being home.

Ring ... Ring ... Ring ... Ring ...

Man, these niggas just not gone let me be. *Fuck*! Haseem thought aggravatingly. He looked at the caller ID. It was Freezo again. He sighed, then pressed talk. "What's up, bruh, you good? Why the fuck you keep blowing my phone up and shit?" Haseem answered agitated as fuck.

"Damn, lil' bruh, curve that nonsense. Where you at?" Freezo asked quickly. Haseem paused momentarily. He didn't know what type of time Freezo was on.

"Bruh? You bullshitting. Nigga, where are you?" Haseem heard the urgency in his voice, so he answered.

"I'm near the Velt. Why, what's up?"

"Get the fuck off that main road, bro, these niggas out lurking for you and ya lil' team."

Haseem instinctively began looking up and down the street for signs of danger. Thankfully, none were present. "Bro, what the fuck is you talking bout?"

"Bruh, just stop being hardheaded and get the fuck off that road. Fatty just called me and told me Torrey on your head." Haseem sighed for a second time. *This nigga had me spooked for a second. I thought it was some different shit.*

"No façade, nigga. I'm not playing. He gave the contract to us to take. Fatty didn't accept your bounty, so the nigga issued someone else to dead you. If you're not willing to come with me for a while, bruh, get missing. I don't know what you heard or think, but nigga... we love you, my nigga. Get the fuck somewhere safe at least for the night," Freezo pleaded.

"Aight, bro. Good looking."

"I'm serious, my nigga."

"I said alright."

"Alright then, hit me in the morning." Just as soon as Freezo hung up the phone, Haseem saw an all-black Crown Victoria creeping down the block, music blasting. He tucked his head into his hoodie and started to walk back down the block, forgetting he was no longer equipped with a weapon. Haseem could hear the car approaching, instinctively he reached for his waist and realized that he was lacking like a muthafucka. *Fuck*! Haseem got nervous. He turned to see where the car was, he needed to know the distance between them. The black Crown Vic was only feet away. *Think nigga, think*. Haseem started to panic.

Before the driver had a chance, Haseem took off full speed into the alley that connected to "Tha Carter." The car didn't follow. Haseem ran up the small hill until he hit the opening of the fence. Once he was through the fence and in the small play yard, he sighed with relief. *Now I know what this nigga Santana talking about.* He didn't know who was watching, who he could trust. Haseem was beginning to realize for the first time since hitting Torrey's spot that he was in grave danger. He needed to get somewhere safe, fast. Haseem pulled out his phone and called Santana. He still didn't want to talk to Zach yet, and he damn sure wasn't going to play and go with any Full-Blooded niggas. Santana answered his phone on the first ring.

"What's up?" Santana answered with a hint of attitude. Haseem hated the fact that he needed anyone right now, but he swallowed his pride and replied.

"What's up, bruh, where you at? I'm trying to slide through, I'm out this bitch naked as hell. Me and Zach just got into it, and I refuse to go back over there. For real, all I need is for you to take me to get my strap."

"So, you telling me this whole time I been talking shit, you been lacking? See the shit I'm talking bout my G. You don't have no regard for life. Where are you, I'll come and get you." Santana exhaled loud enough for Haseem to hear his frustration.

"I'm on the East, if you still over here, I can just slide to you."

"I'm at Kat's with Raven and Niyah. It ain't shit for me to slide ya way."

"Come on, bruh, I been good all this time, I promise I'm straight. I'm on my way now," Haseem assured Santana.

"Alright, bet. I'll just give you the tone I got on me. I have a few stashed around Kat's shit. I just won't be able to grab them until everyone goes back to sleep. Just hit me when you're close."

"Got you, and bro, my ba—"

"Stop, my nigga, that shit ain't for us, son. What is understood should never be explained. Now get the fuck off them streets, you want me to have Kat warm some shit up for you? Before you say no, son, that shit she just made was epic." Santana laughed. "I'm telling you, my nigga." Haseem smiled as he looked around nervously.

"Yeah bruh, she can make me a lil' plate. I'm hungry as a bitch for real. I'm only on Lewis, I'll be there in like five."

"Say less, bro." Haseem flipped his phone shut and came out the shadows. There was no movement or activity going on as far as he could see. Haseem took that opportunity to cross the street and ran along Lewis until he was behind the Roosevelt Center that sat on Ruffner Avenue. As he hit the alley that sat directly behind the Roosevelt Center, in Chamberlain Court, he saw the same black Crown Vic glide past. This time though, Haseem had no worries in the world. He was only minutes away from Kat's side door, but to take precaution he slithered down the alley, hidden deep in the shadows.

Sleeze sat up from his position and looked out the passenger side window. The tint did wonders to conceal his identity. He watched as he seen a dark figure wander into the alley on Chamberlain Court. *That looked like Heem.* He thought about the bounty that was over his head. He looked at Fatty as he drove slowly, listening to Lil' Boosie. Fatty seemed happy as ever to be back into the fold of things and truthfully, Sleeze had to admit, with him being back the hood was moving smoother. Sleeze thought for a second, *what if that was Heem*? Sleeze thought about the conversation Fatty and Torrey had. He remembered vividly what Fatty said to Torrey. He knew Fatty wasn't willing to kill Haseem, but for that fifteen bands, he might have to try his luck. Sleeze didn't have to think long, his mind was made. The money was just too easy to ignore. The opportunity presented itself without him having to search high or low. It was no way he wasn't about to take advantage of this opportunity.

"Bro, pull over, I got to piss bad as fuck!" Sleeze yelled over the music. Fatty looked over at Sleeze and turned the stereo down.

"What you say?" Fatty asked, still rapping to one of his favorite songs.

"I said, nigga, pull over real quick. I have to take a piss." Fatty didn't reply, he just pulled to the side. "I'll be back in a second." Fatty nodded at Sleeze and turned the music back up. Sleeze looked back to see if Fatty was watching him, surprisingly he wasn't. Sleeze could barely see through the tint, but what he saw put him at ease. Fatty pulled a Dutch Master from the glove box and started breaking the cigar open. With that being the cue to do his thing, he flipped his hoodie over his head and slid alongside the nearest house to him. The homes that sat positioned on Lewis Street, also connected to the alley that sat behind the Roosevelt Center.

Ironically, Sleeze creeped slowly past Zach's home and hopped the fence. The commotion he caused made Haseem stop in his tracks and begin to look around. Thankfully, Sleeze wasn't close enough for Haseem to make him. Sleeze stopped completely. He waited until Haseem felt comfortable enough to continue his journey before he moved again. After what seemed like forever, Haseem started to walk again through the alley. Sleeze blew a sigh of relief from his mouth. Sleeze waited a few more seconds before coming out of his hiding place and making his way onto the graveled path. The dark concealed him perfectly.

Honk! Honk!

Sleeze froze momentarily hoping Haseem wouldn't turn around. *Bitch ass nigga, stop hitting the horn. What the fuck?* The thoughts that ran through his head was of pure agitation. Sleeze knew he didn't have much time, so he began to walk faster, he didn't want to let Haseem out of the alley alive. Growing impatient with following Haseem, Sleeze began to trot slowly to his target. Sleeze pulled his XD .45 ACP from off his hip and held it down to his side. He was close enough to get a few shots off, but he didn't want to take the risk of missing his pay day. As he closed the distance between the two, he stepped on a twig, alerting Haseem that he wasn't the only person in the alley no longer. Haseem looked back and saw Sleeze approaching swiftly, without hesitation he took off running. *Yeah, this what I like, nigga.* Sleeze smiled and gave pursuit. He raised his cannon, but didn't squeeze, he wanted every bullet to count. Haseem frantically ran in zig-zag-like motions, making it harder for the person chasing him to get a true shot off.

Haseem's heart thumped through his chest as he ran full speed through the alley. *All I have to do is make it to Kat's,* Haseem coached himself as he made a sharp right into another alley adjacent from the previous one. Haseem picked up speed, knowing that zig zagging in the small ascending alley wasn't possible. As Haseem came to the end of the alley, he turned to see the figure gaining on him. Haseem made a sharp left, slipping but caught himself from falling. Knowing the mistake probably cost him, he became frantic. Gaining his momentum back, Haseem was back on both of his feet and nearing Kat's home on the corner of Jackson Street. When he hit the porch, he felt an instant relief wash over him. He knew he was safe now. Haseem twisted the knob and pushed the door in the same motion, the door didn't budge to his surprise. He tried pushing the door again and again before panic set in. Before Haseem got the chance to bang on the door, the dark figure appeared from around the corner, gun in hand. Haseem looked for an escape route and seeing none, he hoped on a dream to survive.

"Please bruh, don't kill me, my nigga. I'll give you what them niggas promising you to pay. We didn't know who spot we it was that we hit. Please bruh," Haseem pleaded, raising his hands in surrender. The look in the shooter's eyes seemed familiar as hell, he just couldn't place them at the moment, between the night sky and the hoodie the shooter wore, it was too dark for him to recognize. As the shooter stepped on to the porch walking closer to Haseem, recognition set in, it was FB Sleeze. *Fuck, man!* At that moment, he knew his life was over. He knew Sleeze wouldn't spare him. Haseem looked behind him, eyeing the edge of the porch. He didn't know if he could make it, but at this time of life and death, it was do or die. Their encounter had only amounted to seconds, but to Haseem, it felt like a lifetime.

With no more words to be said, Sleeze raised his cannon. Haseem took off and tried to hop the small wall divider. Sleeze squeezed off three rapid shots, hitting Haseem directly in the back of his head. Haseem's limp body crumbled out of the air. His body landed awkwardly on the manicured lawn outside of Kat's residence. Sleeze ran up to the divided wall and squeezed two more shots into Haseem's already lifeless body. Sleeze tucked his gun and took off up Thompson Street towards Shop N Go.

Boc... Boc... Boc...

Santana grabbed Niyah and covered her instinctively. What the fuck was that? That shit sounded close as a bitch.

"Is everybody okay?" Santana asked, helping Raven off the floor. Her hair was disheveled and out of place. Santana swiped at the loose hair that lay across her face, placing it back on her head. The gesture angered Kat. She hadn't moved one bit when the shots rang out, she was too concentrated on being salty over Santana's affection and concern for Raven. The steps creaked as Santana let Niyah go. Someone was descending the stairs. Everyone was present instead of Montez, so it was no surprise when Montez came around the corner yawning, with obvious sleep in his face.

"What the fuck was that? That shit sounded—" Montez stopped mid-sentence when he looked up and saw Santana standing in the middle of the living room with Niyah at his side. The pair hadn't seen each other since the day Santana had shot him in the hand for stealing. Montez gritted his teeth, the anger was visible for all to see, they hated each other. Kat watched the two lock eyes, and it was odd. She took note of it and stored it into her memory bank. She was going to find out what the fuck they were beefing about, but for now she was going to act like she didn't see the obvious. The police sirens snapped Santana and Montez out of their stare down. Montez licked his teeth and walked into the living room past Santana.

"What was that, Ma?" Montez asked, moving the living room curtain so he could look out of it. There was no activity on the street when he looked out. He looked both up and down Thompson Street but saw nothing. But only if he knew a small, guided look towards the ground would have' shown him Haseem's soulless body. Montez closed the curtain and looked at his mother. He noticed something was weighing heavily on his mother's heart, but he left that alone because it was none of his business.

"I know I'm not tripping… those was gunshots. That shit sounded close as fuck, it woke me up in a sweat. I got up and went to close my window, I saw a nigga running up Thompson Street with a hoodie on his head. Of course, that might not mean shit, but still. Am I tripping?"

"Oh shit!" Santana panicked as he ran out the door and opened it. He had halfway expected to see Haseem lying in a pool of blood. Thankfully, he was wrong. Santana walked off the porch and looked both ways. There was nothing going on at this time of night. The sirens began to get closer, as the red and blue lights illuminated the night. Santana hurried back into the house and closed the door. The feeling that consumed him, told him something wasn't right. When he walked back into the living room Kat, Raven, Niyah and even Montez looked at him curiously.

"What's up, you good?" Raven asked with concern written all over her face.

"Yeah. That nigga Haseem was supposed to be on his way from Tha Carter ten minutes ago. That nigga probably got spooked when he heard those shots." Santana opened his phone and strolled down to his contacts and dialed Haseem's number. Haseem's phone just rang and rang, until his voicemail finally picked up. Santana called back. Not receiving an answer from Haseem was odd, but for him to not answer his phone at this very moment worried Santana. The look on his face gave way to worry all around the living room. They were matching his energy.

Bang ... Bang ... Bang ...

The thumping at the door startled everyone. Kat rose from the sofa and advanced to the door, Santana stopped her mid-stride.

"Hold on, ma, let me get this gun off my person first."

"Hurry up," was all Kat said in reply. Santana turned around before ascending the stairs. "My name is Justice Torres. Please don't forget." Santana reminded Kat before running up the stairs to the bathroom. Santana's hands trembled from anger, confusion, anxiety and worry. He walked to the window and peeked out the side of the curtain. When he saw a police officer wrapping crime scene tape around his rental, his heart dropped. *Please God, I know I don't pray to you much, please let Zach and Haseem be alive and well.* Santana looked towards the ceiling hoping God could hear his pleas.

Santana took the 40-caliber Glock .27 off his hip and opened the sink cabinet. Inside the cabinet was dirty, mildewed and unorganized. Santana grabbed a bucket and placed his Glock into the bottom of it. He then started stacking all the other buckets on top of each other to conceal his weapon.

"Justice!" Santana heard Kat call from downstairs. Santana closed the cabinet and ran downstairs. As he descended the stairs, he locked eyes with Charleston's Homicide Detectives Brian Williams and Daniel Schooner. Williams and Schooner were also partners in the investigation of his shooting that took place at Shop-N-Go that left Cameron "N.O." Dukes and Bre-Shawn "Breeze" Saunders dead. The presence of the pair shook him. *Damn, maybe I should have kept my glizzy on me, Santana thought as he slowly made his way down the stairs one at a time.* Santana looked from one detective to the other, then looked at Kat. He searched each of their faces for answers. No one budged, and Kat's eyes teared up as she looked at Santana. She couldn't hold it in any longer. After seeing Haseem's body lying on her lawn, she didn't know what to say or what to do. The image fucked her up. Kat knew from that night forward she would have a hard time sleeping peacefully.

The tears unwillingly dropped from Kat's face, they were coming by twos and threes. Kat's tears signified his worse fears. He didn't know what, but he knew something devastating took place. *Did God even attempt to answer my prayers. Santana's mind was racing a hundred miles per minute.* The empty void that had just washed over him must have been his sign, the answer, from his higher power. Sadness had overcome his soul just like that. As if someone snapped their fingers and it became instant. Kat's tear-stricken face was doing numbers on Santana's heart. Kat was devastated, Santana could tell Kat had seen something she instantly regretted. He shook the chills out of his body and asked the million-dollar question.

"Who got killed? It was Heem, wasn't it?" Before Kat had the chance to confirm it, he knew. Santana just stared at Kat with a look that screamed, "What the fuck do I do now?" Kat wiped her eyes but remained quiet. She was at a total lost over this one.

Damn, God... the lil' nigga was only seventeen, Kat thought angrily. Santana stood in place for what felt like at least five minutes, before reaching for the banister of the staircase. He had suddenly felt dizzy and extremely anxious. Santana sat over on the stairs, he had to gather himself. He was truly fucked up over Haseem losing his life so soon.

Santana just sat and thought. He cried wondering if anything could have been done differently. Not finding any resolution, he put his face into his palms and cried for his friend's lost soul.

Santana looked up, eyes swollen and bloodshot. *How the fuck could this happen?* he thought. He calmly reached into his pocket and dialed Zach's phone number. Santana wanted to be the person to deliver the news about Haseem, that was if he didn't know already. Zach's phone rang for what seemed like forever before it was finally picked up.

"What's good, bruh?" Zach answered groggily. Santana just cried into the phone when he heard Zach voice. He was beat for words. *What the fuck do I say?*

"Bruh, you good? What happened?" From the sound of Santana's crying, it woke Zach up. He was now fully awake andand alert.

"Haseem gone, bro." The words coming out of his own mouth sounded foreign in itself.

"What!" Zach yelled into the phone. "No... no... no... bro, please tell me you're lying, my nigga. Please bro tell me you—" Zach just started crying hysterically. Santana knew Haseem's death would fuck Zach up, but what he didn't know was the guilt Zach consumed in his heart. The argument between him and Haseem played in his head over and over again.

"Where you at, bruh? I'm coming to you now."

"I'm on Jackson at Kat's."

"Say less, bruh, I'm getting dressed now. Don't do nothing irrational. I'm coming." Zach hung up. Santana closed his phone and wiped his tears with the back of his sleeve. He would have time to grieve, the anger he felt inside overrode his heartbreak. Somebody was going to pay for Haseem losing his soul. Santana looked at Detective Williams angrily.

"Fuck you looking at, nigga?" Santana exclaimed venomously. Detective Williams just stood in the foyer, holding on to his cupboard.

"Son, your anger is misplaced."

"Is it? Where the fuck my man at, sir?" Santana rose from his position and walked toward the door. He had to see Haseem. It just wasn't ringing true to him that his dog was really gone. Santana reached for the door, and Detective Williams grabbed for Santana. He pulled away from the detective forcefully.

"Nigga, don't fucking grab me." The look Santana gave him shot daggers through his soul.

"Let him go, Brian," Kat said in a whisper. Detective Williams squinted his eyes in anger. With everything that had been going on, Santana hadn't talked to Darla or Simfany in a few days. He opened the door and stepped into the night air and inhaled deeply, letting the fresh air attack his lungs. Santana exhaled, then sighed. He walked off the porch and walked into the middle of the street. They had half of Kat's porch taped off. Santana looked closer. Blood splattered the small wall that boxed the porch in. Santana lifted the police tape and looked over the wall. Haseem lay crumbled and lifeless with a huge entry wound in the back of his head. Santana looked for other wounds, the holes made them easy to spot. Haseem got hit in his neck, face and back. *Damn, Blood, what the fuck man? I told you they were coming. Why didn't you just listen?* His thoughts were interrupted by a load shout from behind him.

"Aye! What are you doing?" Santana looked up and ignored the officer as he walked off. He knew what the officer wanted, that's why he stopped off with no issue. "You know you can't be over here," the officer still complained. Santana looked at him in disgust.

"Cover my nigga up, you worried about all the wrong shit," Santana replied smugly as he continued his walk to his rental, sitting on the hood, waiting for Zach to show up.

***

Simfany sped through Baltimore County, trying to sober up in preparation for her current mission. She had finally gotten the drop on one of the Brooks brothers and she was ecstatic to be the person snatching his soul. Though the one she craved was Tez-Mo. He was the demon of the two and the one who took Tijuana's life. Both brothers had proven not only to their neighborhood, but to all the surrounding counties how dangerous and murderous they could be. The closer she got, the more she thirsted for revenge. She wanted Tez-Mo's head but was willing to settle for Kevin's. There was no real traffic hindering her from making it to Joppatowne in time to do her.

As Simfany swerved in and around traffic her phone rang. She wanted to ignore it, but the ringtone "Down For You" by Murder, Inc played, the ringtone was solely designed and stored for Santana. Simfany grabbed her phone, footing the gas over Route 40, entering the city of Joppatowne, Maryland.

"What's up, baby boy?" Simfany asked into the phone, looking on both sides of Route 40 in search of the newly built Sheetz gas station.

"They killed Heem, Ma." The words Santana spoke crushed her heart. She knew her son loved Haseem and she knew the loot would set him back tremendously. *Damn, my baby lost Tijuana and Haseem within months of each other*. She mourned for her son's friend.

"How?" Simfany asked, voice laced with deep concern.

"I don't know. I was at Kat's house visiting Raven and Niyah when shots rang out. All I could think to do was grab Niyah until they stopped. Everything after that was slow motion. I just saw son's body, they did my nigga bad, Ma. They did Heem bad. Why didn't he just listen to me?" Simfany could hear Santana crying through the phone. To hear her son so heartbroken fucked her up. Simfany took a deep breath and sighed. She couldn't have this type of shit o her head right before she went on a mission.

"Tang, know I hope you okay. Not everybody is cut for this shit. Right now, I'm on the way to hold Tijuana's memory high, if you catch my drift. I can't be in this kind of mood before go-time. We will talk more about this later, I promise. I'll be back your way in about a week, if not sooner. Think and be cautious. I love you."

Siempre," Santana replied before hanging up. Simafany knew if anyone understood, he did. Simfany put her phone back into the middle console and went back to looking for Sheetz as if nothing happened. When Simfany finally caught a glimpse of the reddish orange gas station, she tapped her blinker to pull off the exit. Simfany picked up speed in hopes she wasn't too late.

***

"Come here, papi." Gloria teasingly grabbed for Kevin's arm.

"You playin' anyway, shorty. What we doing here?" Kevin wasn't going for the games Gloria thought she was going to play. He was uncomfortable, he had been all night. He didn't know what was going on, but he could feel that something just wasn't right. Gloria sucked her teeth and rolled her eyes.

"What do you want from me? I'm trying here. What do you want me to say, Kevin?"

"I'm trying to trust you, shorty, but the killer in me is telling me not to. So... tell me, my nigga, what you really on?" Kevin looked at Gloria sternly. She could see the hate in his eyes.

"Look, I'm sorry for the role I played in your cousin's murder. You know had I known, I woulda never went through with it. I know you want me dead, shit... I would have wanted me dead too, if I was you. I can feel the hate coming from your body. Ya perfume can't mask what's evident. But a part of me feels you may still harbor some kind of love somewhere deep. I don't know. But please let me know what the fuck is going on."

Gloria glared out the window, she hated he was right. She did want him, almost with the same energy. Gloria looked at Kevin one more time, she wanted her decision to be worth the risk. Without another thought in her head, Gloria sat upright and pulled out of the alley they were once parked in. Gloria gunned her SUV up Route 40, drifting further away from Harford County.

Gloria pulled up to her home located in Glen Burnie, Maryland. Kevin looked around at the homes, they were spacious on the outside and greatly cared for by homeowners. He could tell what kind of neighborhood he was in by looking at the landscaping and lawn care. Not to mention, the homes were dope as fuck. He should have been there performing with her. He buried those "has been" dreams years ago. The past was in the past, what he had to focus on was what was happening in present time.

Gloria leaned her seat back, getting a perfect angle of Kevin's face. She had to admit, she still loved him. Gloria always had. She was conflicted between being real with him, or just being happy he wasn't dead. When Gloria looked up, Kevin was staring blankly in her face.

"So, when are you going to tell me what the fuck is going on?" Kevin asked, growing impatient.

Gloria took a deep breath and regained her composure. She started from the beginning, telling Kevin how her life turned out after that fatal night they shot and killed her cousin in cold blood. She went on to explain how she met Rocc and how they clicked over the hatred they shared for him and Tez-Mo. Then she told him about some sexy Puerto Rican chick that had a hard on for him and Tez-Mo mostly, Gloria explained why she took off out the alley so suddenly. She had saved him, now it was time to see if the risk was worth taking.

Kevin looked at her and snarled. "On ya dead, this is your role and only your role?"

"I swear. I'm so sorry, I made it right, didn't I?" Gloria asked excitedly. Kevin smiled.

"Yeah ma, we good. Where is the closest cab or bus station around here?" Kevin asked, looking up and down the street. Gloria looked at Kevin confused. She was lost. *Why is he acting all spooky all of a sudden*, she questioned herself.

"You're leaving? Why?" Gloria grabbed Kevin's arm and rubbed up and down, trying to comfort him. The thirst was real. Gloria could see she was losing him more and more with each minute passing.

"Absolutely," Kevin said as he raised his gun eye level to Gloria's face and pulled the trigger. He had no remorse for opp ass bitches. Gloria's eyes remained open as her brain drizzled over the driver's side window.

"Fuck you thought was gone happen once you told me you lured me to my death, you dumb ass bitch." Kevin rubbed down every surface he thought he touched. He cleaned his side of the car for any sign of company. He looked around the car thoroughly before departing, taking any evidence that could link him in any way, shape or form.

Kevin looked at Gloria's goofy ass again, laughed then walked off. He had a bus to catch and some Crips to flip. *Damn, that was close. Nigga, you slipping.* Kevin shook his head as he peacefully strolled up the street in search of a bus station of some kind.

***

"Nigga, what kind of games are you playing?" Simfany barked into the phone angrily.

"Calm down, calm down. Simf, what you talking about, shorty?" Peedi was genuinely concerned.

"They wasn't there. Shorty faked us out. This that fucking bullshit, nigga. From now on, don't hit my muthafuckin line unless you have flesh for me to hit." Simfany hung up the phone as she pulled back into her driveway in Baltimore County, got out the busted Chevy Cobalt and stretched. Simfany put her keys into her Coach bag and powered her phone off, not taking Santana into consideration. She walked through the darkness of her home, kicking her sneakers off in stride. Simfany stripped down to her bra and panties, climbing into her California king mattress, exhausted from the day's events, so finding sleep was easy for her.

Chapter 12

Both east and west side residents of Charleston, WV, packed the small street. Jackson Street was extremely small to hold so many mourners. Regardless of the fact, the whole city turned out to see Haseem off.

Santana sat in the back observing the crowd. There were too many people to even try and look through, the crowd was building bigger as the minutes passed. Santana couldn't lie, he was impressed by the outpour of support. It was definitely a soldier's way out. *But if you were loved by so many people, how could this happen to you, of all people?* Santana's thoughts were disturbed by a shift in crowd space. People moved to let the gang through. *These bitch ass niggaz ain't even cut like that.* Santana got furious from the lack of respect shown. Santana walked to the abandoned house across the street from Kat's and stood on the porch. It could easily be used as the highest point on Jackson Street, even if it was only temporary.

Santana held his hip tightly, almost applying too much pressure. Santana's eyes followed in disgust as three Full Blooded gang members walked as close as allowed to Haseem's covered body. Santana played attention to one member in particular, he seemed genuinely hurt behind Haseem's death. Santana took mental notes and pictures of each mourner he was able to make eye contact with. Seeing Haseem's body sprawled across the lawn fucked many up, the killing of a kid always brought communities together.

177

Which was sad because that same community promoted the killings.

Santana never once took his eyes off of the FB clan. *What the fuck are you niggaz doing here*, Santana wondered. He just couldn't understand. The only plausible reason could be was disrespect, because the last time he heard, the gang had him, Zach and Haseem on their menu. Just seeing them present heightened his thirst for blood.

Kat rubbed his back as he tensed up from her touch. She had taken him by surprise. Santana looked back at Kat. Kat whispered in his ear.

"Not now, Santana. Not the right time or place. You'll have ya time." Nothing in her words came across as joking, she was as serious as a heart attack. She wanted Santana to handle his business, just not now in front of these crowd of people. Kat licked his ear lobe, sending spasms over his spine.

"I'm out," Santana said as he walked off the porch leaving Kat and her antics behind. One, he wasn't in the mood to be distracted and two, he wasn't into disrespecting Darla. As he moved through the crowd, he realized that in order to have a straight shot at his rental, he would have to pass the gang. Santana gripped his Glock as he pushed his way through the crowd of mourners.

As Santana approached the space the gang occupied, he bit his bottom lip and made his left hand into a gun, shooting each man with his imaginary gun. He wanted each and every one of those niggas to see his face and recognize him, because when the day came to end their existence, they' know what the reaper looked like. Santana's message was loud and clear to everyone with eyes. It was war. The youngest looking member of the crew stepped forward but was stopped by an outstretched arm. Fatty calmed his soldier with the simplest gesture.

Santana stopped and raised his shirt, taunting them further. Santana stood his ground. He prayed that one of the men got froggy. No one moved.

"Man, everything easy, Breezy Blood?" Santana spit back, slyly retracing the death of the man he killed at Shop N Go. The insult definitely hit his target. Fatty Man turned beet red. Santana nodded his head at Fatty, indicating recognition. He studied Fatty a few seconds longer before turning his back to the crowd, hopping into his rental. Santana watched the group of men through his rearview for a few minutes. When he realized they wasn't all shit, he put his car in drive. "Go ahead, I dare one of you niggas. I promise I'll gun ya stupid ass down in front of ya whole city." Satisfied, Santana put his foot on the gas and sped off with murder on his mind.

***

It was the day for Haseem to be put to rest. The funeral was even murkier than the night Haseem was found dead. No matter the static, Santana couldn't miss sending his nigga off right. He was fully prepared for the bullshit. Santana sat in the front pew with Darla, Zach and Haseem's immediate family. He could see the words coming from the preacher's mouth, but his mind was subconsciously elsewhere. Being in a religious atmosphere made him think about the souls he had taken. He wasn't a religious person, but he believed in Karma wholeheartedly. Santana looked at the casket, Haseem seemed so peaceful. The sight of his nigga dead to the world crushed him.

The only loss Santana had experienced was his best friend, Justice, and recently Tijuana, but he wasn't able to attend either funeral. His circumstances at the time of their deaths prohibited him from being able to see them off for the last time. Haseem's homegoing was his first and he prayed it would be his last. Santana's thoughts ran rapidly through his head, he was fighting his inner demons. He didn't want to be in the church anymore, but he knew leaving would be like spitting in the face of Haseem's family and that he couldn't do, so he just sat idle until the service was over.

Every time he looked up, at least one person in the church was looking at him. Santana's mind was so consumed by the bullshit he hadn't realized the preacher was no longer talking and people were moving about. He was looking and he knew immediately when he felt a tap on his shoulder. Santana looked up from his seat into the eyes of a brown-skinned man with beady eyes.

"Santana, right?"

"My nigga, who the fuck is you?"

"What lil' nigga, who the fuck you talking to like that?" the man said offensively.

"Nigga, we don't have to talk at all, whatsoever." Santana dismissed him. That brought a smile to the man's face.

"Yeah ight, lil' nigga. Do you," the man said, before sliding off into the crowd of mourners. Santana watched the man until he disappeared out of sight. As if on cue, another hand landed on his shoulder. Santana shrugged it off aggressively and turned around, ready to snap. Darla's soft features looked back at him. She stood next to him concerned at his anger.

"What's wrong?" Darla asked, taking the empty seat next to him, rubbing the side of his face tenderly.

"Nothing ma, this atmosphere fucking with my head. I'm ready to go. I need some fresh air. All the crying and shit fucking with my mental. How you holding though, ma? I know you grew up with Heem, this shit has to be hard on you." Santana shook his head from side to side, trying to keep his own tears from spilling from his eyes. He had cried enough. It was time for somebody to die for their actions. Darla saw the look she had been seeing for days wash over Santana's face.

"Stop feeling down, you know what needs to be done to correct this. Haseem didn't have to get done like that, and you know I don't promote violence, but enough is enough. I couldn't even fathom the thought of you being hurt again. We need you, Tana, we need you to get back to being you. Stop letting this consume you. For real. Santana, look at me." Darla pulled his chin towards her so they could be eye-to-eye.

"It's time you stop playing. You have a load of responsibilities about to land on ya plate and I need you here with me." Using her fingers to say, "eye to eye." I love you and Melquan loves you. Daddy, we need the old you back. It hurts, I get it, I lost Nessy not to long ago, now this. Come on, baby, it crushes us all. But if it was you, they would be celebrating in ya name. So, about all that, you're gonna drive yourself insane. I need my man back. Take whatever time you need, but please restore me my king." Darla kissed Santana's lips tenderly. "I love you, baby," Darla whispered, playing with Santana's ear lobe. Santana laughed and pushed Darla off his ear.

"Chill out, ma, you playing and shit." Santana smiled and then just burst out laughing. "Chill... chill... chill..." Santana laughed, trying escape Darla's fingers.

"Oh, so you ticklish? Oh, okay. I got something for that ass," Darla replied, pulling her hands back from Santana's head. She didn't get up, she just laid on him. Darla looked up and stared Santana in his eyes. Darla tried to see his soul through his. All she could see was pain. She wanted to be his and only his for the rest of her life. Darla was elated to have a man like Santana.

"What's up... what you thinking about? Tryin' see my soul, are you? What you see when you look me in my eyes?" Santana kissed Darla's lips. Darla then looked away and ducked.

"Down!" Darla yelled, pulling Santana to the ground. Santana rolled, willingly hitting the ground on his back. Darla crawled on her knees until she reached Santana.

Bang! Bang! Bang!

Three loud shots rang out, causing the church employees to run. Everybody started running for the exit.

Boc... Boc... Boc... Boc...

Darla covered her head as the shots went off and began crying.

Boc... Boc... Boc...

Darla jumped at another series of shots. *Man, what the fuck? Them too close*, Darla thought as she looked for Santana. Santana was standing over top of her shooting his Glock. The fire that spit from the mouth of the gun fucked Darla up. *I have this nigga*, Darla thanked God for Sanana and ended up raising to her feet beside Santana. She looked across the church to see who was shooting. The little niggaz she saw peeking in and out of the front door.

"Bae, get down. I got these niggas. Where the fuck is this nigga Zach at?" Santana asked, loading another mag up into his Glock, this time the capacity in the mag was extended.

Bang!

Santana flinched at the loud bang. Santana raised the Glock at shot at the door. The shots no longer scared her, they now gave her comfort. Darla thought quick and pulled her purse out. She searched her phone for Zach's number, finding it, she called him immediately. He answered his phone in one ring.

"Yo," Zach sang into the phone and laughed.

"Nigga, what the fuck you so happy for? Where the fuck are you?" Darla asked frantically.

On the west, I had to leave the funeral early because my moms passed out. I have Heem and he knew it, so not being around those fake ass people was a blessing. Why you sounding all crazy? Where Tana? Ight look, what the fuck…"

Darla dropped her phone as Santana pulled her from the ground.

"Hurry up!" Santana pulled on Darla, getting her to her feet.

"Wait, my phone." Darla pulled from his grasp only long enough to reach and grab her phone.

"Here." Darla handed Santana the phone. He scrunched his eyebrow up to ask who the caller was. Darla stopped walking and looked Santana up and down, lips pressed together and rocking her leg up and down like she always did when she was mad. Santana laughed because he knew her little mean baby face was on its way.

"Not now, okay… come on. I'm leaving your ass, come on." He laughed. *This bitch is crazy.* He couldn't stop laughing. Darla wasn't smiling. She didn't find his humor to be funny, not one bit.

"It's Zach," Darla finally said and walked behind Santana the whole way out the church.

"Yeah, I'm on the corner of Lewis and Beauregard. Ight, bet." Santana hung the phone up and rushed to the rental across the street. He popped his trunk and moved the spare tire to the side and pulled the carpet back. A small safe was hidden there that stored his smaller caliber guns. Santana grabbed another Glock and filled his pockets with many extended clips for the Glocks.

Santana ran back across the street as he saw a Gray Jeep Cherokee hit the corner and speed towards Santana. Santana positioned himself and raised his gun. *You bet not, you bet not.* The Jeep Cherokee was getting closer. Before Santana had a chance to let a shot off, the car stopped suddenly. It parked, Santana looked down the street and pushed his gun down when he saw it was Zach talking shit. Santana waited for him to come down the street. Darla loaded into the car first as Santana and Zach watched both sides of the church's back door. Santana let Zach hop in before him to make sure they were safe. Satisfied, Santana hopped in the back seat with Darla. He held her close, rubbing up and down her arms, trying to warm her up.

"You good?" Zach looked into the back seat and asked.

"Yeah bro, we good. Take me to the hospital." Zach looked at Santana with worry in his eyes.

"Why, you good?" Zach asked, praying Santana didn't get hit by any bullets.

"Yeah, I'm good. Gotta make sure the baby ight. Just go to the hospital." Santana waved Zach off.

"What baby? Nigga, I'm lost," Zach said as he turned back around in the seat and put the car in gear. Santana reverted his attention back to Darla. She was beaming. He didn't have a problem becoming the dad. *Thank you ... Thank you...* she thought then regained her composure.

She smiled, then asked, "How did you know?"

"Really? Usually we are together twenty-four-seven, how the fuck can I not recognize when my baby got a crazy glow about her? Them hips don't get wide and them beautiful breasts of yours are so perfect. I watch the motion. I watch with you hate about me and what makes you love. When I figured that out, I knew I would be a perfect match for you. Not in a million years could I have thought that I would be here with you. This was fate at its best. When I found out about you being pregnant, I freaked out at first. And it wasn't because you were pregnant, it was because I was scared that I wouldn't be able to provide. But of course, I knocked them thoughts out my head and thought about how lucky I really am. Thank you for always having my back. That's real shit. But I do wanna have a serious talk with you later once we get home. Darla looked at him, she was trying to read his face.

"It's Zach. We good, baby. I don't think I can wait that long, if it's that serious so cough it up. Talk." Darla locked her eyes with Santana. He smiled.

"Ma, what you want? What you mean, ask hun..." Santana started tickling her. She laughed, trying to escape. She was on his lap, so she knew escape was impossible.

"Ok... baby... ok!" Darla laughed.

"I'm serious, Santana, what are you talking about? Talk. What is it? Why can't you tell me?" Darla was getting emotional. The corners of her eyes watered. Santana rubbed her forehead back and forth. He rubbed her hair as he admired her beauty, her flaws, just her period.

"I could be going to jail for a while once my run is over. I can't stay away from this shit now. I have to make sure we all are good, everybody. When I was thirteen, I shot a nigga over some shit with my mom. The nigga I was beefing with got killed one day in the city and automatically made me a suspect, so I'm on the run for that body."

"Did you do it?" Darla was interested immediately with this topic. *I knew it. I fuckin' knew it.*

"I already knew. Come on Darla, just because we in the middle of the mountains don't mean, we not a part of the living," said Santana, trying to avoid her Q&A.

"Boy you better stop. It's your persona, Santana. One, you make commands. And two, ya swag is crazy as fuck. Come on, you don't even know what this life with me will do for you. All I ask for is a faithful husband. I wanna feel like you're the only one. I don't want to be stuck raising kids alone. I wanna be loved, Santana. I've been hurt badly my whole life, so the scars are still fresh. I don't know, ever since your mom mentioned you to me, I've been curious ever since. I just observe how you carried yourself. And your ass was a problem, still is. But I'm pretty sure you wouldn't be hollering rape." She smiled be showing off her beautiful pearly whites.

"Are you that man, Santana Vasquez. Are you my man?" Darla searched his eyes, they softened almost immediately. He leaned down and kissed her lips.

"I love you, my beauty, I'm all yours. I show you that. Have faith, we good. The faster I get these licks back over here, I'll be able to sleep better, knowing I sent one of them niggaz with him. It don't matter who they with, or who's around because I'm gonna definitely be masked of course. Fuck talking about that. Let's talk about this baby in your stomach." He tickled her for a few seconds and she giggled.

"Ok, baby... wow... ok." She laughed uncontrollably. She calmed down and was trying to catch her breath. *This nigga is so silly,* Darla thought, still trying to catch her breath.

"So, how long you been hiding this from me and why? Are you used to being in relationships like that? Well, if you are, you better change that. Because I don't play about my family and will not think twice to kill any and everyone bout you. I thought my actions already showed you that daily. I can be looking into too much. What do you wanna name our son?"

Darla looked away playfully and looked at him and said, "Boys are yours and girls are mine. I just want you to know that because when you try it, we gonna be beefing for at least a week."

"Damn, over a name... a week without this?" he asked, putting his finger through her pants and rubbing her clit through her panties. Darla moaned and closed her eyes.

"Baby, stop before I embarrass us in here today," she replied, rubbing on his dick through his jeans.

"See, look at you what you doing?" Santana watched her go up and down on his dick. "Alright, what about going to make sure you're ok?"

"I am ok, Santana, and I'm safe. I don't ask for nothing more than that. You are perfect. I don't know why you think this shit again, we forever. I thought about it and I don't think I could ever share you with another woman besides your mama. This my badge so she get a pass." Darla laughed. "I love you, Tana."

"Siempre."

"Siempre?"

"It means forever, always."

"I like it, I like the way it sound when it rolls off your tongue. You are so beautiful. I know our babies are going to be the bomb." Darla beamed as the car came to a stop. Darla looked up at smiling Zach.

"Let me know when you want me to come back and get you. I'll be around for a minute. Just hit me," Zach said before parking at the entrance of the hospital's emergency room.

"Good looking, bro. Make sure you watch yourself. Are you strapped? If not, go get ya gun now. Stop walking around this bitch like you can't be next. Right now, you a free body. What are you doing anyway? You wanna go legit or something?" Santana asked, he needed to have a serious talk about his lacking abilities. Santana knew you could go to jail behind being caught with them, but if he had to pick from the two, best believe he was picking the lesser and slower route. It's called getting a job.

"Man, I just been working trying to pay these bills. Mom Dukes found that money in my room and put it in the middle of my bed. She of course didn't take the money, but she was surprised at how much money I had made without her knowing the wiser."

Santana reached in the car and dapped Zach up.

"Be safe, my nigga. Go home and strap up. Be prepared for anything. For real, bro, no more being naked out here. I promise if you fall, I'll make sure everything straight. Just stay alive."

"Got you, bro," Zach said, crossing his fingers. Santana busted out laughing.

"Nigga, you stupid." He slammed the door and wrapped his arm around Darla and walked into CAMC.

Chapter 13

It had been weeks since Fatty Man had seen either Santana or Zach. After the funeral shooting, everybody seemed to disappear. Fatty knew who was responsible for killing Haseem but kept it to himself. His loyalty was to Sleeze, though he was mentally frustrated with him at the moment, he kept his secret more or less.

Fatty paced the basement floor, he was pissed. The shooting that took place at the church on the east end, Abundance of Life, left many wounded but only one dead. And that one soul was taken from one of his men. He was getting tired of chasing after Santana and Zach. Their bodies were supposed to be easy to catch, but catching the little niggaz was proving to be more difficult than he thought. Fatty continued to pace from one side of the room to the other. Fatty subconsciously stopped and stared at the spot where Von took his last breath. He smiled, no one in attendance knew he was responsible for the deaths of Nessy, Remy or Von. He was pretty sure Nessy's murder would go unsolved also, but just to make sure all was well, Fatty kept his ear to the streets. He was pretty sure he left no stone unturned, especially when it came to Nessy and Von. He was more hands on with their murderers then he was with Remy's murder, he laughed it off. Instead of running from it, Fatty raced to the bullshit full speed. The night Fatty got the call, he turned himself in the very next morning, to the Charleston Police Department.

The memories flashed through Fatty's mind as he continued to pace from one side to the other. Fatty paced the floor in silence as his soldiers watched him intently. They all knew they were all summoned for a reason. Fatty had just gotten released from CPD only hours before. The meeting he called was a product of the extensive questioning he had to endure.

"So, which one of you lil' niggaz went to the police and told them about the issues me and Remy had?" Fatty rubbed his chin as he paced back and forth. When the basement grew silent, Fatty stopped pacing and looked up.

"Nobody?, So how many niggaz think I killed Remy? Don't hold your tongue. You niggaz gangster, right? We'll keep it real, Fully. How many of you niggaz think I killed Remy?" When Fatty looked around for hands, gestures or sour faces, he saw none so he continued to probe.

"I didn't know we breed hoes, my nigga," Fatty spat venomously.

"Speak now or forever hold your peace. So, I ask one more time, who the fuck thinks I killed Remy?"

Surprisingly to Fatty, he looked on as half of his team raised their hands. Fatty just couldn't help himself, he burst out laughing. He had to look at his men again. *These bitch ass niggas been harboring these faggot ass feelings the whole time I've been back.* So, that alone pissed Fatty Man off, it was no way Fatty would be able to hide his anger, so he turned back to the crowd and addressed the obvious.

"If all you niggas… hold on… put your hands back up. One, two, three, four, five… Damn, you too, Freezo?" Fatty laughed and finished taking inventory of his team's raised hands. The count came to an even fourteen people. Fatty knew the unknown was what kept the remainder of his squad's hands down. No one truly knew what Fatty was capable of, especially if he was the person that killed Remy.

"So, the million-dollar-question is, did I kill Remy? Honestly though, do you really want to know if I plucked bruh's feathers, or do you want the news or the streets to answer your question? Well, if you think I'm gonna get booked for killing Remy soft ass, sorry... Tell them niggaz they have to do better and for the record, I did slaughter that. I haven't ever repeated that until now and if I hear it beyond this point, I will send you with that nigga. Do you niggaz copy? You not feeling how I'm rocking, bounce. This your one and only shot, so leave if you're not ready to deal with it." Everyone had dropped their hands by then, but no one moved. Everyone still wanted to be labeled Fully Blooded.

The fear that Fatty instilled throughout the city was enough for any of them to stay. The love they received from being affiliated was beyond crazy. The gang was damn near like gods of their city. No one had ever posed a threat to their gang, until now. Santana was their top opp. The bounty that sat above Santana's head no longer mattered. They wanted his blood for the soul he snatched that day at Haseem's homegoing. Fatty didn't care about the money, all he cared about was getting his lick back. Fatty Man sat on Von's favorite stool and spun in a circle. He always remembered what Von would say when asked, "What the fuck do you have a stool for?" Von would famously reply, "I keep it around, just in case." *Just in case of what, you fucking weirdo?*

Fatty questioned Von's motives. His thought process dwelled on the negative, if it wasn't negativity, his mind really couldn't make sense of it. Fatty had millions of thoughts in his head at once. He replaced the thought that Haseem got killed many times over, then his mind would jump to the interrogation room, where he was left cold and hungry as he waited on his lawyer to show up. Now his mind was back to the present, he was back surrounded by all his men, sitting on Von's dumb ass stool. Fatty looked around the room, he knew deep down, the majority of his men hated him, but he didn't care. One thing he knew for sure, niggaz would never voice their opinion. Fatty could say he was doing better than most, that's for sure.

Fatty lifted one foot onto the steps of the stool as fun as fast as he could. His team looked at him crazily. Fatty stopped spinning and placed his foot flatly on the basement floor, dust whirled into the air, causing a few coughs around the room.

"Alright look, if anyone knows me, I'm big on niggaz being real. If you don't believe me, then ask around. These niggaz will definitely let you know how I'm giving it up. Enough about that, let me tell you about Remy and what caused his demise. First off, Fully, in the end G talked too fucking much! Long story short, many of you same niggaz was present when Remy tried to get Von to kill me. He told Von I was the reason Breeze got killed. Nigga say I froze up on Breeze that day at Shop N Go. And in all honesty, I think the nigga that helped me stay alive was the witness, claiming I froze on her watch. Of course, we can all guess, it was Nessy. I figured Von took that playbook from Nessy and mixed it with Remy. Bruh put some salt on both of them and let me rock, but not before banishing me from the hood I helped build. I did what I did to shake back. I told Remy before I departed that day, that he was food on a nigga'z menu.

"After I caught Remy, I went to smoke Nessy, but I was already too late. Maybe it was a blessing from God, or maybe from Breeze. You know Fully hated Nessy for many reasons, which I won't really get into. I don't know, all I know was, that shit was taken care of. The rest is history. Now, knowing what caused what, do anybody have any problems that they want to address? I'm telling you to speak now or forever hold your peace." Fatty looked around the basement, seeing no one went for the bait. There wasn't a nigga in the basement curious enough to raise their hand, let alone speak for that matter. Satisfied by the silence, Fatty Man moved on to the next topic at hand... Santana.

"Now, this other issue we have, I hope to be done with this shit soon. There's no way that this little nigga is still running around "our" city doing anything. What the fuck your ass on, bra? That nigga killed one of ours and he still walking around this bitch like shit sweet, why? How the fuck can that even be possible!" Fatty yelled loudly, his voice echoed off the small basement walls, causing the majority of his men to cover their ears.

"Fuck you niggaz covering in your ears for? That bitch ass G needs to be dead now! Him and that light skin nigga Zach. As a matter of fact, whoever catches that lor nigga, I'll shoot a bonus your way. That also comes with stain and keys to a whip," Fatty Man said, enticing his younger soldiers. He knew promising a jump in rank would do the trick. Fatty had even gone as far as giving stain, attached with keys to mobilize the web. Meaning that once promoted to a higher ranking, they would be allowed to recruit others on their own.

Fatty knew he placed a lot on the table, to him it would be just enough to make sure he was taken seriously. Nobody in the basement was paying attention to what Fatty had to say. Their antennas were up, all the majority of them wanted was, to be able to claim a body, hold top rank, and have a few pups of their own. That's all that ran through their heads. Fatty said nothing further, he just let the conversation linger, marinating throughout their brains. Fatty needed soldiers, not niggaz running around in their feelings like bitches.

Fatty chuckled slightly, causing everyone to look up from their own thoughts. The whole gang stared at him. Fatty remained quiet. It was nothing else he cared to discuss. Fatty lifted his presidential Rolex and tapped the big face a few times. The gesture confused everyone, but Sleezey Sleeze sighed and explained.

"Really, Fully? That nigga saying time ticket. Don't make me explain more than I have to." Sleeze shook his head from one side to the next. By the end of Sleeze's smart ass comment, each member left one by one, leaving only Fatty Man and Sleeze present. Fatty walked to Sleeze and dapped him up. It had been days. The last time Fatty could recall seeing Sleeze, was the night he hopped out faking like he had to pee. The pair definitely needed to talk, that was for sure.

Sleeze leaned up against the filthy sofa, coughing a fit when the dust from the dirty sofa began circulating in his airspace. Sleeze couldn't help himself, he coughed, damn near spitting up lung particles. Sleeze rubbed his nose with the back of his hand, until the tingling sensation finally subsided. Sleeze's allergies heightened every time he stepped foot into the basement.

"Come, my boy, sit down. We need to talk. Because that shit you did the other night was foul. I told you not to get involved with Haseem whatsoever. Why the fuck didn't you listen to me and respect what the fuck I had asked of you? Huh, what was so hard to comprehend?" Fatty asked Sleeze, confused as hell. Fatty started feeling like he spoke another language, because every time he spoke, either no one seemed to process the information or more then half the time, they just ignored his nonsense.

"I asked you to take a seat, bro." Fatty sounded serious.

"Nigga, you just saw what that shit did to me. I'm not sitting on that mf couch, my dude. No disrespect intended."

"Fuck it, you good, that shit not really important. What is important, is why do you continue to ignore the shit I keep shooting ya way. Look, all that hinting and beating around the bush shit, I'm done with it. Why the fuck did you kill Haseem when I blatantly told you not to?" Sleeze looked at Fatty and clenched his jaw. It was one of Sleeze's many telltale signs of frustration or building anger. Fatty saw the gesture but honestly couldn't care less. The only thing Fatty had on his head was Haseem and the soldier they had recently lost. Sleeze's actions had caused a hell of a chain reaction. The only reason Fatty even went through the hassle was for two reasons. One, he loved Sleeze to death and two, he wanted every excuse in the book to ignore the betrayal. He just needed a good reason to.

"Do you really want to do this shit, Fatty? Like for real, my nigga, you sure this what you want?" Sleeze asked seriously, putting his phone in his pocket. Fatty stood erect, he was on point now, he was down for the bullshit. Sleeze didn't move, he just watched Fatty preparing for a confrontation. He laughed inside. Sleeze didn't realize how his words could be taken and twisted. Sleeve just watched Fatty look stupid, he knew he coulda told him the words he spoke was meant differently. but it amused him to continue to watch Fatty gear up to fight.

Once Fatty was done stripping his excessive clothes off, he stood in the middle of the floor, hands to his sides.

"Bro, what the fuck are you doing?" Sleeze laughed. *This nigga done lost all his marbles*, Sleeze thought. "What, now you want to shoot the fade with me about Haseem?"

"Bruh, stop playing word games with me. I know what you just said, my nigga. I might be off, but I'm not that off. This what you've been wanting, lil' bro, let's get this shit over so I can get to the bottom," Sleeze interjected.

"Nigga, I'm not fighting you. Period. So, miss me with that. You looking silly as fuck and now when I said you don't want to do this, I wasn't talking bout fighting, dick head. I was talking bout telling truths, about unspoken shit."

"What the fuck you talking about, nigga?"

"You keep talking bout Haseem, inquiring about bullshit. I do know you and Torrey the only niggas know I smoked buddy, but nigga, I know shit about you too that no one else do. That's why I asked that, you want to bring all the shit to light, we can. I've never not confronted my demons, are you ready is the mufuckin question."

"What secrets you know about me, lil' nigga?" Fatty was confused. He usually didn't have secrets, so he definitely wanted to know what the fuck Sleeze was barking about.

"First off, my nigga, understand it's only us in here. You good, regardless. I want you to speak ya peace about Heem and we'll move on. You wanted to speak about that one shit so bad, that when I tried to ignore you regarding it, you kept poking at me. Now's the time to address it. After tonight I'm not speaking about Haseem no more. So…" Fatty finally loosened up and took a seat on the couch only feet away from where Sleeze leaned on the wall. Fatty ran his hands away down his jacket pocket and pulled put a box of Swisher Sweets.

"You tryin' smoke, Fully?" Fatty asked Sleeze as he pulled one of the pre-rolled blunts from the box.

"Nigga, is pussy pink? You know I am. This don't change shit though, big homie, I want to speak about what's on ya mind. I'm being serious, because once that sun come up in the a.m., I'm not talking about that little nigga Heem no more."

"Bet. Now forget about that for a second and ease ya mind." Fatty Man lit the blunt, he pulled on it a few times before passing it to Sleeze. The smell of the weed captured Sleeze every time without fail. Sleeze grabbed the blunt and hit it a few times before handing it back to Fatty. The silence was beginning to make both Fatty and Sleeze uncomfortable. The higher they got, the more awkward it got. Fatty broke the silence.

"Look, lil' bro, I don't want you to think I hate you or no shit like that, because that's not the case. I'm mad as fuck though, but don't confuse the two. That decision you made caused a chain reaction. Now, Lil' Bandy got to be buried behind it. I asked specifically for you not to get involved with Heem, but yet you spit in my face behind it."

"Alright… I smoked Haseem, yeah… but nigga, stop saying you asked me to stay away from dude because my nigga, you lying. I was there when you spoke with Ty about it, but my nigga not once did me and you have a conversation regarding that. Do I need to refresh ya memory of the night all this happened?"

"Nah, I remember and you right. I told that nigga Torrey that 'I' wasn't gone take up the bounty on Heem because I wasn't trying to—"

"Be the one that broke ya nigga'z heart in that fashion," Sleeze finished Fatty's sentence.

"Yeah, that I do recall, but knowing that, why did you go through with that shit? Look at what that shit did to Bandy. Not only did he have to bury his cousin, but now the lil' nigga being buried himself. All this behind your actions. This shit could have been avoided." The frustration in Fatty's eyes was evident.

"I understand, big bro, wholeheartedly. But, my nigga, you really got ya nerve. You know that?" Fatty looked at Sleeze brazenly. Sleeze ignored the look and continued.

"Ironically, you have fell in love with the word 'foul' for some odd ass reason. What I did wasn't nowhere close to me being foul. I just did what I'm paid to do. Now, you on the other hand, my nigga justified nonetheless, so I don't know.

"Man, fuck all these riddles, Fully. What the fuck you talking bout, foul? How am I foul?" Fatty rose off the couch bringing a small cloud of dust with him. Sleeze covered his face, trying to keep from coughing.

"My bad, nigga, tell ne whet the fuck you talking bout. You starting to get me out of my element, Sleeze." Fatty waved his hands wildly, trying to get the dust particles out of the air so Sleeze could talk. Fatty did that until no more dust was visible.

"Good looking on that, bro, that shit liable to kill me. But anyway, I'm not playing no games. When are you planning on telling niggas you're responsible for the death of their big homie? And I'm not talking bout Remy, bruh. You know what you did, and I know why. As I said in the beginning, foul but justified. The look that sits on ya face is telling me you thought a nigga was lacking. When you underestimate me, ask yaself, why am I your only pup? And when you do, you'll realize I'm one of a kind. What you used to say to me when I first got jumped in… 'You a rare breed.' Nigga, I pride myself on that. I pay attention. I listen. I watch. Can a nigga get credit where it's due, damn. Before I go any further, I do want you to know I love you, fool. And what we talk about will stay here. I just wanted to address this shit at once. Back to Von, why didn't you tell me? If anything, I was supposed to know. I've never shown signs of disloyalty or treason. I hate when you try to lil dog me."

"Can't front, I'm lost. How do you figure I killed Von? I've always trusted you, my nigga, don't make me start questioning that with these weird ass theories," Fatty stated with finality. Sleeze laughed, he knew Fatty wasn't going to admit to killing Von and he was okay with it. But his reaction wasn't going to stop Sleeze from probing.

"I was the one Von called the night he was killed. I knew I was on speaker, bro. When I answered I heard you talking briefly. Do you even remember what I said to Von regarding the way he did you in front of everyone?" Fatty didn't answer, but it's no way he could ever forget Sleeze's words on that day. Fatty beamed with pride when Sleeze told Von he deserved to be killed behind embarrassing him in front of all their men. There really was no reason to keep beating around the bush, Sleeze knew more than he was given credit for. *Fuck it*, Fatty thought before he answered Sleeze's question truthfully.

"I remember both of your replies. I appreciate you holding it down for the most part. I just don't understand, what the fuck I—" Fatty just couldn't understand.

"Von called. I answered and agreed to bring you back. I did, I brought you back stronger than ever. You, my nigga, are the reason that I'm here, in this role. You have shown me a lot. I have shown my love and loyalty to you on many occasions. Now, show yours and let them hot ones lay with Heem little ass. Now, with all that extra shit out the way, do you want ya cut, or will you continue to cry over spilled milk?" Sleeze asked as he pulled is neatly counted stacks from his jacket pocket. He counted out several of the fifteen and reached them to Fatty. Without hesitation, Fatty grabbed the money and placed it on the table next to the couch.

"I take it our secrets will go to the grave?" Sleeze asked as he popped the rubber band on one of the stacked bills. He counted out five hundred dollars and stretched it to Fatty. Fatty waved him off.

"I'm good, bruh, you did all the work with ya crazy ass. Now, as far as all that other bs, we are definitely to the grave wit it. I don't wanna hear you speak about any of them again, especially around me. Not ever. Them cases all still open, that's all I'm gone say. Ight?" Fatty looked at Sleeze seriously.

"Fully, this me you talking bout. I've known for a while and haven't said not one word. So, no need to remind me, big bro. I'm solid! I say that to say this… If I begin to feel like you on bullshit, we will have a problem. So, please hear me say this again. You have nothing to worry about. That's on dead homies. I'm solid, my nigga. We good?" Sleeze searched Fatty's eyes for deceit. He didn't see none at the moment.

"Say less. FB till my cold slab," Fatty said, twisting his fingers proudly.

"FB, till my cold slab." Sleeze smiled and followed suit, throwing his gang up proudly. Sleeze walked over to Fatty and peaced him up. They interlocked their fingers until it came to five sharp points.

"I love you, big homie," Sleeze said, really meaning every word.

"I love you too, fool," Fatty replied, ashing the blunt he had just lit. Sleeze sat next to Fatty. They smoked and laughed, smoked and laughed. They were both seven bands to the good and not a care in the world, but to kill. And even that at the moment was put on pause.

Fatty feel asleep, the constant rotation of blunts and Henessy took ahold of them. Sleeze could barely keep his eyes open, but a fear of being snaked kept him alert. Or so he thought at least. He ashed the last blunt and tapped Fatty. Fatty jumped fearfully and woke up.

"What?" Fatty asked suspiciously. Sleeze had one eye open, and one eye closed as he laughed. It was crazy how much they loved each other, but in the same breath, doubted each other's loyalty.

"You good, bro. No need to look like that. I always got your back. Swear, bruh. I just wanted to know before I bounce if you staying here, or sliding with me?" Sleeze said, checking the magazine in his 9-millimeter Springfield XD.

"Yeah, I'm out too. Put that gun away with ya goofy ass. I told you no guns are allowed past some stairs." Fatty slurred his words badly.

"I hear you, bro, but I can't go nowhere without my cannon. Especially down here. The last nigga wasn't so lucky. Won't be me, nigga," Sleeze said to himself as he got prepared to leave.

Fatty got up from his spot of comfort and stretched. He stumbled forward, Sleeze caught him.

"You good, fool?"

"Yeah." Fatty finally got his balance and replied, *Damn, I'm slipping. I got to get home. I have to get home ASAP*, Fatty thought as he closed his eyes and his head spun. Fatty tried to shake the feeling, but he really couldn't. He was fucked up. Out of nowhere, Fatty opened his eyes in a panic. A thought had washed through his mind. All he could think about was that Sleeze drugged him. When Fatty looked up to confront his friend, Sleeze was sleep on his feet too, erasing the thought almost immediately from Fatty's head.

"Sleeze!" Fatty shook Sleeze's arm until he woke him.

"Yo."

"Bro, we have to get ourselves together. We fucked up. We gone get pulled for sure if we don't together. Go put some water on ya face." Fatty tried giving some advice.

Both Fatty and Sleeze washed their faces in an attempt to sober up. Though it didn't take away the drunkenness completely, it helped tremendously. They could make it home now. They were in a better place to do so than before. Fatty grabbed his money and keys off the coffee table and looked to his partner in crime.

"Ready Flully?"

"Yeah, been waiting on ya drunk ass." They laughed in unison. Fatty just stuck his middle finger up. He really didn't have the energy to talk shit. Fatty just wanted to get home to his bed, felt like he hadn't slept in days. Fatty didn't say much more, he just walked out the basement with Sleeze in tow. His next destination was home.

***

Santa sat crouched down in the stolen 2003 Crown Victoria, while Zach laid across the back seat with an AR-15 held across his body.

"How much longer do we have to wait?" Zach whined.

"Bruh! Shut the fuck up. Just be on point, these niggas have to be on their way out soon. Everybody else left already." No sooner than the words left Santana's mouth, he saw Fatty Man's head pop out from behind the bushes that sat directly in front of the stolen Crown Vic. Santana's heart leaped from his chest, he was instantly shook. He didn't want to alert Zach because he knew if Zach had any kind of clue that Fatty Man was that close, he would most likely do something stupid and get them caught or even worse, killed.

"Bro, wait for me," Sleeze yelled after Fatty.

"Nah, my nigga, this a dolo mission," Fatty said halfheartedly. Fatty was way too tired to go back and forth with Sleeze.

Santana watched as Fatty Man sluggishly walked past the Crown Vic in search of his own car. Once all activity seemed to subside, Santana tapped the back seat. Zach rose like Frankenstein from the back seat, holding the AR-15. Zach was ready to shed some blood in Haseem's name. Not only was the FB nigga claiming Haseem's body, but they were also responsible for shooting Haseem's funeral service up.

Zach looked through the back window, Fatty and Sleeze was walking through the streets like they didn't have a care in the world. That made Zach mad as fuck. Santana could see the fire in his eyes. *Yeah, my nigga, crave that hunger.* Santana smiled at the sinister thoughts that ran though his head. Santana rose slightly and peeked out the back window. The sight of Fatty and Sleeze lacking pumped his heart to the core. He was ready. He looked in the rear-view mirror at Zach. Zach was too pre-occupied to see Santana eyeing him. Santana saw all he needed to see.

"Watch them, make sure I'm good," Santana said, before opening the door and creeping out. He wasn't trying to alert Fatty, Sleeze or any nosy neighbors. Santana reached into the car and grabbed the Glock 27 he had resting on the floorboard. The Glock he had with him on the mission was different from all his others. This was a new toy Doug had blessed him with after Haseem got killed. The Glock came equipped with a green beam, a scope, which Santana took off, and 2 thirty-round magazines. Santana had fifty-four shots to give if needed. He filled each magazine with twenty-seven shots. For easy reload, he tapped the cups opposite to one another. The regular extended cup was scary by itself, taped together, he could only imagine what kind of damage he would do.

Santana waved Zach from the back seat, all the while keeping his index finger over his lips so Zach wouldn't forget to be quiet during this process of their mission. Santana knew subconsciously that he was going to have to hold Zach's hand throughout the mission. He just prayed they weren't put in a bad spot. With this being Zach's first time, he knew shit could get all bad real fast. Whenever the outcome, he will protect his neck till his dying breath.

Zach opened the left rear side door and crawled out backwards. Before clearing the door, Zach remembered Santana told him to cut the interior light off. The bright lights that illuminated the car was now gone. Both the driver's side and back seat door set ajar, for an easy get away. Santana just hoped they hadn't wasted too much time.

Santana pulled his ski mask down over his face and rolled from behind the car. He ran lightly to the corner of the block and peeped around the van. Thankfully, Fatty and Sleeze was they are, leaned up against the truck talking. Santana ran back to Zach to report back to what he saw.

"Alright look, both of them niggaz posted at the middle of the block talking. We go run up as close as we can, then fire. Aim for chest, neck and head. You hear me?" Zach nodded in agreement.

"You take away whoever closest to you and I'll do the same. This for Heem nigga, remember that. And remember, if you confirmed ya kill…"

"Double back and help team," Zach finished Santana's statement.

"You ready?" Zach nodded. "I can go by my lonely, son, ain't no pressure. Once we go, ain't no turning back. You sure?" The look Zach gave him spoke volumes. Santana could see Zack was ready to fly. Zack wanted to hold the same flame Santana did. He wanted to be equally experienced.

Ironically, not even Santana was properly equipped with the skill to lead their current mission. Unbeknownst to Zach, the only confirmed kills Santana had were caught in the spur of the moment. The only body that was planned was Hood Ru's. Piru and Stacks happened in the spur of the moment, If Simfany hadn't started tripping it was a possibility that Piru and Stacks would still be alive. The shooting that took place at Shop N Go was no different than any other kill, it was a spur of the moment reaction that saved his life.

Santana didn't show it, but he was nervous as hell. He looked back at Zach as he followed close by. They both hit the corner smoothly and crept along the parked cars. The sound of a car door slamming alarmed them both. Santana rose and looked through the window of a parked car. FB Sleeze was the only one left on the block. The car that pulled down the street had to have Fatty in it because he was nowhere in sight. Santana crouched and explained to Zach what happened.

"We can't let this nigga slide, get ready." Zach already knew he was ready and loaded, but for good measure he popped his clip out and checked anyway.

"I'm ready."

"Bet. No matter what happens tonight, I love you, my G."

"Tell me that when we make it to sis spot," Zach replied and nodded towards the spot where Sleeze was last seen. Without further words, Santana began walking along the parked cars, closing the distance between him and Sleeze. When he got one car away from where Sleeze stood, he stopped and waited on Zach to catch up.

"How you wanna do this? You can walk across the street and as soon as you grab his attention, I can start bangin' him and then we can be out. What you think?" Santana asked in a whisper. Zach looked offended.

"No, we gone smoke this nigga together. Rumor is he killed Heem, I want that nigga's blood on my hands. So come up with something else," Zach whispered back, never taking his eyes off of FB Sleeze.

"Fuck it, let's rock." Santana rose from behind the car and directed Zach to play the middle of the street. Zach nodded and raised the AR-15, locking the stock against his shoulder. Santana walked around the car Glock raised. Sleeze was too occupied with his phone, he didn't see Santana walking up. It was a mistake he would regret.

Boc… Boc…Boc…

Santana fired, hitting Sleeze in his chest three times, shattering the silence of the night. Sleeze jerked from the impact, but never lost his step. He dropped the phone from his grass and reached for his hip. The AR-15 shells that ripped into his chest knocked him into the car behind him violently.

Fsst…Boc…Boc…

Falling to the pavement, surprisingly to both Santana and Zach, Sleeze was still alive. Barely, but still amongst the living. Sleeze gargled the blood that clogged his throat, he was drowning. Though Santana rather him drown himself by suffocation, he took no chances. Both he and Zach advanced towards Sleeze.

Santana kicked Sleeze in the face as hard as he could, then raised his Glock and said, "This for Heem, pussy!" And squeezed the rest of his clip into Sleeze's face and torso.

"Come on, bruh!" Zach yelled, pulling Santana's shirt. Santana smiled as he ran off knowing that FB Sleeze was no more.

They ran full speed back to the car and pulled off. Santana could hear sirens in the distance. They pulled their masks off simultaneously. The silence in the car was teary. Santana looked over and watched Zach's hand tremble. He was shook, Santana understood wholeheartedly what Zach was going through. He had been there. Santana said nothing and focused on the road. He needed to be on point. They don't need unwanted attention right now.

Santana parked the car on Homer Street. The destination was picked solely because of convenience. The Westside hill was known for eluding police, so he chose a spot where if shit got hectic, he could at least have a chance of escape. But thankfully, there wasn't a sign of police or sirens in the distance. They were in the clear.

Santana pulled his phone out and dialed Darla's number. Darla answered halfway through the first ring.

"Hey baby!" Darla said excitedly.

"Quannie ready," that's all Santana said before hanging up the phone.

"Reach into the glove box and hand me those gloves in that bleach."

"Hold on." Zach said putting the AR-15 in the backseat. Zach reached into the glove compartment and did what he was asked to do. He watched Santana put the gloves on and began pouring bleach on everything.

"Nigga, you just got sit there? Get your ass out so we can wipe this bitch down. Hurry up, Darla on her way." Santana stated in a hurry. Zach got out the car and reached back into the glove box and grabbed two more gloves and went to work helping Santana wipe down the Crown Vic.

"I got the rest my G, get out and make sure don't no cars sneak up on us. If I'm not done by the time baby girl come, still warn me of any oncoming lights."

"Bet." No sooner Santana said his peace, Zach knocked on the car door to inform him that a set of lights was climbing the rapidly Santana grabbed his block and slammed the door. They both stepped away from the car and nonchalantly began to walk up the sidewalk. When the car stopped, Santana looked over the face that looked at them put a smile on both Zach and Santana's face. It was Darla. Santana signaled for her to pull over. He ran to the car and kissed her lips.

"I have to finish wiping down the whip, I'll be back in a second. I love you, mama."

"I love you too, daddy." Santana ran back to the car and finished the task at hand. He erased their existence from the car, Santana grabbed the bleach, rags, gloves and AR-15 out of the car and high tailed it to Darla's car. Darla pulled off as if she belonged.

"Down." Darla reminded the pair.

Zach dropped out of sight first and Santana followed, placing his head in Darla's lap as she drove. Darla lifted her free hand and rubbed Santana's chest in an attempt to calm his nerves.

"Thank you, sis," Zach said from the back seat.

"Don't thank me. Thank Nessy for telling me about where them niggas met. It was a long shot, but I hope it paid off. It did pay off, right?"

"You better know it, that nigga a mu'fuckin' beast, sis. Just know that. That nigga Tana a fucking beast," Zach assured her.

"Oh, believe me, I seen him in action," Darla replied as she pulled on to her residential street. "We're here y'all. Don't look…"

"Spin the block once to make sure nobody is looking out windows or creeping around lying in wait." Darla did as she was told, not seeing anything or anyone out of place, she pulled into her driveway and parked. She looked down the street both ways before giving them the ok to depart.

"Call me when it's done," Santana said, leaving the Glock and AR in the car with Darla. Zach looked at Santana dumbfounded. Not willing to chance his fate, he wiped his prints clean from the AR-15 and made a mental note to talk to Santana about thinking with his dick.

Darla watched through the rearview as Zach wiped both guns down, she didn't know why it angered her, but it did. She sucked her teeth loud enough for Zach to hear. Zach looked up unapologetic. *Fuck ya lil' attitude, bitch. Don't nobody got time to be trusting your dingy ass*, Zach thought bluntly. He wasn't willing to bet his life on her making sure all evidence disappeared.

Santana didn't blame him, so he said nothing. He kissed Darla and got out the car. Zach followed suit. Before he closed the door, he said...

"I'm sorry, sis, just being cautious." This sincere look calm turn anger. Darla pulled out her driveway, leaving Santana and Zach in the driveway of her home.

***

Darla pulled up to the bridge that separated Charleston East End from the Westside. She grabbed both guns and the cloth used to clean the inside of the Crown Vic. She looked every way before tossing each item one by one over the bridge into the Kanawana River. It was too dark to see, but as each item found its mark, the splash of the water confirmed a job well done.

After all items were discarded, Darla hopped back in her car and pulled off. Darla pulled out her phone and sent Santana a text message as she waited on the light to turn green.

You ready to play in this wild and wonderful?

Darla smiled, knowing the text would entice him. Darla's phone beeped almost immediately.

Come home and find out!

Darling bit her bottom lip and texted Santana back.

I'm cumming now, daddy.

That'll get his ass. Darla laughed turning her phone completely off as she excitedly raced back home to make love to her king.

Chapter 14

Santana sat in his mother's Tahoe as he watched mourners place teddy bears, flowers, candles and bandanas around the place Shamir "Sleeze" Stokes was found slain. He had been present for hours, just watching from a distance. The streets was clueless, no one knew who really responsible for killing Full Blooded's most prolific shooter. Though many people had an idea, no one knew for sure. But, Santana was definitely about to change that, he wanted everybody to know he wasn't playing and that Sleeze's soul was his and his alone.

Santana waited patiently for the police to dissolve and disperse from the vigil spot. Once the last cop car pulled off, Santana grabbed his Glock 17 out the center console and opened the door. The sun shined brightly. The day was one of the hottest of the year. Santana dressed appropriately for the weather. He was dressed in an all-white tank top, with a black Kevlar vest pulled over to protect all his vital parts. He had a pair of ash gray Rocawear denim jeans on, With a pair of ash gray and black retro Jordan 11's to match. From a distance it was just an outfit, but it all reality, it was a sign of war.

Santana approached the block vigorously, with his Glock 17 concealed behind his back. He studied the crowd of mourners closely. He recognized a few FB members in attendance, a host of different females and who seemed to be Sleeze's mother and siblings. The crowd wasn't as big as it would have been days ago when his memorial was first set up. As Santana approached the memorial, he raised his Glock at the crowd and spoke, demanding their attention. All he heard was a gasp from those paying attention.

"Why the fuck y'all out here? Nigga, I dare you," Santana said, biting his bottom lip, itching for one of them FB niggas to act bad.

"Nigga, stop moving. Where Fatty at? Huh? Where that fat bitch hiding at? We out here drowning his niggaz and he hiding. Ol' bitch ass nigga. Tell that nigga I'm outside." Santana paused, searching everyone's eyes. All he could see was anger and hate. He smiled, loving every minute of the torture he was dishing out. He was giving Charleston what they were asking for. They were fucking with the right one, that was for certain.

"This ya only pass. I catch you again, I'm freezing you where you stand. I put that on Haseem Briggs, you heard. You folks have a nice—" Sleeze's mother interjected.

"Why are you doing this?" Sleeze's mother asked through her tears. Santana looked at her and contemplated if he wanted to entertain her question. He couldn't help himself, he had to indulge.

"This what that faggot ass nigga deserved. Why you ain't ask him these questions when he knocked my nigga skull all over my porch? Or when him and his niggas shot son funeral up? Where was a questions at then, bitch?" Santana was met by silence.

"Yeah, I mu'fuckin' thought so. If only I was five minutes earlier, he would have been a mu'fuckin' memory too, nigga." Santana hit the beam on his gun and pointed it at the crowd, landing on Sleeze's mother. The fear that consumed them all boosted Santana's ego. Sleeze's mother and sisters began crying hysterically, while Sleeze's fellow gang members gritted their teeth in anger.

"What's up, y'all niggaz feel some type of way? Y'all been looking for me, right? Nigga, I'm here. What's up?

Fuck this bitch ass nigga." Santana hog spit on Sleeze's picture and kicked his candles over.

"Nigga!" One of the men went to advance but was pulled back by Sleeze's mother. Santana looked up momentarily before he finished kicking over Sleeze's candles.

"Keep playin' with me, lil' nigga. This what y'all wanted, right? Y'all killed my nigga, right? Well, nigga… I'm out here. Come kill me. Ohh and this fair warning to all you FB niggas. You lucky I didn't know ya ol' ass was this sexy, I would have fucked you before—" Santana stopped midsentence when he looked up and saw Fatty Man's Chevy Impala turn onto the block. *Yeah, now this is what I've been waiting on.* Santana smiled but to his surprise, Fatty threw his car into reverse and sped off. The crowd followed Santana gaze and witness Fatty's departure, causing chatter within the crowd.

"And that bitch ass ya savior? Yeah, ight." Santana jogged backwards down the block until he put some distance between him and the vigil. Santana watched as the men scrambled around in anger, reaching for their weapons.

Unbeknownst to Santana's position, Fatty sped blindly back around the corner ready for whatever. Santana stopped and watched Fatty's stupidity with a sense of humor. He wasted no time running back up, Santana opened fire.

Boc… Boc… Boc… Boc… Boc… Boc…

He fired rapidly into Fatty's Impala, taking him by surprise. With no other options Fatty ducked. The back windshield busted, giving Santana a better view of his target. The thirty-two-round clip Santana had hanging from his Glock gave him comfort as he continued firing menacingly at Fatty Man. Fatty was a sitting duck, everyone could see it. Santana continued to advance aggressively. He wanted to end the threat once and for all.

Boc…Boc…Boc…Pat…Pat…

Return fire stopped Santana in his tracks, especially when he heard a bullet whiz by his head. *Oh shit,* he thought as he ducked low and fired back into the crowd of mourners. Loud screams pierced the air. Santana ran for the Tahoe as multiple guns fired at him. The impact of a bullet hitting his vest knocked him forward. The pain was almost unbearable, but Santana kept going. He fought through the pain as he took cover behind the Tahoe. *Fun!* Santana thought as he reached in between his vest to see if the bullet had gone through. Thankfully it didn't. The spot just ached and throbbed with its own heartbeat. He peeked around the truck and saw Fatty being pulled from his Impala unharmed.

"Man, fuck!" he yelled in frustration. He reached around the Tahoe and fired at Fatty and his men. They returned fire. Santana could hear the bullets connecting with the metal of the truck. Santana reached around and fired back. With no cover to take, the Full Blooded members stood their ground in the middle of the block. The sound of metal being hit again made Santana reevaluate his situation. The gunfire stopped, causing him to look around the Tahoe. He couldn't see anyone, there was no movement. Santana popped his magazine out while he had the chance, he wanted to see what kind of ammo he had left to survive with. His heart sank when he saw the clip indicator showed he only had five shots left to give.

Before he was able to restore his clip back into the gun, a royal blue GMC Yukon speed up. The back door on the driver's side was wide open. Santana's heart dropped. He knew he was caught dead to rights. He was surprised when the driver said, "Hop in!" Santana looked up from his position and recognize the face of the man he dismissed at the funeral only weeks prior. "Bruh, hurry up, they advancing. Hurry the fuck up!" Rasheed yelled once again. Gunfire erupted again, both Santana and Rasheed ducked instinctively. Rasheed reached his arm out the window and returned fire.

Boom... Boom... Boom...

The cannon Rasheed let go seemed to stop time, no return fire came.

"Get in or I'm gonna leave you, nigga," he stated calmly raising the 50-cal Desert Eagle and firing. Shaking the city streets.

Boom...Boom...Boom...

Santana took that opportunity to hop into Simfany's Tahoe. The bullet holes visible in the window and interior angered him. He knew he would have a lot of explaining to do. Simfany wasn't going to be happy, that Santana knew for sure. He started the engine and put the truck into drive.

Boom... Boom... Boom...

Santana ducked again, the bark from the Desert Eagle was deafening. Santana honked the horn repeatedly, trying to catch Rasheed's attention. When Rasheed finally looked over, Santana waved him on. Without further hesitation, Rasheed sped off, clearing the path for Santana's escape. He sped down the block closely behind the Yukon. Once Santana was sure no imminent danger lurked, he breathed a sigh of relief. He had to admit, shit had gotten out of hand quick. He thought he was prepared for all scenarios, but in all reality, he wasn't prepared at all.

Santana didn't know why, but he followed the Yukon until it came to a stop outside of Charleston city limits. Rasheed had pulled into the driveway of a small, abandoned house. Rasheed shut his Yukon off and hopped out. He looked at Santana and asked, "You coming inside, bruh?"

"Nah, I'll be out here," Santana replied. He was still trying to make sense of everything. Santana just sat in the Tahoe. He powered his phone back on, he didn't have any calls or messages, so he put his phone on vibrate and put it in his pocket. He knew it was going to be a matter of time before it would be blowing up.

After waiting for what seemed like forever, Santana cut the Tahoe off and hopped out. It was a must for him to know what was going on, and how Rasheed fit into it all. Because right now he was lost. Tana didn't feel like he was being snaked, because if Rasheed wanted, he could have just killed him when he had the chance. He was literally caught with his clip out of his gun, to say he was lacking would be an understatement. So, with that out of the equation, it had to be more to it, and he wanted to know what the fuck was going on.

Santana walked to the door and twisted the knob, opening the door to a fully furnished home. *I should have known*, he thought, closing the door behind him. It made sense a little, this home was obviously a hideaway spot for Rasheed.

"Sit down, my nigga," Rasheed said, reloading the Desert Eagle. Santana stood and leaned against the wall.

"So, what's the story, why did you help me?"

"Because of Heem," Rasheed said flatly.

"Heem never mentioned you to me before, who are you, moe?"

"My name's Rasheed, I tried to holler at your lil' ass at the funeral, but you was on bullshit. I could understand partly because you just lost your homie and all," Rasheed explained.

"Yeah," Santana replied flatly. He felt Haseem's absence daily. His suck ass comments, and crude jokes was what Santana missed most about Haseem's personality. It fucked him up, knowing the last word spoken to one another was wasted. He wished he could get a redo. Santana knocked the memories away and got back to the topic.

"That still ain't telling me shit, my G."

"I just felt like I owed Heem that much," Rasheed answered as he thought back to the day when he ran into Haseem at his baby mother house.

After Haseem left, he curiously searched the couch to see what it was to seem was so desperately looking for. As soon as Rasheed felt the warmth still pushed deeply into the cushions of the sofa, he knew Haseem was no longer armed.

"Nigga, I'm talking to you," Baby said, walking up to him.

"My bad, what you say?" He turned to look at Baby.

"Why did you do that to him? You know he has looked up to you since he been a young nigga."

"I understand, but come on, niggaz know when they cross the mu'fuckin' line. And him sleeping here fucking you is one of them."

"But I never even fuc—"

"Man, shut that shit up. Baby, you know what the fuck you doing. Stop it. You could have found someone else than him, man. You know you—"

Baby pulled him into her and kissed his lips, finding his tongue. He cursed himself for being so weak for her. Baby pulled at his belt, loosening his jeans. She never broke the lip lock she had him captured in. She knew what needed to be done. Baby pushed her hand into his pants and found what she was looking for. She grabbed on firmly to his dick and stroked him until she felt him stiffen in her hands.

"Baby, stop!" Rasheed asked, barely audible. Baby ignored her baby daddy's plea and dropped to her knees. Rasheed made a feeble attempt to push Baby away. He closed his eyes when he felt the warmth of her mouth wrap around his shaft. Baby knew how he liked his dick sucked so she swallowed him whole, then stroked him slowly back and forth with her palm.

"Nah, watch out." Rasheed pulled back, slipping his wet dick from Baby's mouth. They locked eyes, she was visibly pissed, but he didn't care. He was tired of being seduced by her. Rasheed got himself together and walked back to the couch. He reached in and retrieved Haseen's Glock. When he put the gun in his Carhart jacket, he looked back, Baby was still on her knees like the bird she was. Rasheed never spoke another word to her, he opened the door and left with only one thing on his mind, returning Haseem's gun and apologizing for the attack.

"Bro!" Santana snapped, breaking Rasheed from his daydream.

"Yo."

"Make this shit make sense." Santana needed answers, he needed to understand more. Santana's phone buzzed in his pocket. He pulled it out, it was Darla calling. He answered knowing that she was about to lay into him for what took place earlier.

"What's up, ma?"

"Bitch ass nigga, you know what's up." Santana 's heart sank when he realized the caller's voice wasn't Darla's. It belonged to Fatty Man.

"Babbbyyy…" he heard Darla scream.

"Shut up, bitch!"

"Nigga, I swear, if you—"

"If I what, nigga, this on you."

Boc…Boc…Boc…

For The Love Of Blood 5 (Survivors Guilt)

Lock Down Publications and Ca$h Presents
Assisted Publishing Packages

BASIC PACKAGE	UPGRADED PACKAGE
$499	$800
Editing	Typing
Cover Design	Editing
Formatting	Cover Design
	Formatting
ADVANCE PACKAGE	**LDP SUPREME PACKAGE**
$1,200	$1,500
Typing	Typing
Editing	Editing
Cover Design	Cover Design
Formatting	Formatting
Copyright registration	Copyright registration
Proofreading	Proofreading
Upload book to Amazon	Set up Amazon account
	Upload book to Amazon
	Advertise on LDP, Amazon and
	Facebook Page

***Other services available upon request.
Additional charges may apply

Lock Down Publications
P.O. Box 944
Stockbridge, GA 30281-9998
Phone: 470 303-9761

Submission Guideline

Submit the first three chapters of your completed manuscript to ldpsubmissions@gmail.com. In the subject line add **Your Book's Title**. The manuscript must be in a Word Doc file and sent as an attachment. Document should be in Times New Roman, double spaced, and in size 12 font. Also, provide your synopsis and full contact information. If sending multiple submissions, they must each be in a separate email.

Have a story but no way to send it electronically? You can still submit to LDP/Ca$h Presents. Send in the first three chapters, written or typed, of your completed manuscript to:

LDP: Submissions Dept
P.O. Box 944
Stockbridge, GA 30281-9998

DO NOT send original manuscript. Must be a duplicate. Provide your synopsis and a cover letter containing your full contact information.

Thanks for considering LDP and Ca$h Presents.

NEW RELEASES

BLOODLINE OF A SAVAGE **BY PRINCE A. TAUHID**

THE MURDER QUEENS 4 **BY MICHAEL GALLON**

THE BUTTERFLY MAFIA **BY FUMIYA PAYNE**

KING KILLA 2 **BY VINCENT "VITTO" HOLLOWAY**

BABY, I'M WINTERTIME COLD 3 **BY MEESHA**

THESE VICIOUS STREETS **BY PRINCE A. TAUHID**

TIL DEATH 2 **BY ARYANNA**

CITY OF SMOKE 2 **BY MOLOTTI**

STEPPERS **BY KING RIO**

THE LANE **BY KEN-KEN SPENCE**

MONEY GAME 2 **BY SMOOVE DOLLA**

THE BLACK DIAMOND CARTEL **BY SAYNOMORE**

CRIME BOSS 2 **BY PLAYA RAY**

THUG OF SPADES **BY COREY ROBINSON**

LOVE IN THE TRENCHES 2 **BY COREY ROBINSON**

TIL DEATH 3 **BY ARYANNA**

THE BIRTH OF A GANGSTER 4 **BY DELMONT PLAYER**

PRODUCT OF THE STREETS **BY DEMOND "MONEY" ANDERSON**

Coming Soon from Lock Down Publications/Ca$h Presents

BLOOD OF A BOSS VI
SHADOWS OF THE GAME II
TRAP BASTARD II
By **Askari**

LOYAL TO THE GAME IV
By **T.J. & Jelissa**

TRUE SAVAGE VIII
MIDNIGHT CARTEL IV
DOPE BOY MAGIC IV
CITY OF KINGZ III
NIGHTMARE ON SILENT AVE II
THE PLUG OF LIL MEXICO II
CLASSIC CITY II
By **Chris Green**

BLAST FOR ME III
A SAVAGE DOPEBOY III
CUTTHROAT MAFIA III
DUFFLE BAG CARTEL VII
HEARTLESS GOON VI
By **Ghost**

A HUSTLER'S DECEIT III
KILL ZONE II
BAE BELONGS TO ME III
TIL DEATH II
By **Aryanna**

KING OF THE TRAP III
By **T.J. Edwards**

GORILLAZ IN THE BAY V
3X KRAZY III
STRAIGHT BEAST MODE III
By **De'Kari**

KINGPIN KILLAZ IV
STREET KINGS III
PAID IN BLOOD III
CARTEL KILLAZ IV
DOPE GODS III
By **Hood Rich**

SINS OF A HUSTLA II
By **ASAD**

YAYO V
BRED IN THE GAME 2
By **S. Allen**

THE STREETS WILL TALK II
By **Yolanda Moore**

SON OF A DOPE FIEND III
HEAVEN GOT A GHETTO III
SKI MASK MONEY III
By **Renta**

LOYALTY AIN'T PROMISED III
By **Keith Williams**

I'M NOTHING WITHOUT HIS LOVE II
SINS OF A THUG II
TO THE THUG I LOVED BEFORE II
IN A HUSTLER I TRUST II
By **Monet Dragun**

QUIET MONEY IV
EXTENDED CLIP III
THUG LIFE IV
By **Trai'Quan**

THE STREETS MADE ME IV
By **Larry D. Wright**

IF YOU CROSS ME ONCE III
ANGEL V
By **Anthony Fields**

THE STREETS WILL NEVER CLOSE IV
By **K'ajji**

HARD AND RUTHLESS III
KILLA KOUNTY IV
By **Khufu**

MONEY GAME III
By **Smoove Dolla**

MURDA WAS THE CASE III
Elijah R. Freeman

AN UNFORESEEN LOVE IV
BABY, I'M WINTERTIME COLD III
By **Meesha**

QUEEN OF THE ZOO III
By **Black Migo**

CONFESSIONS OF A JACKBOY III
By **Nicholas Lock**

JACK BOYS VS DOPE BOYS IV
A GANGSTA'S QUR'AN V
COKE GIRLZ II
COKE BOYS II
LIFE OF A SAVAGE V
CHI'RAQ GANGSTAS V
SOSA GANG III
BRONX SAVAGES II
BODYMORE KINGPINS II
By **Romell Tukes**

KING KILLA II
By **Vincent "Vitto" Holloway**

BETRAYAL OF A THUG III
By **Fre$h**

THE MURDER QUEENS III
By **Michael Gallon**

THE BIRTH OF A GANGSTER III
By **Delmont Player**

TREAL LOVE II
By **Le'Monica Jackson**

FOR THE LOVE OF BLOOD III
By **Jamel Mitchell**

RAN OFF ON DA PLUG II
By **Paper Boi Rari**

HOOD CONSIGLIERE III
By **Keese**

PRETTY GIRLS DO NASTY THINGS II
By **Nicole Goosby**

PROTÉGÉ OF A LEGEND III
LOVE IN THE TRENCHES II
By **Corey Robinson**

IT'S JUST ME AND YOU II
By **Ah'Million**

FOREVER GANGSTA III
By **Adrian Dulan**

GORILLAZ IN THE TRENCHES II
By **SayNoMore**

THE COCAINE PRINCESS VIII
By **King Rio**

CRIME BOSS II
By **Playa Ray**

LOYALTY IS EVERYTHING III
By **Molotti**

HERE TODAY GONE TOMORROW II
By **Fly Rock**

REAL G'S MOVE IN SILENCE II
By **Von Diesel**

GRIMEY WAYS IV
By **Ray Vinci**

Available Now

RESTRAINING ORDER I & II
By **CA$H & Coffee**

LOVE KNOWS NO BOUNDARIES I II & III
By **Coffee**

RAISED AS A GOON I, II, III & IV
BRED BY THE SLUMS I, II, III
BLAST FOR ME I & II
ROTTEN TO THE CORE I II III
A BRONX TALE I, II, III
DUFFLE BAG CARTEL I II III IV V VI
HEARTLESS GOON I II III IV V
A SAVAGE DOPEBOY I II
DRUG LORDS I II III
CUTTHROAT MAFIA I II
KING OF THE TRENCHES
By **Ghost**

LAY IT DOWN I & II
LAST OF A DYING BREED I II
BLOOD STAINS OF A SHOTTA I & II III
By **Jamaica**

LOYAL TO THE GAME I II III
LIFE OF SIN I, II III
By **TJ & Jelissa**

IF LOVING HIM IS WRONG…I & II
LOVE ME EVEN WHEN IT HURTS I II III
By **Jelissa**

FOR THE LOVE OF BLOOD 4 | JAMEL MITCHELL

BLOODY COMMAS I & II
SKI MASK CARTEL I, II & III
KING OF NEW YORK I II, III IV V
RISE TO POWER I II III
COKE KINGS I II III IV V
BORN HEARTLESS I II III IV
KING OF THE TRAP I II
By **T.J. Edwards**

WHEN THE STREETS CLAP BACK I & II III
THE HEART OF A SAVAGE I II III IV
MONEY MAFIA I II
LOYAL TO THE SOIL I II III
By **Jibril Williams**

A DISTINGUISHED THUG STOLE MY HEART I II &
III
LOVE SHOULDN'T HURT I II III IV
RENEGADE BOYS I II III IV
PAID IN KARMA I II III
SAVAGE STORMS I II III
AN UNFORESEEN LOVE I II III
BABY, I'M WINTERTIME COLD I II
By **Meesha**

A GANGSTER'S CODE I &, II III
A GANGSTER'S SYN I II III
THE SAVAGE LIFE I II III
CHAINED TO THE STREETS I II III
BLOOD ON THE MONEY I II III
A GANGSTA'S PAIN I II III
By **J-Blunt**

PUSH IT TO THE LIMIT
By **Bre' Hayes**

BLOOD OF A BOSS I, II, III, IV, V
SHADOWS OF THE GAME
TRAP BASTARD
By **Askari**

THE STREETS BLEED MURDER I, II & III
THE HEART OF A GANGSTA I II& III
By **Jerry Jackson**

CUM FOR ME I II III IV V VI VII VIII
An **LDP Erotica Collaboration**

BRIDE OF A HUSTLA I II & II
THE FETTI GIRLS I, II& III
CORRUPTED BY A GANGSTA I, II III, IV
BLINDED BY HIS LOVE
THE PRICE YOU PAY FOR LOVE I, II ,III
DOPE GIRL MAGIC I II III
By **Destiny Skai**

WHEN A GOOD GIRL GOES BAD
By **Adrienne**

A GANGSTER'S REVENGE I II III & IV
THE BOSS MAN'S DAUGHTERS I II III IV V
A SAVAGE LOVE I & II
BAE BELONGS TO ME I II
A HUSTLER'S DECEIT I, II, III
WHAT BAD BITCHES DO I, II, III
SOUL OF A MONSTER I II III
KILL ZONE
A DOPE BOY'S QUEEN I II III
TIL DEATH
By **Aryanna**

THE COST OF LOYALTY I II III
By Kweli

A KINGPIN'S AMBITION
A KINGPIN'S AMBITION **II**
I MURDER FOR THE DOUGH
By **Ambitious**

TRUE SAVAGE I II III IV V VI VII
DOPE BOY MAGIC I, II, III
MIDNIGHT CARTEL I II III
CITY OF KINGZ I II
NIGHTMARE ON SILENT AVE
THE PLUG OF LIL MEXICO II
CLASSIC CITY
By **Chris Green**

A DOPEBOY'S PRAYER
By **Eddie "Wolf" Lee**

THE KING CARTEL I, II & III
By **Frank Gresham**

THESE NIGGAS AIN'T LOYAL I, II & III
By **Nikki Tee**

GANGSTA SHYT I II &III
By **CATO**

THE ULTIMATE BETRAYAL
By **Phoenix**

BOSS'N UP I, II & III
By **Royal Nicole**

I LOVE YOU TO DEATH
By **Destiny J**

I RIDE FOR MY HITTA
I STILL RIDE FOR MY HITTA
By **Misty Holt**

LOVE & CHASIN' PAPER
By **Qay Crockett**

TO DIE IN VAIN
SINS OF A HUSTLA
By **ASAD**

BROOKLYN HUSTLAZ
By **Boogsy Morina**

BROOKLYN ON LOCK I & II
By **Sonovia**

GANGSTA CITY
By **Teddy Duke**

A DRUG KING AND HIS DIAMOND I & II III
A DOPEMAN'S RICHES
HER MAN, MINE'S TOO I, II
CASH MONEY HO'S
THE WIFEY I USED TO BE I II
PRETTY GIRLS DO NASTY THINGS
By Nicole Goosby

LIPSTICK KILLAH I, II, III
CRIME OF PASSION I II & III
FRIEND OR FOE I II III
By **Mimi**

TRAPHOUSE KING I II & III
KINGPIN KILLAZ I II III
STREET KINGS I II
PAID IN BLOOD I II
CARTEL KILLAZ I II III
DOPE GODS I II
By **Hood Rich**

STEADY MOBBN' I, II, III
THE STREETS STAINED MY SOUL I II III
By **Marcellus Allen**

WHO SHOT YA I, II, III
SON OF A DOPE FIEND I II
HEAVEN GOT A GHETTO I II
SKI MASK MONEY I II
By **Renta**

GORILLAZ IN THE BAY I II III IV
TEARS OF A GANGSTA I II
3X KRAZY I II
STRAIGHT BEAST MODE I II
By **DE'KARI**

TRIGGADALE I II III
MURDA WAS THE CASE I II
By **Elijah R. Freeman**

THE STREETS ARE CALLING
By **Duquie Wilson**

SLAUGHTER GANG I II III
RUTHLESS HEART I II III
By **Willie Slaughter**

GOD BLESS THE TRAPPERS I, II, III
THESE SCANDALOUS STREETS I, II, III
FEAR MY GANGSTA I, II, III IV, V
THESE STREETS DON'T LOVE NOBODY I, II
BURY ME A G I, II, III, IV, V
A GANGSTA'S EMPIRE I, II, III, IV
THE DOPEMAN'S BODYGAURD I II
THE REALEST KILLAZ I II III
THE LAST OF THE OGS I II III
By **Tranay Adams**

MARRIED TO A BOSS I II III
By **Destiny Skai & Chris Green**

KINGZ OF THE GAME I II III IV V VI VII
CRIME BOSS
By **Playa Ray**

FUK SHYT
By **Blakk Diamond**

DON'T F#CK WITH MY HEART I II
By **Linnea**

ADDICTED TO THE DRAMA I II III
IN THE ARM OF HIS BOSS II
By **Jamila**

YAYO I II III IV
A SHOOTER'S AMBITION I II
BRED IN THE GAME
By **S. Allen**

LOYALTY AIN'T PROMISED I II
By **Keith Williams**

TRAP GOD I II III
RICH $AVAGE I II III
MONEY IN THE GRAVE I II III
By **Martell Troublesome Bolden**

FOREVER GANGSTA I II
GLOCKS ON SATIN SHEETS I II
By **Adrian Dulan**

TOE TAGZ I II III IV
LEVELS TO THIS SHYT I II
IT'S JUST ME AND YOU
By **Ah'Million**

KINGPIN DREAMS I II III
RAN OFF ON DA PLUG
By **Paper Boi Rari**

CONFESSIONS OF A GANGSTA I II III IV
CONFESSIONS OF A JACKBOY I II
By **Nicholas Lock**

I'M NOTHING WITHOUT HIS LOVE
SINS OF A THUG
TO THE THUG I LOVED BEFORE
A GANGSTA SAVED XMAS
IN A HUSTLER I TRUST
By **Monet Dragun**

QUIET MONEY I II III
THUG LIFE I II III
EXTENDED CLIP I II
A GANGSTA'S PARADISE
By **Trai'Quan**

CAUGHT UP IN THE LIFE I II III
THE STREETS NEVER LET GO I II III
By **Robert Baptiste**

NEW TO THE GAME I II III
MONEY, MURDER & MEMORIES I II III
By **Malik D. Rice**

CREAM I II III
THE STREETS WILL TALK
By **Yolanda Moore**

LIFE OF A SAVAGE I II III IV
A GANGSTA'S QUR'AN I II III IV
MURDA SEASON I II III
GANGLAND CARTEL I II III
CHI'RAQ GANGSTAS I II III IV
KILLERS ON ELM STREET I II III
JACK BOYZ N DA BRONX I II III
A DOPEBOY'S DREAM I II III
JACK BOYS VS DOPE BOYS I II III
COKE GIRLZ
COKE BOYS
SOSA GANG I II
BRONX SAVAGES
BODYMORE KINGPINS
By **Romell Tukes**

THE STREETS MADE ME I II III
By **Larry D. Wright**

CONCRETE KILLA I II III
VICIOUS LOYALTY I II III
By **Kingpen**

THE ULTIMATE SACRIFICE I, II, III, IV, V, VI
KHADIFI
IF YOU CROSS ME ONCE I II
ANGEL I II III IV
IN THE BLINK OF AN EYE
By **Anthony Fields**

THE LIFE OF A HOOD STAR
By **Ca$h & Rashia Wilson**

THE STREETS WILL NEVER CLOSE I II III
By **K'ajji**

NIGHTMARES OF A HUSTLA I II III
By **King Dream**

HARD AND RUTHLESS I II
MOB TOWN 251
THE BILLIONAIRE BENTLEYS I II III
REAL G'S MOVE IN SILENCE
By **Von Diesel**

GHOST MOB
By **Stilloan Robinson**

MOB TIES I II III IV V VI
SOUL OF A HUSTLER, HEART OF A KILLER I II
GORILLAZ IN THE TRENCHES
By **SayNoMore**

BODYMORE MURDERLAND I II III
THE BIRTH OF A GANGSTER I II
By **Delmont Player**

FOR THE LOVE OF A BOSS
By **C. D. Blue**

KILLA KOUNTY I II III IV
By Khufu

MOBBED UP I II III IV
THE BRICK MAN I II III IV V
THE COCAINE PRINCESS I II III IV V VI VII
By **King Rio**

MONEY GAME I II
By **Smoove Dolla**

A GANGSTA'S KARMA I II III
By **FLAME**

KING OF THE TRENCHES I II III
By **GHOST & TRANAY ADAMS**

QUEEN OF THE ZOO I II
By **Black Migo**

GRIMEY WAYS I II III
By **Ray Vinci**

XMAS WITH AN ATL SHOOTER
By **Ca$h & Destiny Skai**

KING KILLA
By **Vincent "Vitto" Holloway**

BETRAYAL OF A THUG I II
By **Fre$h**

THE MURDER QUEENS I II
By **Michael Gallon**

TREAL LOVE
By **Le'Monica Jackson**

FOR THE LOVE OF BLOOD I II
By **Jamel Mitchell**

HOOD CONSIGLIERE I II
By **Keese**

PROTÉGÉ OF A LEGEND I II
LOVE IN THE TRENCHES
By **Corey Robinson**

BORN IN THE GRAVE I II III
By **Self Made Tay**

MOAN IN MY MOUTH
By **XTASY**

TORN BETWEEN A GANGSTER AND A
GENTLEMAN
By **J-BLUNT & Miss Kim**

LOYALTY IS EVERYTHING I II
By **Molotti**

HERE TODAY GONE TOMORROW
By **Fly Rock**

PILLOW PRINCESS
By **S. Hawkins**

FOR THE LOVE OF BLOOD 4 | JAMEL MITCHELL

SANCTIFIED AND HORNY
by **XTASY**

THE PLUG OF LIL MEXICO 2
by **CHRIS GREEN**

THE BLACK DIAMOND CARTEL
by **SAYNOMORE**

THE BIRTH OF A GANGSTER 3
by **DELMONT PLAYER**

BOOKS BY LDP'S CEO, CA$H

TRUST IN NO MAN
TRUST IN NO MAN 2
TRUST IN NO MAN 3
BONDED BY BLOOD
SHORTY GOT A THUG
THUGS CRY
THUGS CRY 2
THUGS CRY 3
TRUST NO BITCH
TRUST NO BITCH 2
TRUST NO BITCH 3
TIL MY CASKET DROPS
RESTRAINING ORDER
RESTRAINING ORDER 2
IN LOVE WITH A CONVICT
LIFE OF A HOOD STAR
XMAS WITH AN ATL SHOOTER

www.ingramcontent.com/pod-product-compliance
Lightning Source LLC
Chambersburg PA
CBHW071147260626
47162CB00003B/951